https://www.brindlebooks.co.uk

SUMMER AT TANGENTS

BY

RODERICK EASDALE

Brindle Books Ltd

Copyright © 2024 by Roderick Easdale

This edition published by

Brindle Books Ltd
Wakefield
United Kingdom

Copyright © Brindle Books Ltd 2024

ISBN 978-1-915631-16-9

Chapter 1

"Blast it – Benton!"

"Sorry, Secretary?" the Secretary's secretary said, looking up distractedly from her paperwork.

"Blasted Benton Snivelgate. Should've known. Martin Cowmeadow has just scratched from the Shackleton Cup. I've just been looking up the sheet – guess who his opponent is!"

"Billy Down, Bert Duffield, Arthur Tillotson?"

"What? No! Why did you say that?"

"You asked me to guess. Those three play in every competition, so they seemed as likely as any."

"No, Benton Snivelgate."

"Oh I wouldn't have guessed him. Robert Musgrove or Jim Baker maybe."

"It is a wonder he doesn't win every knockout. No sod ever wants to play him."

"Is there a reserve slot?"

"No, everyone who wants to play gets in. Well, that's another bye for blasted Benton."

"Perhaps if you went in the bar and told people there was a spot available you could find someone?" suggested his PA. "There'll be a lot of people in there as it's Captain's Day."

"No point. Anyone keen enough to play in Captain's Day is going to be signed up for the Shack already. And if they aren't they'll quickly twig why there is suddenly a slot free."

"Perhaps if you tell people the draw hasn't been made?"

"Everyone knows it has. Been on the noticeboard for weeks. Half the first round ties have been played."

"Benton Snivelgate? He came in when you were out, selling raffle tickets."

"Which fool organisation has entrusted him with that? Glad I was out."

"He said he'd come back."

"Oh hell."

"Only to sell you some tickets."

"Oh double hell."

"But I put a stop to that."

"Well done. How?"

"I bought some for you there and then. I thought it'd stop him coming back and pestering you to buy some."

"What's the prize? Oh don't tell me, I won't win, not if Benton is involved. It will be dodgy somehow. Probably write his name on all the stubs or something."

"I thought of that. He said he'd fill in the stubs for me, but I said I'd do it. He wasn't happy about it, but I did."

"Oh well done." The Secretary looked at his PA approvingly – her moments of shrewdness always brought from him a mix of admiration and surprise. "I still can't believe somebody would be so daft as to let him sell their tickets. Who has, as matter of interest?"

"The club."

"Which club?"

"Us."

"What!"

"He said the raffle was raising money for club funds."

"This club? Our club?"

"Yes."

The mixture of surprise and admiration for his PA, Miss Murtle, was replicated towards whatever unseen hand had set up this raffle. The club needed to increase its revenue, but he could never get the committee interested in doing something sensible about it. Not, admittedly, that letting Benton Snivelgate be involved was remotely sensible.

"Why didn't anyone tell me about this? I am only the Secretary after all."

"Quite."

He thought to himself, not for the first time, that when something is wrong with the loos it is the Secretary who runs the club; when it's anything important to the strategic business planning of the whole enterprise suddenly it is the committee who runs things and the Secretary can go hang.

"Wait a minute, I have bought tickets to raise money for club funds?"

"I thought you would be pleased. You were saying funds were so low that you did not know if there would be enough to pay all the salaries by the end of the financial year."

"True," admitted the Secretary grudgingly. But he had been wildly over exaggerating; well, lying, to make the point to his PA to be less extravagant with the petty cash.

"But now there will be more money coming in."

"But don't you see, I am giving over some of my salary so as to ensure club funds have enough in them to pay my salary."

"Yes, clever isn't it."

"No, it's not. I am in effect paying my own salary with my own money."

"Hardly, it was only a few raffle tickets."

"S'pose so – a book of raffle tickets won't cost that much."

"Oh I bought two books."

"You got one for yourself, too? I suppose you had no choice – bad luck."

"No, I didn't get one for myself. I'm not going to pay money to the club. Its job is to pay me. I bought the two books for you."

"Two! Oh well, the deed is done now. What is it, a quid a ticket I suppose?"

"That is usual isn't it?"

"Yes."

"Oh good, I thought so. That's why I bought two books for you. Only when it was too late did I learn that the tickets were five pounds each."

"A fiver! Each! That's £50 for the two books."

"Well no, it isn't actually."

"Isn't it? There's a discount on two books – buy one get one half price sort of thing?" he said hopefully.

"No, it's £50 for one book."

"No, a book of five tickets at a fiver each" – he couldn't help groaning at the reminder – "is £25, and so two is £50."

"The books are of ten tickets."

"Ten? That's a hundred quid!"

"Yes, it is a lot isn't it? He should raise a lot of funds shouldn't he at those prices."

"A hundred quid," said the Secretary again, sitting down absent-mindedly on a nearby chair. "A hundred pounds. What is the first prize anyway, anything good? Something blagged I suppose? Or more likely stolen."

"It's £75."

"And the chances of winning won't be high."

"Could be – he said he was finding it hard to sell tickets. That's why I agreed to buy two books for you. Thought you'd want the raffle to be a success, seeing how it is for a cause close to your heart. Maybe you will win both prizes – there's a runners-up one of £25."

"Not selling many tickets is he? Well as I now have 20 of the darn things that must give me some chance. Wonder how many books he will sell."

"Said he hadn't sold any. No wonder at those prices – what idiot would pay £50 for a book of raffle tickets?"

The Secretary looked as if he was going to say something, but let out a quiet groan instead. "If anyone wants me, I'll be in the back office." For the umpteenth time since he had taken the job of Secretary, he wished that he hadn't. It wasn't the golf club that was the problem. Golf clubs were fine. It was the blasted members. He slumped into a chair in the back office, his place of retreat, and looked across to where the fish tank had been. He missed the fish, especially at times like these. The tank had been the idea of his predecessor, as a soothing presence in the office.

Well that hadn't worked out too well for him.

So when he took over he soon got rid of it. He had liked the fish at first, they swam contently round and caused him no problems and if they thought something should be done better they didn't say anything about it. He rather envied the lifestyle of a fish – and that was the moment he realised the tank had to go. What had happened to his predecessor was not going to happen to him.

One of the things that the committee had impressed upon him at his interview was that they needed to drive more revenue into the club. The Secretary had tried but, although everyone agreed more revenue was needed – well those that took any notice of the club's finances that is, which was precious few – no-one would agree how.

The members wanted more revenue coming into the club, but not if it meant their subscriptions going up, societies playing the course when a member wanted to, or raising bar prices; nor, indeed, if it meant doing anything sensible and effective to actually bring in this extra revenue. The only thing the members had agreed upon was the one option the Secretary had been opposed to: the introduction of a joining fee. But, to the members, this had the happy consequence that none of them would pay it. That such a fee could be a bar to others joining was not something they had considered important. Only when the feeble trickle of new members joining had dried to an occasional drip did it occur to people that the Secretary might have been right.

Another meeting was held to debate whether therefore to do away with the joining fee. Opinion was divided and the meeting ended up agreeing that the joining fee would be retained but not charged. This was a decision which made no-one totally happy yet no-one totally unhappy. Committee decisions tended to be like that.

What the club needed were new members, but where was he to conjure them from? They were a small golf club on the outskirts of a large village in the middle of nowhere. Golf club membership was no longer fashionable. Younger players did not have time to spare to play regularly. Society had changed: fewer husbands and fathers could leave wife and children for half a day each weekend to spend this time instead at their golf club. Most golf clubs now allowed non-members to play their course, so golfers wanting only an occasional game no longer had to join a club to get it.

His ponderings reminded him of something and he went out to speak to Miss Murtle: "We have a prospective new member coming at 4. Name of Larry Keene."

"It's almost 4 now," she replied. "Have you done the preliminary paperwork?"

"What, oh yes, it's in that folder there," said the Secretary pointing. "You will need to fill in some of the details – I only took brief ones on the phone as the line was so bad. In the folder marked new memberships," he prompted.

"You haven't forgotten I have to leave at 4.15 today?" Miss Murtle reminded him.

"No, I'd not forgotten," he lied.

"Oh I meant to say – you need to replenish the petty cash."

"I can't, I put a hundred pounds in there only yesterday. How much is left?"

"None."

"None of it?"

"No. I had to borrow £100 on your behalf so that you could pay for your raffle tickets. So you owe petty cash £100."

"A hundred quid," the Secretary groaned softly.

At the moment that the Secretary was groaning 'a hundred quid' to himself for about the seventh time, a young man was hesitating nervously outside the door. The Secretary's office was a separate single-storey building off a courtyard, the central feature of which was a small pond adorned with a fountain. He had been staring at the pond for some while now, trying to discern whether there were fish in it, as a way to eat up time. Eager not to be late, and create a bad impression, he had come too early.

He felt strangely intimidated by his surroundings. It didn't really seem to be part of his world. There had been one space left in the car park, but when he parked there an old buffer had come up to him and said hadn't he seen the notice that that space was reserved for the Lady Captain and was he the Lady Captain? He could not find another space so he had parked on a patch of waste ground nearby instead.

He had never been a member of a golf club before. He fancied he would rather like it. He was looking for new society, and the club could provide it. He was new to the area and if he was going to be working on his own from home it would be nice to get away from being hunched over a computer screen to go out for fresh air and exercise and look at different horizons. Not that he had played much golf, or knew much about it. But he was keen to learn, had played a few rounds and had some lessons and had enjoyed it.

He checked his watch again. It was now bang on 4. He knocked and entered. "Hallo," he said to the gentleman in a blazer he found behind the counter. "I phoned earlier."

"Oh, hallo, hallo, yes do come in. You must be Keene I take it. We have been expecting you. Delighted to welcome you to the club."

"Thank you. Yes, I'm keen, jolly keen," the other replied, somewhat taken aback at the question but feeling he ought to replicate the other's enthusiasm. Or had he got the time wrong and arrived too early?

The Secretary laughed at what he thought was the other's little joke. "Yes Mr Keene, I've already prepared some of the paperwork. Er, oh flippitydoodah I had it here somewhere."

"I am not Mr Keene."

"Oh you don't have to be that keen; some of our members only play a few times a year. Entirely up to you."

"No, I am not this chap you appear to be expecting. I am Mr King – Harry King."

"You are not Mr Keene?"

"No."

"Are you sure?"

"Yes, quite sure."

"Oh sorry, my mistake. It was just that I was expecting a Mr Larry Keene as he phoned earlier and said he would come at four o'clock. As that is now, I had thought you must be him. Never mind, not your fault. Sorry, I am very busy at the moment waiting for Mr Keene, but Miss Murtle will deal with whatever it is you want I am sure. Is it directions? To Paddock's Farm? We get a lot of that.

Don't worry it is quite simple – it's very near here, but it's terribly easy to miss the turning. You have probably gone right past it without noticing. My secretary, Miss Murtle, will be able to help you. She lives just by Paddock's Farm as a matter of fact."

He called his PA over, and retreated to the back room with the explanation to Harry: "Sorry, ordinarily I would happily stay and deal with you but it's just that we have a new member coming in any moment now and, as I am sure you understand, I need to be free to deal with him. It is important to make new members feel welcome. We pride ourselves on being a most welcoming club."

"Hallo, can I help you?" asked Miss Murtle breezily, as the Secretary retreated.

"Yes, I hope so. I'd like to become a member please."

"Yes, of course, are you Mr Keene?"

"No."

"Oh, are you sure?"

"Yes, I checked only recently. I phoned earlier and the Secretary said he would start an application form for me."

"In which case it will be in the new members' folder," said Miss Murtle rummaging in the folder. "Ah, here we are. Are you Larry Keene?" she said brandishing the form that the Secretary said he had mainly completed for the new applicant. Surveying it, she noticed that he had written 'Larry Keene' in his spidery handwriting next to the name, but everything else – address, telephone number, email address, previous clubs, membership category, handicap, county card and all the rest had been left blank.

"No, I am not Larry Keene."

"Oh, sorry. I don't appear to have a form for you here. No problem, I can do one now. Now Mr um – sorry I don't know your name?"

"Call me Harry, do."

"Thank you." She looked through some paperwork in an increasingly flustered way, "No, I definitely can't find a record of your application, Mr Do, but don't worry we can sort that."

"No I'm not Mr Do – King."

"King?"

"Yes."

"You're a king?"

"No not A King," said Harry trying to peer over the counter at the handful of papers Miss Murtle was shuffling through to see if he could help, "H King – Harry. Do you have an application form for me there?"

"You're King Harry?"

"That's it. So you have found it?"

"Er, no. Er, if you don't mind me asking, where exactly are you king of?"

"I'm not royal, my surname is King. My name is Mr King. Harry King."

"Oh, silly me – you must think me very silly."

"No, not at all."

"But I imagine it happens to you all the time doesn't it?"

"No, not at all."

"King Harold. That's one in the eye for me. Sorry, you must also get that all the time?"

"Yes. Our family are not good at choosing names. I have a cousin called Joanna, but everyone calls her Jo."

"Oh I have always liked Joanna as a name. Don't you like it? I've always thought it a pretty name."

"Yes, but that meant she was Jo King? Get it?"

"Oh she wasn't really called Joanna, she just joked that she was?"

"No. Her Christian name was Jo, as in Joanna, and her

surname was King, which makes Jo King – joking, geddit?"

"Oh yes," said Miss Murtle finally getting it. "Oh dear. Still I suppose a blessing is that if you are a girl when you get married you change your name so she needn't be straddled with it for life. Well, so long as you get married," she added wistfully.

"She did. Unfortunately it was to Mr Kerr."

"Oh dear, wasn't he very nice?"

"No, that then made her... oh it doesn't matter."

"What sort of member do you want to be?"

"Of this golf club."

"Yes, I had presumed that. But there are lots of different memberships available. Do you want to be a Full Member?"

"Er, is there such a thing as a half member?"

"I don't think so. But there are all sorts of other memberships available," she said fishing a folder out from under the desk to look them up. "For instance there is Highwayman 5, Highwayman 6, Highwayman 7."

"Er what are they? What's the difference between them?"

"Well it depends on what days you can play. Highwaymen 5 members can play on Wednesdays, Fridays, Tuesdays, Mondays and Thursdays. Highwayman 6 on Wednesdays, Mondays, Fridays, Tuesdays, Sundays and Thursdays. And Highway 7 members can play..."

"All week round?" suggested Harry.

"Yes, that would appear to be correct," said Miss Murtle surveying the description.

"And what is a Highwayman? In this context I mean."

"He is someone who can play in all Highwaymen competitions for free, but if he wants to play in a silver trophy competition he has to pay a green fee of two thirds of the going green fee for that day, except for the Shackleton, where the cost is a half of the going green fee, or the Club Championship for which there is no green fee payable, only an entry fee. Oh, and you have to be at least 55 years of age."

"I am 23!"

"Well you cannot be a Highwayman then. Sorry. But don't worry, we have lots of other memberships that you might like. There are Junior 5, Junior 6 and Junior 7 memberships for example."

"And what is a junior please? I mean how does one qualify for that?"

"Someone under 18 years of age at the start of the subscription year or, if joining part way through a year, under 18 years of age at the beginning of the calendar month in which he or she joins, so long as the first day of the month is a weekday. Otherwise it is the first available weekday, with the exception of bank holidays, in which case it is the second available weekday, so long as that is not also a bank holiday, in which case it will be the third available weekday. Or if joining in June it will count as the first day of the month regardless of what day of the week this is."

"I am 23," he reminded her.

"Well you can't be a junior member then. Sorry did you want to be one – I don't think they can make any exceptions but I can ask if you'd like?"

"No. Let's scrub the Junior option shall we. What other options are there? What about Full Membership – what does that entail?"

"That allows you to play the course at any time and enter all competitions without extra charge except for whatever entry fees may be in operation as determined by the Competitions Committee or sanctioned by them."

"That sounds ideal, I think that's the one I want please."

"We also have Intermediate 5, Intermediate 6, Intermediate 7 memberships," said Miss Murtle ploughing on.

"How does one qualify to be an Intermediate Member?"

"That category is open to members who are aged 18-24."

"Bingo! I am 23."

"Are you 23?"

"Yes."

"Well that's alright isn't it, 23 is between 18 and 24."

"Yes, so perhaps this is the one for me?"

"You also have to have been a Junior Member of the club for the two seasons preceding your application to be an Intermediate Member."

"Okay, let's scrub that one, too."

"Oh no, you don't necessarily have to be a Junior Member for the two seasons preceding your application to be an Intermediate Member."

"Oh good, so I could be a Junior Member then? I mean an Intermediate Member, sorry."

"You don't have to have been a Junior Member for the two seasons preceding your application to be an Intermediate Member if you have been a Junior Member for the preceding season and in at least two of the five seasons preceding the preceding season. Years spent as a family member are to count as two-thirds of a full year for the purposes of calculating how many years qualify in determining the figure of seasons to be counted as preceding the application to be an Intermediate Member."

"Let's scrub that one too, shall we?"

"Are you interested in a Family Membership?"

"No I am single." He winced at the reminder. His main motivation for moving to Tangents had been to forget a girl.

"There are various ladies' memberships available."

"But I am not a lady."

"I had to ask otherwise I could be had up for sexual discrimination. Health and Safety regulations you understand."

"Perhaps, I should just become a Full Member?"

"Don't worry, there are other categories. There is an Armed Services one for instance."

"I am not in the armed services."

"You don't have to be in the armed services to have an Armed Services membership."

"Oh, don't you?"

"No. You can be a firefighter, an ambulance driver, or a coastguard. Or in the navy."

"I am a writer."

"Sorry," said Miss Murtle scanning the list, "we don't appear to have a membership category for writers."

"Perhaps I should just become a Full Member then?"

"There is also Country Membership."

"How does one qualify for that?"

"You have to live more than 30 miles away and be a member of another golf club at least 40 miles away unless you were previously a junior member of said club in which case that club needs to be at least 25 miles away."

"I have never been a member of a golf club. Also, I now live in Tangents."

"So you won't want to be an Overseas Member then either?"

"Probably not. I think I would like to be a Full Member."

"We also have Husband-and-Wife memberships."

"I am not married."

"I am sorry Mr Do, Mr Doodah er um Mr King I can only offer you Full Membership I am afraid."

"Can I enrol as a Full Member then please?"

"Yes certainly and well – welcome to the club. I hope

you will be very happy here. I don't play myself, but people who do tell me it is a very nice course. Well a nice course anyway."

The Secretary came bustling out of the back office, an idea having just occurred to him. "Ah excellent you are still here," he said seeing Harry. "We are raising money for the club by selling raffle tickets, I thought you might like to buy some as a thank you. We have some nice prizes available and it could be a way for you to say thank you for us giving you directions – and of course it's a chance to win some wonderful prizes."

"Er, for the club you say? This club?"

"There is of course also social membership," said Miss Murtle, "but you don't want to be a Social Member do you?"

"Don't I? I want to socialise with other members. That is one of the attractions of joining – I am new to the area you see and don't know anyone round here."

"Could I interest you in a book perhaps?" prompted the Secretary.

"On what? The local history?" said Harry, struggling to follow two conversations at once.

"No, a book of raffle tickets."

"Oh, sorry, of course. How many in a book – five? And what are they, a pound each?"

"Well something like that," replied the Secretary.

"Oh well I might as well..."

"The books are of ten tickets and the tickets themselves are a fiver each," cut in Miss Murtle. The Secretary gave her a daggers look.

"Oh, are they?" said Harry, "in which case I will just have the one ticket then please if that's all I get for my five pounds."

"What about two?" suggested the Secretary.

"Two pounds? But I can't get anything for two pounds if tickets are five pounds each. No I am happy to spend a fiver. Consider it a bonus three quid for club funds."

Feeling he had somehow been outsmarted, the Secretary handed him a ticket and accepted a five-pound note in return which he slipped into his wallet.

"Er, Mr Secretary," said Miss Murtle thrusting the petty cash tin at him. "That belongs in here I think?" The Secretary took out the note and placed it in the tin with bad grace and retreated into the back office.

"Is that it then?" said Harry handing over the completed form to Miss Murtle. "Am I now a member of the golf club?" He felt a slight thrill as he said these words.

She scanned the form as she said, "Yes apart from the payment bit at the bottom, I will have to get the Secretary for that. Please excuse me a moment."

She went into the back office. "I need you for a payment please, Secretary."

"I have paid! You just saw me. I put the fiver in the petty cash tin – you saw me. The rest will have to wait, I don't have a hundred pounds on me. Well, ninety-five now."

"No, it's not that, I need you to authorise a subs payment out here please."

"Oh excellent, Mr Keene has arrived has he? Most excellent," he said, rushing out to the front office. When he saw Harry he said. "Oh it's you. I thought Miss Murtle had said Mr Keene had arrived. Is he here also?"

"No, sorry. Just me."

"Never mind, not your fault." Then, a happy thought having just occurred to the Secretary as to why he was needed for a payment: "Oh, are you looking to buy some more raffle tickets? Delighted to, would you like another one, maybe a couple this time – they are only five pounds each, a real bargain, and there are some lovely prizes and all the money goes to help an important village resource. The girls at Paddock's Farm – where you are going – are members here. Only Social Members, but still part of our happy family."

"Social members?"

"Yes."

"Do you have anti-social members?" said Harry perplexed.

"We also have Golf Members."

"Golf members are not social?"

"No they're not, they are Golf."

"Mr Secretary, Mr King would like to become a member and I just need you to complete the payment formalities please," prompted Miss Murtle.

"So you don't want any raffle tickets?" said the Secretary to Harry.

"No, thank you."

"Sure?"

"Yes, thank you. I already have one."

"If you had two you would double your chances of winning."

"Mr King would like to become a member, and we just need you to complete the payment formalities," Miss Murtle reminded him.

"A hundred pounds!" the Secretary groaned to himself loud enough for Harry to hear.

"It will cost a hundred pounds to be a member?" said Harry.

"What? No. We don't have any memberships at that rate. The subs list is here," said the Secretary distractedly passing it over. "What type of member do you wish to be?"

"A Full Member please."

"Okay," said the Secretary handing Harry the new

members' application form that Harry had just filled in. "Just write the sum in there please next to where it says annual subscription and sign in the space indicated – where it says candidate's signature."

"It also says joining fee here," said Harry having filled in the box for subscription fee.

"A hundred pounds!" groaned the Secretary.

"The joining fee is a hundred pounds?"

"What? No, the joining fee is calculated at one and half times the annual subscription based upon your subscription category."

"Gosh I wasn't expecting that," said Harry. "That's a lot."

"Yes it is. Sorry, what?" said the Secretary.

"The joining fee sounds a lot. I wasn't expecting that."

"Joining fees can be spread over three years if the member so elects. But there isn't a joining fee."

"Oh I thought you said it was one and half times the annual subscription."

"It is."

"But you just said there isn't one."

"No there isn't."

Harry decided he would quit while he was ahead. He didn't understand what the Secretary was saying, except that it seemed to be that he didn't have to pay some extra money that he hadn't known about and hadn't been expecting to pay. "Well that's that all completed," he said handing the form to the Secretary.

"Thank you. You said you were interested in buying a book on the club's history. I am afraid we don't have one, but there are lots of interesting things about this club which I am sure the members can tell you about."

"But not the anti-social ones," Harry joked nervously.

"Pardon?" said the Secretary still brooding on other matters.

"Nothing."

"Oh, yes," a happy thought having just occurred to the Secretary, "would you like to sign up to play in the Shackleton? It's one of our major competitions, singles match play. I could get you into that if you like?"

"Well it might be a bit early to start taking part in club competitions – I am not an experienced golfer and so I might need to learn a bit more of the ropes first."

"Nonsense, nonsense. Ideal way to get integrated into a club – join into everything you can, that's my advice. Get yourself known. I'll put you in the Shackleton, now let me see where is there a vacancy? There's bound to be one. Ah, I have found one. Your first round tie will be against a chap named, let me see, Benton Snivelgate. One of our longest members in fact."

"Oh, okay then."

"There you are," said the Secretary Tippexing out Martin Cowmeadow's name and writing in Harry's.

"Oh, I don't want to knock anyone out of the competition," said Harry seeing what the Secretary was doing.

"Isn't that the point of a knockout? Still, it will make you a popular opponent, I suppose."

"No, what I mean is that I don't want to push anyone else out who was expecting to play. You seem to be deleting someone's name to put mine in."

"Oh don't worry. It's Martin Cowmeadow, he had to drop out."

"Oh, why?"

"Er, um he's keen on rugby, moved here from a rugger town and I think he might be organising a club tour or something. He manages a side, the Bentleys I think they're called. Nice chap – you'll like him. He's very recognisable round the club – wears plus fours and plays with persimmon woods. You know what persimmon woods are don't you?"

"No."

"Yes, he says the old ways are the best," continued the Secretary ignoring Harry's answer. "Well, I am sorry, I would normally take a new member into the clubhouse and introduce you to some of the members, but I have got to wait here for Mr Keene. But please go across and introduce yourself. Or do you not have time – do you have to hurry off to Paddock's Farm? I will try and come across to the clubhouse later once I have enrolled Mr Keene. It's Captain's Day, one of the most important days in the club calendar, so there's a bumper crowd in. Do you know the tradition of the Captain's Drive In?"

"I'm sorry about that. I didn't realise that space was reserved, I didn't see the sign. But someone explained it to me so I moved my car. Sorry."

"Eh?"

"In the car park when I drove into the Lady Captain's space."

"Oh no the Drive In has nothing to do with the car park. Talk to Mr Ramsbotham about it, he'll be delighted to tell you all about it. He's here today. Oh and Benton Snivelgate, your opponent in the Shack, that is the Shackleton – he's here, too. Or was anyway. You'll want to see him to fix up your first-round tie. Do you know where the clubhouse is, it's just over there," said the Secretary opening the door and pointing. "Well nice to meet you."

Once he had dispatched Harry, he turned to Miss Murtle. "First thing Monday morning get that cheque into the bank account."

"Oh dear, are the club's finances as bad as that?"

"Oh no, it's not that, I want to get it cashed before he

plays Benton. Just in case that makes him change his mind and he stops the cheque. Oh, gosh," he said looking at Harry's completed membership form. "I've just seen where he lives – have you?"

"No."

"Winnie's Place."

"Oh no."

"That was a terrible business wasn't it."

"Yes it was. Quite awful. Still no reason why it should happen to him as well."

"No quite. But, just in case – definitely make sure to cash that cheque first thing Monday. I wonder where that Mr Keene's got to? He said he would be here at 4."

Chapter 2

Harry walked into the bar of the clubhouse to a hubbub of noise, fragments of conversation assailing him from all sides: "I should have taken a 6-iron... I hate that hole... there's too much sand in the bunkers... left a few out there for sure... your driver was working well today... have you heard poor old Jimmy Walton has had to go for another operation... you've got to play right of the flag when they put the pin in that position... got a really good deal on this winter's skiing... twice I lipped out, twice... there were some tough pin positions today... there's not enough sand in our bunkers..."

The room was heaving with people, all in groups talking away to one another. He looked around nervously to see if there was some opening to join a group, or to find a singleton he could chat to, or just someone making eye contact, someone alone at the bar waiting to be served who he could sidle up alongside and make conversation with. There didn't seem to be anyone. He looked for somewhere to join in, with something, anything. He thought perhaps it would be best to try to make contact with, what was his opponent's name, Benton Snivelgate.

He picked a well-upholstered middle-aged man of friendly countenance who was standing on the edge of a group near him to ask. "Please excuse me for butting in, but I am looking for Benton Snivelgate."

"My word," the man replied, looking him up and down, "they say policeman are getting younger, but I hadn't realised how young."

"No, I'm not a policeman."

"Bailiff?"

"No. I'm a new member, Harry King."

"Pleased to meet you Larry, I'm Willoughby Cornwallis. Benton? Doubt he'll be in here – he doesn't venture into the clubhouse, thank goodness. He was playing today – tried to interest me in some raffle tickets, I should cocoa – so he might still be floating around somewhere. But what on earth do you want him for if you are neither a policeman nor bailiff? Are you an unemployed cat burglar looking for work?"

"No, I don't steal cats. I am a writer. Or rather," he stuttered, "I want to be."

"What are you now?"

"Well I suppose I am not really anything. I have just graduated from uni. I have rented a place down here, and plan to write."

"Well I wish you good luck with that Gary. Why d'you want Benton?"

"I have been drawn to play him in the Shack." At the use of the slang term for the competition Harry felt a slight thrill. He realised his feeling of nervousness was a bit like a new boy at school and lapsing into the lingo of the place made him feel a bit more as if he belonged in this society by feeling and understanding, not just by enrolment.

"Bad luck. Oh – I've just spotted him through yonder window, walking towards the car park. You might catch him if you're quick."

"Thanks," and with that Harry was off.

"I'd be slow if I were you," said Willoughby as he turned back to the group.

"Who was that?" asked one of that number.

"Bod who wanted Benton."

"Policeman or bailiff?"

"Neither apparently."

"Too much to hope he is a hitman?"

"New member. Said his name was Gary. Or was it Larry? Perhaps it was Barry. He was called something anyway, I distinctly remember that."

"A new young member? We should have him stuffed and displayed."

"Wouldn't that rather defeat the benefit?" pointed out another in the group.

"Pirbright has made him play Benton in the Shack. That might defeat the benefit anyway," said Willoughby. "Wonder if we will see the poor lad again."

"Poor sod. Perhaps he will play so well that even Benton won't be able to find a way to cheat him out of victory."

In the car park Harry had caught up with who he presumed must be Benton Snivelgate, as he was the only man there. He wished he had asked what he had looked like. "Excuse me, you Benton Snivelgate?"

"You a policeman?"

"No."

"Bailiff?"

"I'm Harry King, a new member. I have been drawn to play you in the Shack." Again Harry felt that thrill of the lingo, the false impression that he already belonged in this society.

"Oh yes, I am he. Sorry at my ah, ahem, little joke. But I thought I was playing Cowpatch? And then Sheep's Bum, if I win."

"No, he had to scratch if you mean Mr Cowmeadow – I have been drafted in as his replacement."

"Drafted in? When?"

"Today, I joined the club this afternoon."

"Today?"

"Yes."

"That seems most irregular."

"Oh it is all above board, I saw the Secretary this afternoon, paid my fees and everything," said Harry, confused and a bit taken aback.

"Not that: I am sure your membership is all above board. But being drafted in after the competition has begun. All sounds most irregular. I have been drawn to play Mr Cowmeadow, I can't see how the draw can be changed after it has been made. It all sounds most irregular."

"I was asked if I wanted to play," said Harry, "by the Secretary. Obviously I said yes."

"I am not saying it is your fault. Just that ah, ahem, it might look bad for you if you, as a new member, start off by doing something unethical. You might get a bad reputation at the club and you don't want that do you? Not as a new member. I can see it is not your fault, you probably didn't understand the rules, the unspoken rules of the club, the ah, ahem, conventions of the club. All clubs have their ways and traditions, which are not written down but are unspoken."

"Well the Secretary led me to think it was alright."

"Yes, well he is not actually a member is he? He is an employee. I have been a member here since before you were born."

"Well if there is a problem, should we not sort it out now with the Secretary?"

"We don't want to embarrass the man do we? Or rather, you don't want to embarrass him on your first day. You don't want to fall out with the Secretary do you? Not at the start of your membership, could be very awkward."

"I can't see how I would be falling out with the Secretary by doing what he said. I would surely be more likely to do that if I, a member of ten minutes' standing, told him I knew more about the club rules and conventions than him?"

"Are you saying I, who has been a member for more years than you have been alive, do not know the club's conventions? I ah, ahem, could also point out that I own part of this course."

"As I said, I feel it is something better sorted out between you and the Secretary. Shall we go and see him now?"

"He won't want to be bothered on Captain's Day. I don't want to embarrass you or cause you to get a bad reputation, so how about we just agree, for the sake of argument, that the tie is valid but you give me a walkover and I progress into the next round? Be less embarrassing for you. It is only you I am thinking about here. I would happily play you, but other members might feel your behaviour a bit off, and I wouldn't want you to suffer that. It wouldn't be fair on you – I am ah, ahem, thinking of your reputation here."

"I think we'd better see the Secretary," said Harry, keen not to upset anyone and not sure that he wasn't going to end up upsetting everyone somehow.

"I don't think that would be appropriate," said Benton. "You do not want to embarrass him, as I have just said."

But, without saying anything else, Harry turned heel and walked to the Secretary's office. He realised after a while that Benton was not following, but he carried on anyway, and went into the office.

The Secretary looked up, "Ah, you I take it are Mr Keene; we have been expecting you. Oh it's you," he said, his face falling. "Never mind, not your fault. How can I help? Still trying to find Paddock's Farm are you? It's quite simple really, I don't know how you've got confused, what you need to do is turn left when..."

"No, no, it's not that," cut in Harry. "Mr Snivelgate is saying I can't take part in the Shackleton," he didn't feel able to use its apparent nickname at so early a stage in his membership when speaking with the Secretary, "as the draw has already been made."

"He is wrong. If someone pulls out from the first round a replacement is summoned from the top of the reserve list. You were head of the reserve list. It's in the club rules. If he has a problem, tell him to put it in writing to the Competitions Committee."

"He was saying that there was an unspoken rule that the person called up waives his place, as it were."

"He is right that this is unspoken. No one has ever said such a daft thing. This is a golf club and exists for people to play golf."

"Thank you, just thought I'd check." Harry left to tell Benton, and met him coming towards the Secretary's office. "I have just had a word with the Secretary, and he says there is neither a written nor unspoken rule to prevent me playing."

"The Secretary is relatively new here after the previous one had some, ah, ahem, fish trouble. I was just going to have a word with him myself actually."

"Shall I come in with you?"

"Best you do not."

Harry was left standing outside, thinking that he had never realised becoming a member of a golf club was going to become so political so soon. All he wanted to do was play some golf, get to know people and make friends. He had already decided that Benton was unlikely to be one of those friends.

The Secretary heard the door open "ah hallo, do come in," invited the Secretary, "I take it you are Mr Kee... oh blast it."

"Ah Mr Secretary," said Benton, "I was hoping to have a word with you."

"I hear you have been telling Mr um, our newest member that he isn't allowed to play in the Shack?" said the Secretary. "Not true. If someone pulls out from the first round of a competition a replacement is summoned from the reserve list. Mr er um, well he was top of the reserve list so he now plays you."

"I think he was a little concerned that he might be doing wrong by entering the competition in an unorthodox way. I tried to reassure him that I was fine with it. He's a new member you know and so anxious to start off on the right foot with someone so senior in the club. I'm glad you have managed to reassure him it is alright. I had told him it would be quite in order but I could see he wasn't convinced. Good work, Secretary. No, I just popped in so you could get some raffle tickets. We are raising money for club funds."

"I have already bought some."

"No, I sold some to Miss Murtle, but you weren't in, so I said I'd come back when you were. We are raising money for club funds."

"Miss Murtle bought some for me."

"No, she only bought some for herself."

"No, she bought some for me – two books."

"You want two books for yourself? Certainly."

"No I do not."

"Quite right. If Miss Murtle bought two you feel to ought to buy three being her boss. Quite understand, very fair of you. It's what makes you such a good Secretary; well, better than that fish fellow anyway."

"No. I do not want to buy any more books, thank you. I already have plenty."

"More? You haven't bought any so far."

"This office has already bought two books. Oh excuse me, I hear the phone in my office, please excuse me. I think this might be Mr Keene – we are expecting a prospective new member today." The Secretary hurried through to the back office to answer the phone there which he had just called surreptitiously from his mobile. It was a technique he had perfected as a way to avoid talking to members.

Benton found Harry still outside the office. "Ah I, ahem, have spoken to the Secretary and although he agreed you should not have been allowed in to the competition by such means, as I was so keen to give you the chance to play, he has agreed that I can indeed play you on my insistence."

"Oh," said Harry, by now thoroughly confused.

"Have you played here much?" asked Benton.

"I haven't actually played the course at all. Don't even know it, to be honest."

"Don't you?"

"No. I'd better play a few rounds before our match so as to know where I am going, shouldn't I? Perhaps we could fix up our match for sometime the week after next maybe? Give me a chance to get acquainted."

"Another thing the Secretary said was, in the view of the ah, ahem, exceptional circumstances of our fixture that it better be played as soon as possible. That way it would be by way of a *fait accompli* and so not attract attention. He ah, ahem suggested it were best if we play our match tomorrow."

"Er, that is a bit soon, how about later in the week – as it'll give me a chance to play the course and know where I'm going."

"I can't make any day next week other than tomorrow. Don't worry, I can talk you round the course if you like as we play. It's all quite simple and obvious."

"Well we better make it tomorrow then."

"Tomorrow? Oh good. How about we tee off at 8 – are you an early riser?"

"Yes, I am as a matter of fact."

"Oh, on second thoughts be better to play at 11. Be, ah, ahem, less crowded then. Ah well see you tomorrow," and with a rather nervous, gauche wave, Benton was off.

Harry, retreated back to the bar. Willoughby greeted him: "Find him?"

"Yes, thank you."

"Bad luck."

"I'm playing him tomorrow morning."

"Bad luck."

"Oh, is he a good player?"

"Not really, no. But he's hard to beat, shall we say. I daresay you need a stiff drink after that."

"Yes, thank you, I think I do."

"Splendid. If you're going to the bar, you can get one for me, too, there's a pal. I'll have a large whisky. Then I'll introduce to you some of the faces. Well you don't want to meet the faces, fish-faced gargoyles most of them, but they're attached to some decent coves in certain cases."

"The Secretary suggested I speak to a Mr Ramsbotham."

"Rambo? Gosh he does have a funny idea of how to show a chap a fun time, our Secretary – first Benton, then Rambo. Rambo's not as bad as Benton though, just don't let him near a milk jug."

"Er, I won't then," said Harry not sure what to make of this statement. He guessed it was a golf term that he was not familiar with. He knew little as yet of the language of golf. "He suggested I ask him about the tradition of the captain's driving. Is Mr Ramsbotham the club historian or something?"

"Of those two options I would plump for the latter. But I suppose you could say he is an amateur local historian. Loves his history."

"Does this place have an interesting history?"

"I don't know – I have only had it told to me by Rambo. But it might. The Captain's Drive In you mean? Oh I can tell you about that – and quicker than old Rambo will do – if y'really wanna know."

"Oh please do," said Harry. Then as an afterthought he asked: "What exactly is the Drive In?"

"Ceremony to usher in the new captain. He drives a ball off the 1st tee and thereupon becomes captain and everyone watching applauds. That's it basically."

"Right," said Harry, not a lot the wiser.

"It is a bastardisation of the way captains were appointed in days of yore when the club captain was the winner of the club championship. Golf club captains don't lead the side against other teams, so ability at golf isn't important. What they did was run the club; still do to a certain extent, though now it's a combination of Captain, committees, Secretary and whatnot."

"It dawned on people," continued Willoughby, "in badly run clubs that the best golfer was not necessarily the best administrator, chairman, man-manager, financial expert, after-dinner speaker and whatnot. Plus, as club champions can often be the same people year after year, those who got landed with the job year after year naturally began to resent it. So clubs started appointing their captains instead from those who had the time, inclination and ability to do the job. Well the last one perhaps not so much."

"But to maintain the tradition that the captain is chosen through golfing merit, clubs devised a competition in which only the captain-elect took part, and once he had teed off, in the absence of other competitors, he was the winner and hence became club captain."

"Oh ingenious," said Harry feeling some comment was required of him.

"Or a way to maintain a tradition that was unwanted and make something more complicated than it need be. One or the other. But we have turned the Drive In into a bit of an occasion here – we have a fun nine-hole competition afterwards of the captain's devising. This year's captain chose a three-club competition," then, seeing that Harry may not have comprehended what this was, he added: "whereby you can only use three clubs plus your putter all the way round. As it's a way of making a difficult game even harder, I sat that one out."

He took Harry on a partial tour around the bar introducing him to some of the people there. Although the gesture was kindly meant, Harry did wonder whether Willoughby was the ideal person to do it. One of those he introduced Harry to he described as Thingummybob and another as Old Hoojameflip. Names, it was clear, did not rank high in importance in Willoughby's world, such that he was not sure even when a name was given if it was the right one. Harry got into the habit, after being introduced, of proffering his hand to shake and saying 'Harry' hoping the other person would reciprocate and confirm their name. This also helped to correct the times when Willoughby had wrongly introduced him, normally as Larry; sometimes as Barry and, once, as Gary.

Harry thus moved from group to group, never really being absorbed by one, but, the ice having been broken for him, he was able to conduct desultory conversation with various strangers. Often it was to answer where he normally played, or what was his previous club; questions he didn't have satisfactory answers to, or rather it was 'nowhere' and 'didn't have one.'

One member, the one he had been introduced to as Gary had even replied "pleased to meet you Barry. So what brings you to our neck of the woods, Larry?"

"You play golf?"

"Yes, well I have just started."

"Play any other sport?"

"At university I played Real Tennis."

"Is there fake tennis?"

"There is also Lawn Tennis, which is the younger game. The original version of tennis was indoors and had an irregularly shaped court which originated from medieval courtyards. Henry VIII was a keen player and it's from him we get the word service."

"Is that so?"

"He reckoned it was infradig for a monarch to start a rally, so got a servant to do so, who then had to beetle off the court as soon as he had done that – a door was built into the court by the serving area to enable the servant to exit proceedings pronto. That is why you start tennis with a serve."

"Oh, interesting."

"Do you play any other sports?" asked Harry.

"I used to race cars."

"Did you? Why did you give up?"

"The cars were much faster than me. Well nice to meet you Barry, see you around no doubt. Welcome to the club."

Shortly afterwards, as Harry was talking away to someone, the room suddenly became almost silent. He looked around just in time to see probably the most attractive girl he had ever seen glide into the room. He found himself temporarily unable to speak. Then following her came a girl even more attractive than the first, something he would not have believed had he not seen it with his own eyes. She was definitely, unquestionably the most attractive girl he had ever seen. The first girl seemed aware of the impact she was making, and welcomed that many eyes were on her; the second seemed oblivious as she came into the room, something that, to an instantly smitten Harry, only added to her loveliness.

"Close your mouth!" he heard a lady's voice bark. Guiltily, Harry tried to shut his mouth, only to find it was already closed.

"Ah, things have looked up around here," remarked the member he was talking to. "Well not for Wilko – that was Mrs Wilkinson you heard telling him off," he explained.

"Sounded more like an order to me," replied Harry.

"Sorry," said his interlocutor, leaning forward, "like what?"

"Like an order."

"Oh yes, thank you, Very generous of you to be ordering them in. I'll have another pint, thanks – very kind of you."

"Oh, er, right."

"Oh, are you getting them in Larry? That's very good of you. I'll have a pint, too," said the third of the group. "Very civil of you, cheers."

When Harry returned from the bar with the drinks, the third chap, feeling the need to make conversation, said: "So you're just joined the club then have you?"

"Yes, today."

"Live locally do you?"

"I do now, I have rented a cottage in the village."

"Oh, which one?"

"Winnie's Place."

"Oh... have you," he said hurriedly moving away.

Harry wondered what to do next, then he spotted a man

wandering across the room towards him looking a bit lost. He saw his chance to make an introduction.

"Hallo," he said holding out his hand "Harry."

"Oh hallo, but I am not..."

"Not what?"

"Sorry?"

"You apologised and said you were not, but you didn't say what you're not."

"Oh dear, sorry. My wife criticises me for not finishing um."

"For not what?"

"Um what?"

"You said your wife criticised you for not finishing something..."

"Does she? So does mine. Mine criticises me for not finishing my sentences. What does yours criticise you... um.... I am looking for someone, a new person."

"A baby?"

"No, an adult. A new member called um..."

"Harry?"

"Who? No, um, no it's not Harry. I am Chairman of the Membership Committee and it's part of my role to welcome new members and I was told there was a new member over here called um..."

"I'm Harry."

"Pleased to meet you Harry. I don't think we've met before. I'm Brian, I'm the chairman of... um... No the chap I am looking for is um..."

"Harry? I'm a new member."

"Oh are you? Then perhaps you might know him as he's a fellow new member, called um Larry."

"I think that's me."

"I thought you just said that you were called Harry."

"I am."

"Then how can you be called Larry? Is it some sort of nickname?"

"It seems to be this afternoon."

"Curious, I always thought it was short for Lawrence. I knew a chap called Lawrence once."

"Did you?"

"Did I what, sorry?" he said distractedly looking around the room.

"Know someone called Lawrence?"

"Oh, are you looking for him, too? Well if I find him I'll tell you. But I don't think he's here, everyone in the room I seem to recognise. Perhaps he has been playing here a while as a guest, but has only just become a member. Well nice to..." and with that he wandered off.

Chapter 3

Harry was back at the bar buying more drinks. His attempts to get to know people had resulted in this happening too often for his liking. He felt he was, albeit unwittingly, that chap at the school tuck shop trying to buy friends, a process that rarely brought the desired friendship. However, unlike that chap, he was not going round offering to buy people things; it was just that somehow he got manoeuvred into it in various ways. Perhaps it would have been better if he had started off by just playing in some club competitions as the Secretary had suggested. Mind you, the Secretary had also suggested he go into the bar and meet people.

"Oh heck, I don't have enough," said Harry looking in his wallet. He had taken out lots of cash last time he went to a cashpoint, as there wasn't one in the village. Now it was almost all gone.

"You say you have no money, Sir?" said the Steward.

"Well I did," stammered Harry, embarrassed, "I had lots of it, I thought, but with raffle tickets and drinks for half the room I don't seem to have any left. Can I pay by card?"

"No, Sir, we do not take cards. But, if you are a member, you could open an account."

"Oh excellent, could I? I am a member."

"It will be five pounds to open an account, Sir."

"Heck, will it? Can you just put that on the account as well – I don't even have a fiver on me. No, I don't," he said checking his wallet more for the show of it than in expectation that money would suddenly have materialised there. "Can I please put the five pounds on the account?"

"If you don't have five pounds, I regret you cannot open

an account, Sir. So I will have to ask you for the money now. It is £21."

"But I don't have the money. That's the point."

"Is there a problem?" asked a gentleman walking up to the bar.

"Well yes," said Harry. "I have ordered a round of drinks, and as I don't have the cash for it on me, and I'm a new member, I wanted to set up an account. But I can't as that requires me to have five pounds to give this gentlemen, but I don't have any money on me, hence why I needed to open an account in the first place."

"Oh that's not right. I'm Ramsbotham by the way, Chairman of the House Committee. Chairman."

Harry looked at the person now standing alongside him. He was, he estimated, someone in their late fifties, maybe early sixties; grey of complexion; knock-kneed; wearing a pair of cords designed for someone of another shape, certainly someone shorter of leg, the effect enhanced by one of the trouser legs being caught in the top of his sock; also of someone slimmer, for his pocket insides were forced outwards, as too much waist was crammed into too little space. His trousers were winning the fight to contain an extensive waist, but the solitary button at the front looked under considerable strain in so doing. He was peering at Harry through a pair of thick glasses worn lopsidedly. The part of his appearance he had obviously paid most attention was his greying hair which he had combed over an extensive bald patch, or rather over only half of it as the strands were only long enough to go partially across the crown, thereby drawing attention to his baldness. On his top lip, either a moustache had come to die or some bristles had bumped into one another without much sense of collective spirit. This was, Harry reflected, the person they called Rambo.

"No that's not right," repeated Mr Ramsbotham, with an air of mildly peeved belligerence that Harry was to learn was the other's default setting.

"That's what I was thinking," said Harry.

"I am Chairman of the House Committee, the chairman," he replied in a way that made Harry feel that he was being chided for venturing an opinion which was not his place in the presence of such an eminent club personage. "Steward," commanded Mr Ramsbotham calling the Steward over. "I hear there is a problem that this gentleman, a new member, wants to open an account as he has run out of cash and has drinks to buy, but he cannot so do as he needs cash to do so, but he cannot do so as he has no cash to so do."

"Yes, Sir, that is indeed the situation. Opening an account requires a cash payment of five pounds to be made."

"I see where the problem is," said Mr Ramsbotham to Harry. "We have a very obvious problem here don't we?"

"Well I didn't like to say so, being my first day as member here – but yes."

"Yes, I spotted it at once. I spotted it at once. Don't worry, Harry, I will sort this. I am the Chairman of the House Committee, so the bar comes under my remit."

"Thank you," replied Harry.

"Here, here's a fiver, so now you can open an account. Don't worry, you can owe it me. Better still why don't you just buy me a drink and we'll be all square. Get me my usual."

"Oh yes um, thank you," he said to Mr Ramsbotham and then to the Steward: "Oh and can you add a drink for Mr Ramsbotham here, please."

"He doesn't want a pot of tea does he?" asked the Steward, looking anxious.

"I'm not sure. He just said he wanted his usual."

"Oh good."

"Oh," said Mr Ramsbotham walking up to Harry again, "I forgot I was in a round with Todd so better get him a drink, too. He'll also have his usual."

"Oh, okay," said Harry reluctantly.

"Oh and another thing, I suggest you try a packet of our crisps, Harry, they do good crisps here, bit of a speciality of the house – have you tried some of our crisps yet?"

"No I haven't."

"Two packets of crisps too, please Steward for Harry, here," he called out. "Yes, you must try the crisps in here, Harry."

"If I can just ask you for some details, Sir," said the Steward, thrusting a form towards Harry, "then I can set up your account for you."

"So, you are a new member are you," said Mr Ramsbotham. "Did you watch the Captain's Drive In?" Harry said he had not. "You must be wondering then what our little do here today is all about. It's the Captain's Drive In. Do you know the tradition behind the Captain's Drive In?"

"Yes, I do actually, the gentleman over..."

"It's quite an interesting story," continued Mr Ramsbotham oblivious to what Harry had said for he had not listened. "Well originally in the mid-18th century, when golf clubs were first founded, although, of course the game of golf had been played for many years, centuries indeed, before that, although how many centuries is a matter of some dispute among the historians as quite when what we would now term, or describe as some may prefer to say, although I prefer the term 'term', what we may term as golf started is disputed making us in what you might call us in golf history circles disputatious because golf evolved like all sports so what counts as golf and what..."

As Mr Ramsbotham ploughed on, Harry filled in the form and handed it to the Steward. "Thank you, Sir. Now if I can just ask you to sign for these drinks, it's £33.50."

"I thought it was £21?"

"It was, Sir. But then you ordered two more drinks and two packets of crisps."

"Oh, of course. He said the crisps here were famous," said Harry looking at the two packets in front of him. They looked like any old bog-standard crisps you could buy in a supermarket or corner shop. "I thought they were going to be handmade or something. Is it true that the club is famous for its crisps?" asked Harry dubiously of the Steward, looking at the mass-produced packet of crisps.

"I understand the cheese-and-onion crisps have become much talked about. I claim no credit for it myself, Sir, for I did not select or buy these crisps you understand. But Mr Ramsbotham certainly seems to value them highly – he has bought lots of packets."

Harry opened one of the packets and munched on a crisp. He then took another. Both tasted just like any other crisps as far as he could tell, neither better nor worse. Well, if anything, marginally worse.

"Would you like some crisps?" he said thrusting the other packet towards Mr Ramsbotham, who was still in full flow.

"No thank you, I don't like crisps myself," said Mr Ramsbotham briefly breaking from his monologue which he promptly resumed. "So in 1806 I think it was, or was it 1805, anyway it doesn't really matter, it doesn't really matter, no it was 1805, or was it? It doesn't really matter much as no-one is quite sure of the exact date, but one date has been accepted as the most likely. No it was 1806. Or was it 1805? I have it written down at home somewhere so I could look it up if you really want to know and tell you another time, as I have written in my blue notebook, or is it my green one, no the blue one. The St. Andrews Club as it was known then, decided that rather than award the captaincy of the club to the golfer who had won the Silver Cup or of the Challenge for the Silver Club as it was more formerly known, but which we nowadays more commonly refer to as the Silver Cup and when I say 'we' what I mean that by that is..."

"Are these our drinks, Harry?" Harry realised that he had not given the people who he had been originally talking to, and had been buying drinks for, their drinks.

"Oh sorry, yes. Would you like some crisps?" Harry asked proffering a packet to them.

"Cheese and onion?" one of them laughed.

"Yes."

"No thanks."

"I was told they were a speciality of the club."

"They have become so, yes. Well thanks again for the drinks, Harry – very good of you." And with that the trio of gentlemen sidled away, leaving him alone again with Mr Ramsbotham. As Mr Ramsbotham pressed on with his lengthy monologue, Harry's attention wandered, his eyes tracking the movements of the girl who had bustled in after the other girl. She was obviously well known to Willoughby Cornwallis, for she had bounded up to him and given him a big hug and a kiss. Harry found himself strangely envious. He wondered what the relationship between them was. They were across the other side of a noisy room, so he had no idea what they were saying, all he could do was guess from body language. Their age difference automatically sent him away from the idea that they were husband and wife, or boyfriend and girlfriend. Or could they be, he thought with a sting of jealousy. No the greeting was not of that, it was more one might give to a favourite uncle or a firm family friend. She looked a bit like him in some ways, so maybe he was an uncle. Or her father? No, it hadn't seemed the greeting someone would give their father. Or maybe it was. And what of the other girl, how did she fit in? He tried to discern the similarities between the girls – they looked a bit alike, not enough perhaps to be sisters, but maybe cousins; perhaps half-sisters? Was it that Willoughby was father to one, uncle to another? Or uncle to both? Or neither of these. He wondered how long it would be before he could escape the tedious clutches of Mr Ramsbotham and find a reason to talk to Willoughby again. Could he indeed really impose himself on Willoughby again, after all he had given him a lot of his time already. Perhaps he should just walk up to the one of the girls – they were, after all, more his age than almost everyone else in the room. Willoughby had given him a lot of his time and introduced him to others in the room; but the one person he wished to be introduced to, Willoughby had not.

"So you see that is why we have the Captain's Drive In. It was quite an interesting story wasn't it?" Harry became aware that Mr Ramsbotham had finally stopped talking.

"Yes, Willoughby Cornwallis had told me about it all," he remarked absent-mindedly. The girl was now going off to talk to another man, and Harry was trying to divine what sort of relationship, if any, existed between those parties. "Who are those two girls behind you?" he asked Mr Ramsbotham.

But Mr Ramsbotham was not listening. He had embarked upon another rambling exposition of a piece of golfing history.

"Now then Rambo." Harry was delighted to find that Willoughby had loomed up over his shoulder. "You must not hog this new young member here. It's important he circulates and gets to know all the crowd, not just its shining lights," he said and Mr Ramsbotham's responding smile was in recognition of the correctness of Willoughby's description of him.

"I was just telling Harry here why golf courses are traditionally of 18 holes."

"Early courses were of any number of holes but then courses began to copy St Andrews in having 18 of them," Willoughby said.

"Well in a way you are right, but it is not as simple as that. It's quite an interesting story actually...."

"Which we have no time for now," cut in Willoughby firmly, "and anyway Rambo are you sure that you should be giving people all these lectures about golf history?"

"Why?" he demanded with his particular blend of peevishness and belligerence.

"I am thinking of that book of yours we hear so much about. If you tell everyone its contents every time you corral someone, what's to make them read the book? It's like those newspaper serialisations – you've read the best bits in the paper so why buy the book?"

"Oh, I hadn't thought of it like that. Don't give the milk away as otherwise they won't buy the cow?"

"I wouldn't mention milk around Anun if I were you. Not after the milk jug incident," counselled Willoughby, who then then had to raise his voice a little to drown out the other's angry splutterings. "Think about it logically, if you can – who is most likely to read a book about a golf club. Why it's the members of that club, but if they already know what is in the book as they have been told it in copious and repetitious detail several times over they won't. If you want your book to be a success, if I were you I wouldn't talk about any of it, or indeed anything about golf history, when you are in the clubhouse. Keep your powder dry."

"Oh are you writing a book," said Harry, now genuinely interested in something Mr Ramsbotham might say, "what's it about?"

Rambo seemed torn between defending himself against what he clearly viewed as an unjust accusation by Willoughby to do with milk jugs, and answering Harry. In the end the chance to talk about himself, one of his favourite topics, won over. "It's a history of the club."

"Oh, I will look forward to reading that. How did you find a publisher for it?" Harry asked from professional curiosity.

"Yes, I have always had a keen interest in history, it goes back ages," said Mr Ramsbotham, again oblivious of what had been said to him.

"Well history does," pointed out Willoughby.

"Yes, it's always been one of my interests since I was child," Mr Ramsbotham ploughed on, oblivious that Willoughby had said anything. "My wife suggested, now that I am retired, that I devote my time to researching and then writing a history of the golf club. The book was her idea. She has become very keen on me writing a history of the area and the golf club. Well in fact she said I might start with a history of the club and when I have finished that move on to do a history of the area. She has been very supportive of the book idea and has converted the shed at the bottom of the garden into a writing room for me. She says all the best writers have a set pattern of work, and so I must do the same and so she makes sure I am down there by nine o'clock every morning and doesn't allow me back into the house until 5pm. She says that way I can focus on my work. I did worry that I would be neglecting her by leaving her alone all day, but she says she will put up with that if it helps me get on with my book. Isn't that selfless of her? We used to have some interesting conversations over lunch, but she fears if I break off from work for lunch I will lose my train of thought, so she now brings me my lunch on a tray for me to eat alone in the shed, so that I don't have to break off from my work. Isn't that kind of her? She is one in a million my wife."

"She must be," said Willoughby. "But you can't be down in your writing hut every day as you seem to be here one heck of a lot. Shouldn't you be limiting your visits to the club so as not to neglect your art?"

"No I don't do art, it's not a picture book I am doing, although of course I plan to include some pictures in it. There are some quite interesting pictures of this club, historical photographs I mean. I have been going through some of the old stuff, for instance, I don't know if you know this, and I confess I didn't, though perhaps I should have though there is no reason I suppose why I should, but did you know that the parking spaces in the car park used to be laid out in a different formation, or a partially different formation anyway, as the main..."

"No, Rambo," said Willoughby sharply so as to cut off what threatened to be another long rambling exposition of interest only to the rambler. "I mean should you not be limiting all this time you have been spending in the club so as to focus instead on writing your book? It seems to be all play and no work with playboys like you."

"Well that is also my wife's idea. She says if I am writing about the golf club I should really immerse myself in the subject matter, and so with any free time left over she is very keen that I am down here rather than at home. She has really got behind my book, you see, been really supportive. Some days I hardly see her at all. But she says me doing the book makes it all bearable."

"How did you find a publisher?" Harry asked again.

"Oh I haven't got a publisher for it. Not yet. I was a bit worried about starting a big project like this without knowing that it had a publisher waiting at the end of it all. I did approach some but none seemed to be interested, and my wife said I was doing it the wrong way. She said no-one was going to commission a book from me as I didn't have a track record in writing books, so the thing was just to get on and do it and then I would have a finished manuscript to show to publishers."

"Well when I say no publisher seemed to be interested," he continued "that is not strictly true as one was. What I meant by that previous statement is that it was the other publishers who were not interested – well those of them that is who I had approached – who were not interested for there was one publisher who I had approached who had been interested. He had seemed really keen. A small publishing house which specialises in local history. I had a meeting with the chap and told him all about my book and my researches. Unfortunately I got a letter a few days after our meeting saying that they had had a corporate restructure and so they were no longer able to take an interest in my work, but he wished me the best of luck in placing it elsewhere. Very nice letter it was – I could see my book idea had made a big impression on him. I don't mind confessing that I had been thinking of abandoning my project, but receiving this letter gave me fresh heart to continue for obviously people in the publishing industry saw merit in my book."

"Oh Rambo," said Willoughby, "there was a chap over there who had a question, something to do with the history of golf. I said I didn't know the answer but I knew a man who probably would."

"Who was this?"

"You."

"I mean the man who wanted to know," said Mr Ramsbotham impatiently, surveying the corner of the room.

"Oh I can't remember – you know how I am with names. He was over in the corner there, other side of the bar," said Willoughby. "I was going to call you over, but seeing you deep in conversation over here, I didn't. But I know he'd appreciate you giving him the answer – I am sure you know it."

"What was the question?" asked Mr Ramsbotham eagerly.

"It was, oh dear, it's slipped my mind. Oh it doesn't matter does it as he can ask you himself."

"If you can't remember his name, can you remember anything about him?"

"Oh let me see, yes, I can remember he said he took a 7 on the 6th, and he was wearing a polo shirt."

"Thanks," said Mr Ramsbotham.

Harry looked around the room. "Almost everyone is wearing a polo shirt," he remarked to Willoughby after Ramsbotham had scurried away.

"Exactly," said Willoughby. "I thought you needed rescuing, Larry."

"Thank you."

"Don't mention it, but if you wish to thank me you could buy me a drink, and I can introduce you to the girls."

"The girls?" said Harry, trying to make his words sound as casual as possible, resulting in the words coming out as an unnatural squeak.

"Yes, Rikki and Anun – I'm sure they'd love to meet you. In fact why don't you buy us all a drink? That will be a splendid way to make their acquaintance. Oh heck, Rambo has nabbed Rikki. That wasn't supposed to happen. She'll definitely welcome you inviting her over for a drink. So long as he doesn't snare Anun, too: she's very nervous around him after that milk jug business. Can't blame her."

Harry now had a name to put to the girl – Rikki. Rikki he told himself over again silently, just as he had been doing when told anyone's name that day. Not that he was going to forget her name in a hurry.

"Well get them in young Larry and I'll call the girls over. I'll have a whisky, and Anun will have a red wine and Half Pint a gin and tonic."

"She wants a red wine and a half pint of gin and tonic?" said Harry, startled.

"No, just a normal gin and tonic."

"Er yes," said Harry. The amount he had drunk he realised, or half realised, must be clouding his thought processes. "Who was the half pint for?"

"Sorry old boy, what's that?" said Willoughby, who had been distracted by looking to see where the girls had got to.

"I was asking who wants a half pint."

"Oh that's very generous of you, Harry," said a member of the group standing behind him, "I'll have a half pint. In fact, why not make it a full pint – save going back for the other half. Very good of you."

"Er yes, okay," said Harry to this gentleman.

"Fine new member this," said the gentlemen to

Willoughby, "a welcome addition to the club. Used to play genuine tennis you know."

"Genuine tennis?" said Willoughby to Harry.

"He means Real Tennis. I was telling him I played Real Tennis and the origins of the word service in tennis – how Henry VIII considered it beneath the dignity for such a lofty figure as himself to be asked to start a rally, so he always got a servant to start it, hence why you start tennis with a serve."

"I never knew that, that's interesting," said Willoughby, making it sound as though he was genuinely interested, which gratified Harry. In fact it was true for Willoughby loved accruing assorted information about words. He enjoyed the English language.

"You were telling me about someone wanting a half pint," Harry said to Willoughby. "One of the girls," he added hurriedly before he ended up buying yet more drinks for others in the room.

"No, a whisky, a gin and tonic and a glass of red wine, and whatever you are having. Oh sorry! Yes, my fault – Half Pint is Rikki."

"So Rikki wants a half pint. Of what?"

"Oh, sorry. No, Rikki's nickname is Half Pint. So that is one gin and tonic normal size for the young lady known as both Rikki and Half Pint. Whilst you rack up the drinks, I better go and extricate said female," announced Willoughby.

Harry turned his attention to the Steward and placing his order. He heard a voice at his shoulder. "Hullo, you Larry?"

He looked around, it was Rikki. Close up she looked even more beautiful than she did from a distance was his first reaction. His second was that he ought to say something, but his breath had been taken away.

"Erm, well it's Harry actually," he eventually managed to stutter out.

"Harry is it? I do apologise, although I am privately impressed that Willoughby has 80% of the letters right. I was half-expecting you to reply that your name was Octavius or Chauncey or something. Or Bert or John if your parents had been less adventurous at the font. I'm Rikki by the way, and I was informed by my admittedly less-than-reliable source that if I came over here you would ply me with alcohol and delight me with your conversation."

"Well your source was half right – I have a gin and tonic for you."

"Well cheers, Harry," she said raising her glass, "and thank you. Now you have got to do the entertaining conversation bit."

"What's Rikki short for?" was all Harry could think of to say, and regretted the lameness of it as soon as he said it.

"Richenda, but everyone calls me Rikki fortunately."

"What does that name Richenda mean?" was all he could think to reply to that.

"Other than that one's mother has a taste for the unusual? Powerful ruler."

"We'd make a great couple."

"That's very presumptuous of you Harry: we have only just met."

"No, gosh, sorry, no. I just meant my surname is King. As I am a King and you are a powerful ruler we would make a great couple. Or are you a ruler as in a bit of wood that you draw straight lines with?"

"Well I like to think my influence causes people to keep on the straight and narrow – though I'm not sure that has always been the case with Willoughby. No, as in the monarch – I am a powerful monarch. Or at least my name is – I have yet to live up my billing I regret. I shan't ask you what Harry's short for."

"No need, it's Chauncey."

"Chauncey?"

"Yes."

"So what does the name Chauncey mean then?"

"It means a person who wants to be called Harry."

"Not Larry?"

"No. Larry also means a person who wants to be called Harry."

"What about Barry, as it will only be a matter of time?"

"I happen to know this one, too. It means someone who wants to be called Larry. Which, of course in turn means he really wants to be called Harry. Well I am glad you have escaped Rambo," Harry added as a way to make conversation.

"Yes, it was quite easy this time as he seemed very agitated at knowing who has taken a six on the 7th. He is going round interrogating everyone. That's good isn't it, a six?"

"Well not really."

"Oh, I thought six was the best score you could get."

"Perhaps it's cricket you're thinking about?"

"Oh, is it?"

"Hallo," said Anun, "is this the Dumbo Avoiding Society, where refreshments are provided to its members – or so it said on the verbal invitation Willoughby issued."

"Oh yes," said Harry, "I have a red wine here for you."

"Thank you, kind Sir."

"This is Anun," Rikki introduced the newcomer.

"But not that sort of a nun. My name is short for Annunciata."

"Oh, I see, like Rikki."

"No, Rikki is not short for Annunciata," she corrected him.

"No, I meant Rikki is, er are you in the club?" said Harry in his embarrassment trying to turn the subject onto different ground.

"Oh dear, does my dress make me look that fat?" she said smoothing her thin dress against her body to show off her shapely form. "Or are you taking the meaning of Annunciata literally?"

"No, no," said Harry even more embarrassed than before. "No, I meant this golf club. This club."

"Not the pudding club?"

"No, no."

"Yes I am a member of this club."

"Oh excellent, perhaps we might play a round sometime?"

"Perhaps we might. But I don't play golf."

"Hallo, what are you youngsters talking about?" asked Willoughby, joining the group, "and will an old fogey like me understand it?"

Rikki replied: "Harry – his name is Harry – wants to team up with me and rule the world as that is what the stars say our destinies are, or rather what our names do."

"Have you any experience of ruling, Harry?" Willoughby asked.

"Well I used to rule lines in maths lessons."

"You seem ideally qualified then. What is life but one big maths lesson. But I thought you wanted to be a writer?"

"I do."

"Won't having to rule over your subjects cut into your writing time?"

"Yes, but it could be good for sales. One of the bestselling books of all time is Chairman Mao's Little Red Book, so all I need do is write my own little red book and ensure my subjects have to have it on their bookshelves whether they want to or not."

"What happens if the bookseller gets the orders muddled and everyone gets Mao's one instead?" pointed out Anun.

"Okay, I will make mine a different colour. I could have a little black book."

"Little black book?" queried Willoughby.

"Is your little black book interesting then?" asked Anun.

"Well of course, it, er no, no I don't mean it like that," said a flustered and reddening Harry, "I just wanted another colour. I'll make it a little blue book."

"So you are going to write blue books are you?" said Anun. "Tell me, how do you research your literary works?"

"Well, I am oh gosh, no, I don't mean that. Not blue books that like," he stammered. "I mean in blue covers."

"Which then have to be placed in brown paper ones from the sound of it?" said Anun. "Well I shall look forward to your literary output. But I suspect from the sound of it I will have to read it in the local lending library wearing dark glasses as I don't think mother will allow such material in the house. Mummy has strict views on what is and isn't appropriate under her roof."

"Oh heck, I've just seen the time," said Rikki, "we have to be going as we have to help Mumsie as Mags Murtle is coming to dinner and she needs some able-bodied assistance. We just popped in to say hello to you," she said, addressing Willoughby.

"And it was a delight to be said hello to," said Willoughby. "I will escort you young ladies part of the way home, if you like, as it is time I pootled off, too."

"In case we get mugged by a gang of field mice hiding in the bushes?" asked Anun.

"You can never be too sure. There are all sorts of things you can see in bushes around here I am led to believe," said Willoughby with a knowing look.

"Pleased to have met you Harry," he said as he left, "no doubt see you around."

"We must play a game some time," suggested Harry to Willoughby.

"Er, yes, yes some time, some time perhaps."

"Yes, look forward to playing around with you," said Anun teasingly to Harry as she left. Rikki, to his great sadness, did not say anything to him as she left.

Harry watched them leave; well, really he just watched Rikki leave.

"Have you seen Willoughby Cornwallis about?" Harry turned round – it was Mr Ramsbotham asking the question.

"He has just left. With Rikki."

"Tcch. He wanted me to answer someone's question, but he couldn't remember who it was who had asked the question other than he took 6 on the 7th, and I can't find who it is."

"It was 7 on the 6th," replied Harry absent-mindedly, his thoughts on other matters, all of them connected to Rikki.

"Tcch. He said a 6 on the 7th. Oh he is hopeless. He gets everything wrong. It's Larry isn't it?" said Rambo.

"No, Harry," said a still-distracted Harry.

"Yes, Larry, I understand you play Real Tennis. Do you know it's from Real Tennis that we get the name serve? It's quite an interesting story actually…"

Chapter 4

Harry was aware of an irritating, persistent noise. He was aware of it because it had woken him. Or had partially woken him at any rate. On the question as to whether he was awake – or indeed even still alive and well – his body seemed to be prevaricating over answering. Or, if it had made a decision, it had not sent the information through to his brain. The noise sounded vaguely familiar.

In his groggy state he reached out to turn off his alarm clock. He groped around. He knocked the glass off his bedside table. Then the alarm clock. The noise continued, a trilling sound. He leant out of bed to try to grab the clock which was now on the floor. He overstretched and toppled out, landing on his head. He cried out in pain.

He crawled across to the chair to where his clothes were strewn, for by now he had recognised the sound as that of his mobile phone tone. He fumbled around, then realised the sound was coming from under the bed where, further researches showed, his trousers were. He crawled under the bed and pulled from one of the pockets his trilling mobile.

"Hallo?" he croaked into the phone.

"Hallo, Percival Pirbright, Secretary of Tangents Golf Club here."

"Yeow." At the other's name, Harry had started, and cracked his head on the underneath of the bed. Panic – as well as the bed – had struck him: what had he done last night that the Secretary was phoning him so early in the morning. Er, was it actually early in the morning, he had no real idea what time it was. Had he been blackballed already? He had clearly drunk too much last night, his head told him that; but he couldn't remember doing anything wrong, but then he couldn't remember much of the later stages of the evening.

"Is everything alright?" asked Harry nervously. Just calm down, he told himself, act natural, the Secretary was probably calling about something about his match. Oh heck, he was due to be golfing today. In his current state he felt like doing anything but play golf. All he really wanted to do was crawl back into bed and let his body come to a considered opinion over several hours as to whether he was half alive or half dead.

"You'd better tell me. You alright?"

Heck, thought Harry. Why is the Secretary asking if I am alright, what on earth have I done, that he was phoning the next day to ask if I was alright? Well as least that's kind, considerate, shows a caring side to the club. No it isn't that – the Secretary doesn't phone every member each morning to ask how they are. Was it sarcastic, or merely a polite formality before the main item of business? No, that is a 'hope you are well', not the more demanding 'are you alright' presuming that you are not. Why would he not be alright? What had he done? Why had the Secretary told him that he better tell him first? What had others said about him and what he had done? What on earth had he done that he was being asked to tell his side of the story?

"Yes, I am fine thank you," he croaked nervously. Not that that was true. He felt anything but fine – his head hurt doubly so now, and he was worried.

"Oh good," said the Secretary, "I just thought I heard you yelp as if in pain."

Oh stop panicking, Harry told himself, it isn't that he had done something wrong, or that he was about to be blackballed or thrown out of the club. Maybe the Secretary was calling to tell him that his tee time had been brought forward, or put back – he hoped it was the latter. It was almost certainly nothing to do with his membership.

"I'm just phoning about your application for membership."

Oh heck what had he done? He was going to be blackballed. After one day of membership. Perhaps it wasn't anything wrong he had done, there was that strange business about the joining fee, perhaps he was due to pay one after all. Or perhaps he had been entered under the wrong category of membership.

"Sorry," said the Secretary, "I take that I am speaking to Larry Keene?"

"Who?" The name sounded vaguely familiar to Harry, where had he heard it before?

"Is that Larry Keene I am addressing?"

"No, Harry King."

"Who?"

"Harry King," he repeated, or a remnant of him, he thought to himself. "We met yesterday afternoon in your office, Mr Pirbright," he reminded him.

"Oh. Never mind, not your fault," and the line went dead.

Harry crawled out from under the bed, inadvertently kicking the clock further across the room. He retrieved it, and saw the time – yes, he had time for a shower and a pot of tea.

The shower partially revived him. Very partially. He would put its effects at one or two percent improvement, but at least it was improving. However, so rotten had he felt when he woke, there could almost only be an improvement. The pot of tea revived him further, as he sat hebetudinously in his small kitchen reflecting on the previous day. He had become a member of a golf club; he had bought, or so it seemed, every member of that club a drink; and he had met Rikki.

He regretted that he had so little time with her, and that he knew hardly anything about her. Did she have a boyfriend, a partner, what were her interests? He had no idea even what her relationship was with Willoughby Cornwallis. All he knew about her was that there was a natural, unaffected, unknowing beauty about her. But that was enough.

He checked his watch. It was time to go, as he was going to have to walk to the club as he had left his car there. He remembered that much. He also remembered he had emptied his wallet the previous night. He kept £20 petrol money in the car. He would have to raid that to partly replenish his wallet. Oh heck, just how much money had he spent last night? He realised he did not know – it was a wallet's worth plus whatever had ended up on his account. Probably best that he did not know.

He went outside and saw the roads were puddled – it had obviously rained hard in the night which, in his state, he had slept through obliviously.

He wished he was wearing Wellington boots. He thought about going back to put them on but that would involve a palaver, as he would then have to carry both his golf shoes and a spare pair of shoes for the clubhouse. He wasn't sure it was the right image to walk round the clubhouse in Wellingtons; indeed, it was probably not allowed.

Carrying his golf bag along the lanes to the club he was on the lookout in case anyone recognised him as a golfer – well they would of course, carrying his clubs, but whether they wished to acknowledge it and him. He wasn't clear who was and wasn't a member of the club. He had met some members last night, but he was not sure he would recognise many of them again; his memory was hazy as to parts of the previous night. No-one was about, which he was partly relieved about.

He got to his car. The bit of scraggy ground near the car park which he had parked on had become a boggy patch. As the car park now had empty spaces in it, he thought it best to move his car, as he had no idea if he would get into trouble for leaving it on that bit of waste ground overnight. It must belong to someone, he reasoned, and that someone was probably not the golf club. He did not want to make trouble for the club, his club, with the neighbours. In particular, as the new boy, he did not want to be one who caused it.

But his attempt to drive the car off this muddy patch just resulted in wheel spinning. The only way in which the car may have moved was deeper into the mud. He was aware of someone shouting 'hey' at him, but he ignored it. He guessed it might be the owner of the land, now probably doubly irate – originally that someone had used his land, and now that it was being churned up.

When the chap who was making the noise tapped on the window instead, he could no longer ignore him. He only wished if he was to have an altercation with an irate landowner that he was not starting at the disadvantage of being so hungover.

"You stuck?" the other man said in that curious way people had in such circumstances of making a statement of the obvious a question.

"I am afraid so, I should not really have parked here yesterday, I am sorry." He had turned to speak to his interlocutor as he spoke, and was relieved that the other was dressed as a golfer. Perhaps it was not the owner of the land or, if it was, at least he was a golfer. Oh heck, maybe that makes it worse – making enemies among the membership already.

"Do you want a push? Should be able to get you out.

You parked it here yesterday then? It chucked it down really hard in the night – bad luck."

"Yes," Harry stammered, wondering if he was admitting guilt in doing so, not only parking there, but leaving it there for over three-quarters of a day. "When I came the car park was full up. The only space left was reserved for the lady captain."

"Oh you should have parked in that. She doesn't drive, so never uses it. You a visitor?"

"Well, no. I am a member. I joined yesterday. That's why I had come to the club."

"Oh, pleased to meet you. I'm Jack Lyon and this is Jerry – Jerry Best," he said indicating someone walking up. "Jerry, you up for giving this chap's car a shove out before it gets foot rot, well tyre rot or whatever?"

"Sure."

The pair of them managed to push the car free. "Oh thank you," said Harry gratefully. "It's most kind. Oh heck, you seem to have got a bit splattered by mud. Sorry."

"Oh yes, never mind, can't be helped I suppose. You can buy us a drink to thank us."

"Well..."

"Don't tell me, you were just leaving."

"No. I am just arriving, well sort of. I am just about to play with Benton Snivelgate."

"You friends with Benton then?"

"No, don't know the fellow, I've been drawn against him in the Shack." Again he felt a thrill at using the lingo. "Don't know anyone here really, I've just moved to the village."

"Oh good. I was going to say if you were friends with Benton Snivelgate we should have left you there. Sorry, but Jerry here won the Hanky Panky Cup this year. Need I say more? You a new member you say?"

"Yes."

"Got an account at the bar?"

"Yes."

"Well that's okay, just pop in and tell the Steward that Jack and Jerry will be coming in later and they're to have a drink on your account. He knows who we are."

"Oh, ah, yes, thank you."

"You just moved to Tangents you say?"

"Yes I have rented Winnie's Place for the summer."

"Winnie's Place you say? Gosh. Oh, well I am sure that will be alright. It was probably just a one off. Possibly. Anyway don't forget – tell the Steward it's Jack and Jerry. Sorry, what's your name?"

"Harry – Harry King."

"Pleased to meet you Harry. Good luck with Benton. Hope you win. Watch out for the bunkers," laughed Jack and with that he and his golfing partner were off.

Harry got out of the car and then remembered the £20 note in the glove compartment. He collected that and gathered up his clubs and shoes and went to the locker room to change his shoes. Then he remembered he had to speak to the Steward so changed back into to his street shoes so that he could go into the bar.

"Ah hallo," he said to the Steward, "I am a new member, I was in here yesterday…"

"Yes, Sir, I remember." Harry was flattered that he was remembered: it made him feel more like a member of the club that the club servant knew him already. Then he panicked – why had the Steward remembered him? What had he done that was memorable? He wished he could remember more of the previous evening.

"I um, set up an account yesterday and er, a couple of members called Jerry and Jack will be coming in, and could you please let them have a drink on my account."

"You want to buy those two gentlemen a drink?"

"Yes, but I won't be here as I have to play golf, but I owe them a drink as a thank you for helping me, so if you could let them charge a drink to my account, that would be great. So if you could let Jack Lyon and Jerry, er sorry I forget his surname but if you could let them have pint on me that would be ace."

"Best?"

"Well a pint of whatever they want, but yes a pint of best if that's what they drink."

"No, Sir. I was not suggesting a drink, Sir."

"Oh, weren't you?"

"No, Sir, I was not."

"Oh, I thought you were."

"So I divined, Sir. But I was not."

"Oh, sorry," said Harry as something seemed to be expected of him.

"I was suggesting that one of the gentleman to whom you had referred and wished me to provide with a drink on the account you have opened is a Mr Jerry Best."

"Oh is he? Thanks, sorry."

"If you do not mind the remark, Sir, you seem as though you may be a trifle hungover?"

"I do not and I am."

"If you would permit me, Sir, I can suggest a cure for when you have a hangover which you may find advantageous to know."

"Chopping off my head? I had already thought of that."

"No, Sir, although I daresay that may also work. However I believe that there would be what one might term as undesirable side effects to such a course of action.

What I was about to suggest was a drink."

"The old hair of the dog you mean? No thank you. I think I have sworn off alcohol for life. Well at eleven o'clock in the morning certainly."

"No, what I would recommend to you is a non-alcoholic cocktail which acts as a remedy. I have known several gentlemen who have perhaps drunk with more enthusiasm than intelligence and long-term planning the night before say it has had pleasing recuperative effects in restoring them to a more optimal physical condition."

"It works you say?" said Harry.

"Yes, Sir. How I understand it is that the combination of ingredients serve to increase the activity of enzymes which break down alcohol in the body. When alcohol enters the body, it gets converted into acetaldehyde. A build-up of acetaldehyde causes the hangover, and the body can't fully recover until this has been digested."

"Ah yes, acetaldehyde. I remember doing something about it at school."

"Do you, Sir?" said the Steward stonily.

"Yes."

"Certain gentlemen have also told me they found the effect of the cocktail is enhanced by eating a plate of cucumber, cheese and tomato."

"Those enzymes again?" said Harry, who was finding the efforts of following what the other was saying strangely taxing.

"I believe that may be the case, Sir. Did you not do that also at school?"

"Okay, well what is this miracle cure of yours?"

"A cocktail made of coconut water, lime juice and pear juice. About two-thirds of the cocktail should be pear juice, a quarter lime juice and you top it up with coconut water."

"Oh excellent, well serve me up one then please."

"Pardon, Sir?"

"Please could you make me one of these miracle cures then. In fact no, forget that."

"Forget it, Sir?"

"Yes make me two instead. I think I may need a double dose. I have got to play 18 holes with Benton Snivelgate and my head really does not feel right."

"If you are to play with Mr Snivelgate then some gentlemen here might indeed say you were not right in the head. But I regret, Sir, I am unable to accede to your request to make you one of these hangover-ameliorating cocktails of which I have just been outlining the components."

"Eh?" said Harry slowly processing this information. "Oh, you mean it is too early and the bar is not open? Well could you make an exception?"

"You make that hypothesis, Sir, but how then would I decide who to make an exception for? If I made an exception for you would I not have to make an exception for everyone else? And then of course it would not be an exception it would be the norm, and so then to make an exception would be to do what had previously been considered the norm and so, to take the hypothetical instance you have just postulated, if it became the norm to serve someone a drink at 10.47am in the morning when it had previously been forbidden then it would be making an exception – which is what you just asked – to be forbidden to serve someone a drink at 10.47am in the morning. So you see that asking me to make an exception would be self-defeating."

"Two beers please Steward when you're free," said a member walking up to the bar.

"Certainly Sir," the Steward replied to him.

"Hey, how come you will serve them but not me?" asked Harry.

"I never said I would not serve you, Sir."

"Didn't you? I thought you had."

"No, Sir. As I would remind you, you yourself said you are not right in the head."

"Oh. Well can I have one of your miracle hangover cures then please?"

"No, Sir."

"Is that not you again saying you will not serve me?"

"No, Sir, it is not."

"Isn't it?" said Harry, wishing he was not having this discussion when severely hungover.

"No, Sir."

"Why not?"

"Because I am not refusing to serve you, Sir."

"Aren't you?"

"No, Sir."

"Well in that case can I have one of your miracle hangover cures then please."

"No, Sir."

"Why not?"

"Because I don't have any coconut water. Or lime juice. Or pear juice."

"Then why did you offer to make me one?"

"With respect, Sir, if you remember I did not. What I told you was that I could suggest a cure for when you have a hangover which you may find useful to know. I was only trying to be helpful. I am sorry if you did not wish me to be helpful, Sir. But I can offer you some cheese-and-onion flavoured crisps."

"Not cheese and tomato, or cheese and cucumber?"

"No, Sir."

"How will that help? The cheese I suppose?"

"The combination of cheese and onion when presented in crisp form aids the activation of ruffleine in the body. No doubt, Sir, you also did the effect of ruffleine at school?"

"Did we? Oh, ah, yes, probably. With Stinks Pinks."

"Stinks pinks, Sir?"

"Yes, the chemistry teacher, known to all as Stinks Pinks as he was always stinking the place out with experiments. His actual name was Pinkerton, but was known to all as Stinks Pinks." For a brief while he was transported to what seemed a simpler, happier time – not that it had seemed so at the time.

"Thank you for sharing that most interesting piece of information with me, Sir. Perhaps you may remember Mr Pinkerton teaching you that the function of ruffleine in the body is in regulating the rhythm of the functioning of the dispersal of benhendrozine so as to prevent bozone blockage?"

"Er ah do I? Yes I probably should, but please refresh the memory as my brain does not seem to be working that well this morning."

"Indeed, Sir. Well this in turn is said to have a beneficial effect on cheering some people up after people have what the medical profession term as got stewed to the gills the night before."

"What cheese-and-onion crisps?"

"So I have heard it said."

"Really?"

"So I have heard it said."

"Well better bung me a packet then."

"I beg your pardon Sir?"

"Please may I buy a packet of cheese-and-onion crisps?"

"Certainly, Sir. But if I remember correctly you were suggesting you needed two doses of the cocktail Sir, such was the degree of discomfort you were experiencing from your unwise behaviour yesterday evening."

"Yes but you don't have any cocktail juice, er, lime juice and pear drops and all the rest."

"No, Sir, what I was hinting at, and will be so bold as to suggest with your permission as I remember you saying something to the effect that your brain does not function well, is that as you thought you needed two doses of the cocktail to improve matters perhaps you may take a line through that logic and decide that two packets of crisps is required on the same principle."

"Oh, ah yes, I see what you mean. Two packets of crisps then please Steward."

"My pleasure, Sir."

Chapter 5

When Harry got to the 1st tee Benton was not around. He looked at the clubhouse clock, which was showing a minute to 11, and gingerly tried a few practice swings. He still felt awful.

The Secretary, who had seen the back of an unfamiliar person on the tee through his office window, came bustling out: "Hallo, we haven't met I think, are you by any chance Mr Keene?" Then, as Harry turned round: "Oh it's you. Never mind, not your fault." Then, seeing that Benton was approaching, the Secretary shot back into his office.

"Good morning Harry, you all ready?" Benton greeted him. "Do you ah, ahem know the rules of golf well?"

"Well I know the basics alright, but no, not in great depth I suppose."

"You will find me a stickler for the rules, I am afraid. But don't worry, anything you are unclear about just ask and if you are a bit vague about the rules – would you say that is a fair statement?"

"Well, yes, I suppose so."

"Then I will make sure we play the game in strict accordance with the rules. It's alright, I can make any decisions thrown up by the rules – don't worry we won't get onto trouble with the committee. You don't want to get into trouble with the committee do you?"

"No," said Harry.

"Quite right, not in your first week as a member. I can give you information so anything you want to know, just ask; but I can't give you anything that may be construed as advice. The rules of golf are very clear about that, and I am ah, ahem a stickler for the rules, I am afraid. It is the only way to be. People don't like me for it, but I always believe in honesty. Makes me unpopular with some, but there it is. You might have heard people talk about me and the rules."

"No I haven't. But, sure, any information you can offer would be greatly appreciated for, as I said yesterday, I haven't played this course before."

"Well the first hole curves around slightly to the left – do you have a scorecard?"

"Yes, thanks."

"Well that gives you the distance so you can tell how far away the green is although you can't actually see it as it's obscured from here by that mound and bush. But you'll see it for your second shot so long as you do not hit too far left. That green can be deceptive."

"In what way?"

"Sorry, I can't answer that, as that might be construed as giving advice, so forget that I said that. I shouldn't have said that. Forget that I said about this green being a bit deceptive and a hard one to hit and requiring a particular type of shot. Well good luck Harry – and I hope you have a good game."

"Thanks – you too."

Benton's opening drive was long and down the middle of the fairway. So, to his great relief, was Harry's. In the state he was feeling, he had not been sure that he would even make contact with the ball. It was not that long a shot, but it was straight and the ball was visible, sitting up on the fairway.

And his head had not fallen off, something he would have given long odds against only a short while ago.

His ball had finished up quite a few yards further from the hole than Benton's had, so it was his turn to play next. The green, now that he could see it, was raised, perched on its own wee hilltop. The green looked, oh only about 130 yards away, but from the size the flagstick must be further, about 160 or 170 yards. He looked back at the tee to try to gauge how far his ball had travelled, but it was not much help to his hungover brain as the curve of the fairway obscured the tee from view.

He pulled his 5-iron from his bag, as he normally hit that about 160 yards. He struck the ball well, to his delight and slight surprise, only for the ball fly over the green.

"Well that was a fine, clean hit," said Benton. "But it was a bit too good – you don't know your own strength," he laughed nervously.

"It must have been nearer than it looked – I thought it was about 150 yards away."

"Only about 120 from where you are I'd say."

"The flagstick looks further away than 120."

"Oh that flagstick is a special short one – that green is exposed and we found a normal flagstick would get blown down. So we have a shorter stick."

"Oh, I didn't know that. You could have told me," said Harry amiably.

"I remind you that you cannot ask advice from an opponent, and he cannot give it. I remind you also that this encompasses any comment or action that is intended to influence another player in making a stroke, choosing a club to use, or in deciding how to play a hole."

"That wasn't advice; that was information."

"That is debatable. I did not think I could tell you after I had so kindly and helpfully informed you that the green can be deceptive. I thought to tell you that this was because the flagstick size can give a false impression to first-time visitors would constitute giving advice and I don't want you to have to be disqualified, not in your first competition. I am ah, ahem, only thinking of your reputation here. Be an awful thing to get a reputation for breaking the rules in your very first competition at the club. That would soon spread around the club and well, I am just making sure you don't start off on the wrong foot. I am only thinking of you here. Just trying to be nice to a new member. If it were a social game I could give you all the advice in the world as it wouldn't matter then."

"If you like," continued Benton, "we could just abandon the match – you could give me a walkover – and we could play a nice social game instead and then I could give you all the advice in the world. It might help you in the long run. After all you are not going to win the Shackleton with all its rounds, are you, not with all the experienced golfers around. So this match is pointless anyway and there are few who know the course as well as I do."

Harry sidestepped the suggestion: "I see the pro offers playing lessons, I was wondering whether to book one. He could give me tips on how to play the course as well as some technical advice with my swing."

"Pah – I wouldn't ask him. He doesn't know anything about the course."

"Doesn't he?" asked Harry surprised.

"He has only been here a relatively short time, and anyway he spends all his time selling Mars bars and golf balls. He is just a glorified shop assistant. He never plays the course. If you want to know the course and its secrets you need to play with a long-standing member. I am one of the most senior members, and I could tell you far more about the course than any pro ever could – I would be cheaper too, as I would do it for half the price, well two-thirds, of what he charges. But only be about half in the end as I obviously wouldn't expect a tip."

"You'd have to tip the professional?"

"You'd tip a caddy for going round with you, wouldn't you, why should going round with a pro be any different? Stands to reason. If you like, we could fix up a lesson for you later this week – be only about £40, well £50, say. I know the course well and as parts of it are on my land I know more about the characteristics of this course than anyone else in the world – the lie of the land, how the drainage affects it and the roll of the ball, the all-important fringe density which so many overlook and don't understand, and so on."

"I thought you weren't free anytime this week? That's why we had to play today."

"Oh, ah, yes, I ah, ahem thought I wasn't; well I wasn't, but things got moved about."

Harry lost the first hole.

"The white tee for the 2nd is over there – competitions off white tees, everyday play off yellows, as I am sure you know," said Benton indicating a tee off to the side of the green, an isolated platform in a small copse.

This white tee for the second hole had caused a stir when it was introduced. Some members had loved it, as it made the hole more interesting, as from the previous tee, and indeed what was still the yellow tee, it was a dead straight hole of no great length, running parallel to the first fairway in the opposite direction for its early stages, before a dense clump of trees and bushes provided a barrier between the fairways. From the white tee, it now required a drive over the 1st fairway to reach the 2nd fairway, and a decision as to how much of the corner to attempt to take on – too much and you end in the rough between fairways, too little and you could end up in the rough on the left hand side of the 2nd fairway.

Benton, having won the previous hole, had honour and

so hit first. His shot, a mild hook, bounced towards the rough on the far side of the 2nd fairway.

"Bad luck, that's gone into the rough," remarked Harry.

"Looks like it doesn't it," replied Benton, "but it can be deceptive the land over there. What looks like it has rolled into the rough can often in fact be on the edge of the fairway, as there is more room out there than it looks like from way back here. Ah well, we will see in due course."

Harry's tee shot was a slice, which landed on the 1st fairway. Fortunately no-one was playing the 1st. His angle in to the green was blocked by trees and bushes so he had no option but to chip sideways to the target to get onto the correct fairway and have a clear route in to the green.

When he had done so and was walking to his ball, he saw Benton standing beside his ball, which was on the edge of the fairway.

"You found it okay and hacked out?" asked Harry.

"No, this ah, ahem, is where my tee shot finished."

"Oh, gosh, I could have sworn I'd seen it bounce into the rough. Could have sworn it."

"As I had said, it can be deceptive like that. The land holds the ball up more than you would expect over here – I no longer have the power to hit the ball far enough to get into the rough," Benton laughed nervously. "I am not a young man like you."

Benton won the second hole as well, Harry unable to claw back the extra shot it had taken him to get onto the correct fairway.

"Tricky hole that," Benton said as they walked off the green, "takes a bit of time to get to know how much of the corner to cut off. The course gets a bit easier from now on. That's me two up."

The 3rd hole was a short one, with the green easily

reachable with the tee shot. The hole played steeply uphill to a green whose surface was obscured from the tee. A shallow bunker was cut into the face of the slope in front of the green.

"The only way to tell where the hole has been cut in the green from here is to look at the colour of the flag," explained Benton, "red it's in the front third portion of the green, yellow in the middle, white at the back. This green is quite deep but flat so as long as you get it on the putting surface you should do okay, although get on the wrong part of the dance floor and you can leave yourself a long putt when the flag is at one of the ends of the green. But what you must do is avoid the tough greenside bunker as it can be difficult to get out."

Benton's ball just made it onto the front of the putting surface. "Well I am on the green at least, but a long way from the flag," he grimaced.

Harry sensed his chance to pull a hole back. The flag was white, so Benton looked to have a long putt, so if he could get his ball on the back part of the green then – if the green really was as long as Benton said – that would give him a chance. Plus aiming for the back of the green gives a greater chance of missing that bunker at the front Benton had warned him about – better to overclub than underclub.

"Oh good hit," said Benton as he watched Harry's tee shot soar away, "just hope you have avoided that treacherous bunker I was telling you about."

"I've cleared it easily," said Harry surprised. He was just hoping he had not hit it too far – it all depended on how deep the green was.

"Not the one at the front," Benton said testily, "the one at the back I was telling you about."

"I didn't know there was a bunker at the back."

Benton let out a sigh of exasperation. "Yes you do, I have just been telling you all about it and saying how treacherous it was."

"Oh, I thought you meant that one there," said Harry nodding to the one at the front.

"Why would I tell you about a bunker you can see for yourself? Anyway you may have avoided the bunker."

But he had not, and he lost that hole as well, the bunker proving as tricky to get out of as Benton had said it might.

"The course gets a bit easier from now on. That's me three holes up," said Benton.

Off the 4th tee, Benton hooked his drive into the trees that lined the left side of the fairway. Harry sliced his drive into the rough to the right of the fairway.

"See you at the green," Benton joked as he and Harry set off in different directions in quest of their balls. As he was hunting for his ball in the long grass, Harry heard the sound of a ball ricocheting off a tree – Benton obviously had found his ball, but had had difficulty playing out. So, so long as he found his ball and could hit it out, Harry knew he would have the advantage on the hole. He found his ball and hacked it out onto the fairway. Just after he did, he heard Benton play again from the woods, and saw his ball pop out a few yards nearer the green than Harry's one, but on the other side of the fairway.

Harry, as furthest from the hole, played next, and found the green with his approach shot. Benton did likewise, both balls ending up about nine feet from the hole.

"You here in how many?" demanded Benton.

"Three."

"You sure – how many shots did you take in the rough?"

"One," said Harry surprised.

"You sure?"

"Yes."

"Oh, well if you say so," said Benton with a disbelieving air. "So we are both here in three."

"Are you sure?"

"Well not really, but if, as you said, you really took only one shot in the rough then we have ah, ahem both taken three."

"I make you four. Tee shot, two in the woods, and then the approach."

"There was only one shot in the woods. I got out first time."

"Did you? I thought I heard a ball ricocheting off trees when I was looking for my ball and well before your ball came out."

"That must have been a shot from elsewhere on the course you heard. Sounds can ricochet off at unexpected angles round this section of the course due to the layout of the trees."

Both missed their putts, so the hole was halved. "I am still 3 up," announced Benton, "don't worry, the course gets a bit easier from now on."

Harry little-by-little managed to get back into the match. Benton was normally steady off the tee, although occasionally he would hook one way off to the left in amongst the rough and the undergrowth. But he always found his ball even in deepest rough. "One of the advantages of playing here for so long – I know the terrain. I ah, ahem, have spent so long looking for balls here that I should be good at it by now," he laughed nervously when Harry remarked upon this.

Neither golfer was good at playing out of bunkers and when Benton had bunker trouble on the 5th that ended up in Harry winning the hole. A freakishly good – for Harry was not normally remotely of that standard – long putt which rattled into the hole on the 8th gave Harry that hole, and left him only one down as it had followed on from two halved holes. The 9th and 10th were also halved.

It was Harry who encountered bunker trouble on 11 and Benton won the hole as result, to send him 2 up.

Harry pulled one back at the 12th, so as to be only one down. But on the 13th he played into a bunker with a sign beside it saying that it was the Captain's Bunker. "What does that mean?" Harry asked.

"It means I think I may end up winning the hole," chuckled Benton. He recognised in Harry a similarly poor bunker player. In Harry's case it was from lack of experience. The municipal course, to which all his rounds thus far had been restricted, had only three bunkers, as they were expensive to maintain, and so he had little experience of how to play from one. Crucially he had not yet learned that the trick with most bunker shots was to play the sand just behind the ball and to scoop the ball out that way, rather than play the ball itself.

"No, I mean the sign saying 'Captain's Bunker'."

"Oh, if you go in that bunker you have to make a donation to the captain's charity."

Oh, another expense thought Harry, what joy. "How much?"

"A fiver I think. I don't know as I ah, ahem have never gone into it."

To his, and certainly Benton's, surprise he got the ball out of the bunker first time, but the ball rolled back down the slope in front of the bunker back into the sand. But, emboldened by his relative success, and having accidentally hit upon the way to do it, he played the same shot again, but with more confidence and force and the ball popped out and rolled right next to the hole. When Benton three putted, Harry had halved the hole.

On the 14th, Benton landed in a bunker which was only a few yards from the front of the green, the deepest bunker on the course. Harry was standing behind Benton as he clambered down into the bunker. To Harry, this looked a tough shot. Indeed, the bunker was so deep that Benton's head was below ground level, although admittedly the ground level was artificially high at that point, as there was a mound just beyond the bunker, which added to the challenge of extricating oneself from that hazard. This mound was larger than the one on the previous hole where Harry had hit his ball onto and seen it roll slowly and agonisingly back into the sand.

Harry was trying not to get ahead of himself, but he sensed a win for him here as he saw scant prospect of a bunker player as poor as Benton getting out of that easily. And even if he did, he was unlikely to end up near the hole – and Harry was already on the green in the same number of strokes as it had taken Benton to get into the bunker.

"Could I ask you please to go ah, ahem round the other side of the bunker," said Benton. "It's just that this could go anywhere with my bunker play and that way you could spot please where it goes. I have had to play out of here several times over the years and sometimes it has flown over the green and no-one knew where it went as everyone else was also on this side. So if you wouldn't mind."

Disappointed, Harry moved away around the green on the other side of the bunker. Seeing Benton try to extricate himself from there could have been entertaining viewing. As Harry was walking to get into position, a ball rolled towards the hole. He looked round to see where it had come from, as he had not heard any blasting of the sand, as he would have expected to if it were Benton's ball. But it dawned on him it must be Benton's as there was no one else around who may had mis-hit their ball from their fairway onto this green.

"Wow, is that my ball," said Benton clambering out of the bunker. "Well get us and our bunker play – you on the last hole, me here. We should be turning pro!" he laughed.

"Yes, splendid shot. I confess I hadn't twigged at first it was your ball, and hadn't got into position as I hadn't heard a shot."

"That bunker is so deep it can ah, ahem muffle the sounds from it. That was half the problem that time I told you about when I blasted out and no-one saw where it went – as no heard the shot no-one was keeping an eye out at that particular moment. Sorry, perhaps I should have called out when I was about to play. But all's well that ends well. Phew, I'm not half glad to get out of there like that. That bunker is known by some here as Hell Bunker, for obvious reasons."

The hole was halved, leaving Harry still one down. Harry then won the 15th to square the match, and the 16th to go 1 up.

"The 17th green is being redesigned," explained Benton, "you can't really see it from here, but the back section is roped off. They are making that part flatter to allow for more pin positions, as the current green is so sloped you can only find a few spots on it where you can cut a hole, which has caused problems with wear and tear. While the redesign is going on, if you hit the ball onto the roped-off portion of green it is Ground Under Repair so you have a free drop from the Drop Zone – a circle marked out in paint by the greenkeeping staff beside the green."

"Where's that?"

"I can't see it from here," laughed Benton,

"Oh sorry, I thought it was in a set place."

"No. Quite obviously the greenkeepers have to move it around regularly as that patch of turf gets worn."

Benton was the first to play his approach shot and overhit onto the closed portion of the green. So, did Harry, albeit only just as he overshot the part of the green still in play by a matter of inches.

"You play first," said Benton surveying what was obviously going to be a tricky shot from the Drop Zone, so severe was the slope on that part of the green.

"Oh, I thought furthest from the hole always plays next," remarked Harry.

"That's you."

"But my ball was nearer the hole."

"No, it wasn't."

"You were right at the back of the green, I was just here."

"Ah, ahem, yes, but once my ball was in the area marked out as Ground Under Repair then it is automatically deemed to be in the Drop Zone. So its position is taken as being in DZ not GUR by R&A RRP after being in a NPZ as defined by E8. You then played your ball to the wrong part of the green. It's your turn to play next."

Harry studied his shot. It was indeed a tricky one. The Drop Zone was at the top of a slope off to the side of the green, and the hole was cut on the flattest part of that section of green, but 'flattest' was indeed a comparative term here, for all that section of green sloped. The topmost part of it most severely, although it flattened out a bit near the hole. Clearly he could not aim directly at the hole as the slope would take it well away from the target. He aimed above the hole. But not by enough. Also he had hit the ball too hard, for it gathered pace down the slope, missed the hole by a wide margin and rolled off the front of the green, eventually coming to rest several yards from the green.

"Bad luck," said Benton. "It's a ridiculous pin position. This part of the green was never meant to have the hole on it. The committee have no idea what they are doing." Armed with the knowledge of what had happened to Harry's ball, Benton aimed higher up the slope and hit the ball more softly. The ball ended four feet from the hole.

Harry decided that putting back onto the green was a safer option than chipping onto such a sloped surface, especially as he was putting directly uphill, the putt golfers like the most apart from the absolutely dead flat one. But the overnight rain had made the area where the water ran off from the green soggy, and soggier than Harry had realised and his putt barely made it onto the green. His next putt just shaved the hole, and stayed above ground, and he conceded the hole. They were back to being all square.

The 18th hole at Tangents has a wide landing area for drives, so the tee shot is relatively unthreatening. The challenge comes with the approach to the green, played uphill and over bunkers, with out of bounds both behind and to the left of the green. To the right is a relatively steep slope, above which is the clubhouse and its terrace. On busy days those putting on 18 have to contend with the hubbub from the terrace, along with the prospect of several pairs of eyes watching them. The 18th green shares with the 3rd the characteristic that the surface cannot be seen by those playing to it from the fairway.

"Right, tricky green to hit this one," said Benton. "Usual format with flags – white front, yellow middle and red back."

"I thought it was red at the front and white for the back?" said Harry, who had already clocked that the flag was a white one.

"That's exactly what I just said," said Benton crossly. "Green relatively flat. You can see the slope on the right down from the clubhouse, sometimes when you land on that it stays up there, sometimes it rolls down onto the green – luck of the gods really. To the left of the green, obscured by the bunkers, the land falls away steeply to a hollow and there is out of bounds – tricky pitch up onto the green from there as the putting surface is above eye level. The coward's way out is to go long when playing from there as you have the slope beyond the green as a backstop and possible aid. But if your chip lands short it just comes back to you or beyond – I've seen people play from there and end up in the out of bounds behind them. Oh yes, and there is out of bounds behind the green. Very tough shot you've got there, Harry. Very tough."

It was Benton's turn to play first. Harry managed to see the ball during the early part of its flight, but lost it later on, and Benton's body language was giving nothing away as to where it had gone. The early path of the ball had suggested it was heading towards the bank to the right of the green, but then Benton tended to hook, so if he had hooked that one slightly then it would curve around to the left and may have landed on the green.

Anyway it did not matter much where Benton's ball was, rationalised Harry, as there was not much of a safety-first option for him to consider. It was a case of hit and hope, avoid the bunkers and, if anything, favour the right side of the green. He hit. His shot felt good, but it was a fade and it looked to be curving towards that bank.

"Not sure where either of those have ended up," he remarked affably to Benton as he turned to put his club back in the bag. But Benton was already marching down the fairway – he had set off as soon as Harry played his shot – and said nothing. Perhaps he had already moved out of earshot, wondered Harry.

When Harry got to the green he saw the two balls. One was on the green and Benton was inspecting the line of the putt. He was bending down behind the ball trying to read the contours, looking to divine whether the ball would roll straight or if there was a borrow he needed to take into account. Benton then walked round to the other side of the hole and looked back at the ball, trying to read the putt from the opposite direction.

Harry's ball was obviously therefore the one on the fringe of the green. Benton's was about ten feet from the hole. His own putt was at least twice that distance Harry reckoned. Plus he had a bit of fringe to putt over before he reached the green. He had a quick look to line up the putt – it looked dead flat. He was surprised that Benton was making such a fuss of lining up his own putt. Benton had walked off the green and was looking at the path of the putt sideways – presumably judging the distance and how hard to strike the ball.

Harry knew that he had to hit the ball straight – no need to allow for any slope as there was none that he could make out. He told himself to just concentrate on how hard to hit it as there's no break to worry about. The fringe of the green was cut quite short so would not slow down the ball's speed too much. Getting the ball onto the green rolling at the right speed would be crucial. He made a couple of practice swings with his putter to the side of the ball as much from nervous tension as to practise exactly how hard to hit the ball. Then he settled down in his stance and pulled the putter head back.

He struck the ball harder that he had meant. But the fringe was wetter than he had anticipated, from water running off the bank, and so was slowing the ball more than Harry had expected. But it was going straight, dead straight so long as no hidden borrow took the ball away. No, he appeared to have read the line correctly for the ball continued arrow straight. But it was slowing rapidly. He felt he hadn't given it enough oomph. The ball had slowed almost to a standstill – from his angle he couldn't see how far it still had to roll. It seemed to have stopped, but then it disappeared from view – it had just enough energy to topple, exhausted, into the hole.

He had made a birdie, the first of his life, and what a time to do it: on the final hole of a tied match. He hadn't won the hole just yet – if Benton made his putt he, too, would have a birdie. But Benton had to make his 10-foot putt to halve the hole – and for some reason reading that putt seemed to be greatly troubling him.

"What have you done?" shouted Benton. "What on earth have you just done?"

"I have made a birdie," said Harry proudly. He looked round to see if anyone was on the terrace watching, and one person in particular. The terrace was empty.

"No, you haven't, you have just lost the hole!"

"No, I have just made a birdie, my first ever. How is that losing the hole?"

"That wasn't your ball. It was mine."

"No, yours is… isn't that yours?" he said pointing with his putter at the only ball now left on the green.

"No, that's yours."

"But you were lining up that putt, that ball."

"I was trying to work out how easy a putt it would be for you. I needed to know how likely it was that you would make it, and so whether I had to be bold and go for the hole from off the green or just play cautiously and make sure I got down in two."

"Oh," said Harry deflated, "I thought this was mine. Ah

well, I know exactly where your ball was, so we can replace it in the exact spot."

"Sorry, no, you have lost the hole. Playing the wrong ball in match play automatically entails losing the hole. I am afraid therefore that you have also lost the match."

"But, but I thought it was my ball. I didn't do it deliberately," Harry's voice tailed off. His sadness at being deprived of his birdie had temporarily eclipsed the realisation that he had also just lost the match.

"So I would hope. It is bad enough that you play someone else's ball, even worse if you did it deliberately," Benton said severely.

Harry was made to feel he had done something terribly against the spirit of the game. "Never mind," said Benton patting him on the back in a gauche way, "no need to tell anyone. Don't want to embarrass you, not as a new member. No need to let anyone on the committee know what you've just done, nor indeed to tell anyone else in the club. It can remain our secret. We'll just say you lost 1 down after an excellent and enjoyable game," he said, smiling in an awkward way. "But you must never do that again," he said firmly. "But I am sure you will not."

"No," said Harry dejected.

"Well bad luck Harry, that was a fine shot of yours and it was an enjoyable game. Oh yes, that money for the Captain's Bunker – I can ah, ahem put it in the kitty if you like as I'm going that way."

"Oh, er, okay, thanks. It was £5 you said?"

"Yes, so that's a tenner, as you were in twice."

"I thought there was only one Captain's Bunker."

"But you went in it twice remember with consecutive shots – remember the one that rolled back in again."

"Oh, does it work that way?"

"'Fraid so".

Harry only had the emergency petrol money from the car in his wallet. "Sorry, I only have a £20 note on me."

"That's all right, I can give change."

"Or we could get some in the bar," suggested Harry. "Do you want a 19th hole? You know, a drink," he added as the other's face looked blank.

"Oh, that is kind of you, but no I don't drink in this clubhouse."

Harry wondered if he had made a bloomer – was Benton teetotal or AA or something? Or was he suggesting that they drink somewhere else? But Harry didn't know of anywhere else locally – not that he was that familiar with the area, but he was pretty confident if there was pub locally he would have come across it.

"Very kind of you, and I don't want to embarrass you, so how about you just give me the money for a drink – that seems fair doesn't it. Say another fiver."

Harry was a bit taken aback by this. "Er I am not sure it really works that way."

"No, you are quite right, you'd also get a drink for yourself so say a tenner then? That's good, that saves having to fiddle about with change – I'll just keep the £20. Well nice playing with you, and I am sorry about the last hole, but you know rules are rules and we cannot change that. And if you ever want a playing lesson here, don't go to the pro as I can give you far better advice about the course and ah, ahem I'll charge less. Oh yes, I imagine you'd like to buy some raffle tickets – would you like a couple, or perhaps a book?"

"Sorry, you have taken my last cash with that £20 note," said Harry with a note of triumph, and with that he turned and walked to the locker room. It occurred to him his dramatic exit may be in vain if Benton was also going there. But it seemed Benton was not.

Harry changed his shoes and went into the bar. He wanted to see if Jack and Jerry were having their drink there; well his drink. If so, he could join them. He wished now he had been less defensive when Jack had hoved up. Also, at the back of his mind was the thought that perhaps Rikki might be there.

She wasn't. He noticed that first; then he noticed that Jack and Jerry were not there.

He asked the Steward: "Did those gentlemen come in who I owed the drink to?"

"Yes, Sir. They took your drinks as a rather nice bottle of wine with their lunch."

"Oh, ah good," said Harry wondering whether 'rather nice' was code for 'expensive'. He rather feared it was. Ah well, too late now. And if it hadn't been for them his car would still be stuck in that quagmire.

"Can I get you a drink Sir?" asked the Steward.

"No, allow me, would you like something Harry?" Harry turned round to see it was Willoughby Cornwallis. "My turn as you bought us all drinks last night – Half Pint, Anun and me."

"I think I have sworn off alcohol after last night. Well I had this morning anyway."

"How about a nice pot of tea then? You could join me in a spot of afternoon tea if you like."

"Oh thank you, I'd love that," said Harry. The talk of Jerry and Jack's Sunday lunch had made him hungry. He hadn't had anything to eat all day bar two packets of crisps.

"How about some scones with jam and cream, Larry? That suit you?"

"Sounds excellent, thank you."

"Steward, please may we have a pot of tea for two and scones with jam and cream for three."

The 'for two' bit had struck at Harry, for he had been hoping that maybe the girls would be joining them; well Rikki anyway. But when he heard 'for three' his spirits rose again.

"Are we going to be joined by anyone?"

"Not that I am expecting. Why?"

"Well you just ordered scones for three."

"Always wise to have a spare scone. Nice putt of yours on the last hole by the way."

"Oh you saw," said Harry disconsolately.

"Don't look so glum," said Willoughby. "You must have won the match, as I saw Benton pick up after you made it. Will make you popular in here, knocking out Benton."

"No I lost."

"Oh were you just playing the last hole for fun with the game already over? Sorry, I had presumed the match was still live. Still, splendid putt."

"No, it was live, but I lost the hole. For playing the wrong ball."

"Well of all the sneaky things."

"I am sorry, please forgive me – it was an innocent accident."

"I saw Benton lining up the other putt – you mean he was lining up your ball?"

"Yes."

"Well, that's a new one. Oh Martin," Willoughby hailed a passing member, "I have got a new one for you. Oh this is Larry, our newest member."

"Harry," Harry said.

"Pleased to meet you Harry," said Martin, proffering his hand, "Martin Cowmeadow."

"Yes, young Barry here has been playing Benton in that match you scratched from."

"Oh yes," Martin said to Harry, "sorry about that, I was er, I was too busy to able to play it. Did you win?"

"Did he heck," scoffed Willoughby. "Putting up a fresh-faced young lad against Benton. You know what he did?"

"Got into Hell Bunker and sent you round the other side where you couldn't see him throw the ball out?"

"No. Or did he?" said Willoughby looking at Harry.

"Gosh, er, well yes he did and he did send me round… oh gosh, I remember remarking at the time I didn't hear his shot… he told me it was the unusual acoustics."

"No, this is a new one on me. Oh you tell him Harry." Harry told the story of the putt on the 18th green.

"Oh my, that is indeed a new one," laughed Martin. "Oh I am sorry for you Harry. Please be assured we are not all like that. Most of us are splendid chaps and I hope you will give us another chance and find that this is true."

Harry's feelings had moved from one of embarrassment for seemingly doing something completely beyond the pail, to one of relief, to one now of anger that he had been tricked out of victory.

"So, Benton is a cheat?" said Harry to Willoughby, as Martin moved off.

"Careful, you can't say that of a fellow member. No, no. You can say that he is a prattling gabler, a lickorous glutton, a freckled bittor, a mangy rascal, a shite-abed scoundrel, a sly knave, a curdled cur, a mendacious heel, a lousy louse, a stinking scoundrel, a wretched worm, a base blackguard, a devious dog, a grubby good-for-nothing, a slithering snake, a dishonest toad, a double-dealing stinker, a loathsome wretch, a vile varlet, a yellow dog, a shifty sorner, a deceitful dalcop, a loathsome lubberwort, a crafty conman, a disgusting doddypoll, a mephitic maggot, a serpentine snollygoster, a murky mumpsimus, a putrid poltroon, a feculent fustilarian, a scurvy slubberdegullion, a filthy borgait, a grasping grupelgrinder, a tilly tosser, a rancid ransenhansen, a trandled strendelbarn, a runctuous snodgrater, a ratgalled durmaid, a suddled ninnywhoop, a dileaky griffdender, a wurnocked sidikitulip or a watboddled dumpelrump, but you cannot say that a fellow member is a cheat. Even when he is, like Benton."

Harry was not sure what to say to this, so switched the subject. "Er, might Rikki be coming in this afternoon?"

"Doubt it, but maybe. She can normally nose out food from a hundred yards. Just depends whether she comes within a hundred yards I suppose. You do mean Rikki, the younger one, not Anun?"

"Yes, Rikki."

"Ah, often it's Anun boys ask about. No, I doubt we shall see Rikki. Why?"

"Oh, no reason, just that I met her last night and well, be nice to see her again. Forgive me for asking, but is she a relative? Your daughter?" asked Harry nervously.

Willoughby gave him a long look, scrutinising his face. "My wife and I do not have any children. We had tried for them in the early days of our marriage but the Lord giveth and, well, sometimes the Lord does not."

Harry felt embarrassed now at his question. "Oh, sorry. I had just thought you two look a bit similar in some ways," he said then wondered whether he was not putting his foot further in it.

"That is very flattering, Barry. Well to me, to be compared to such a rare beauty. But make sure you never say so in front of Rikki as I am not sure she would take kindly to being compared to a crusty old gargoyle such as myself. In fact, she would not. Rikki is my Goddaughter. She and her sister Anun are down from university for the vac – arrived yesterday so they popped in to say hello."

"Oh, what's she reading?"

"History of Art at St Andrews. Have you played our course before?"

"No."

"What d'you make of it?"

In truth, Harry did not have a lot to compare it with as he had only previously played one other course. "I like it," he replied, as a safe answer. "But it has more bunkers than I am used to. I am going to have to learn how to play out of them."

"The main thing with bunkers is to avoid going into them in the first place."

"I think I failed at that rather. Cost me £10, too."

"How come?"

"I went in the Captain's Bunker twice."

"Twice? How on earth did you manage the other one?"

"Well I hit out onto that mound thing and it rolled back in."

"Hmm, I am not sure the R&A have a ruling about captains' bunkers but I would make that only once myself. But anyhow it's only £2; or a quid if you agree with me. The jar's over there, if you want to pop it in."

"Oh, I gave the money to Benton."

"Why on earth did you do that?"

"He said he would put it in the kitty for me as he was going that way," he said.

"Hah, he never comes in here, thank goodness. He stiffed you for a tenner did he as well as the match? Here, have the spare scone, you look like you need it."

Chapter 6

A week or two after his Shack setback, Harry walked into the club bar and, as had become his habit, immediately scanned the room to see if Rikki was there, but no. However Willoughby was, sitting with a man in a dog collar, so he made for him. "I was wondering if I could ask you for your opinion?"

"Hallo Larry old boy. Yes of course – draw up a pew. Be delighted to. Well, you can ask me for anyone's opinion. But probably wisest to ask for mine, as I am more genned up on that. Though other people's opinions may be more informed than mine, so perhaps you'd be better asking me for their opinions after all. But then I might not be informed of what their informed opinions are, so their informed opinions may become uninformed through me. Or was it the padre you wish to ask? He after all has a hotline to a higher authority."

"Er, yes, quite," said Harry trying to process this and thinking that maybe it would have been better had he approached the vicar. However vicars, in his limited experience, said bland things with gentle smiles, whereas Mr Cornwallis was likely to be more forthright. Also, as Mr Cornwallis had termed it, a higher authority was not needed on this matter, just someone acquainted with the machinations of the club and club life and Mr Cornwallis was, he had gleaned, one of the longest-established members. "I would welcome both your opinions. Someone has suggested that I ought to consider standing for a committee to help integrate myself. I hear there are elections hoving up."

"Well this club certainly does not lack for committees. There are committees for this, committees for that and committees for a bit of the other. Well not so much the last one, I admit," replied Willoughby.

"No, quite," said the vicar.

"But almost everything else. This club has far too many darn committees in most people's opinion – well when I say most people I don't actually mean that of course, I mean very few people. Most people have no views on the subject: Iranian picture framers, the Anthophile Association of Armenia, the philatelists of southern Greenland, or indeed of western Greenland..."

"A few years ago there were plans to prune the number of committees here," cut in the vicar before his good friend could list any more groups.

"What happened?"

"Oh, they formed a committee to look into the matter."

"Can I offer you some scones and jam?" asked Willoughby of Harry. "No? I could offer you fruit cake, but yonder steward has very strict ideas about the dishing out of fruit cake, and is insistent that it cannot be served until four o'clock."

"Why?"

"Why indeed. One of his rules, well the rules of the club he claims. Fruit cake counts as afternoon tea, and afternoon tea will not be served before the hour of four. Scones, however, under the strange system of apartheid that seems to exist here, count as general foodstuffs and so may also be served at select other times of the day, hence why we have scones in front of us but no cake as yet. Jolly good fruit cake you get here, nice and moist and rich," and at this he went into a mild reverie.

"I am sure the club would benefit from someone of youth and vigour adding their deliberations to a committee," said the vicar, recognising that his friend's attention, as so often when it had found a tangent to explore, had wandered contentedly along it. "If you felt able to contribute your time to a committee I'm sure it would be welcomed. A club depends on its members as I'm sure you know."

"Well I've never been a member of any sort of club before, so it's all rather new to me. But yes, I imagine that must be so. I am keen to play an active part in the club."

"Oh look, old Pirbright has just come in," remarked Willoughby. The sight of the Secretary had jolted him from his cake-related musings, which had meandered on from fruit cake via angel cake to Madeira cake by this stage. "*Cave* – he has that walk of his, the man-of-action about to sort out the pesky natives. Some poor soul is in for it – pray for him padre. This perisher makes one long for the days when Pike was Secretary, even if one did risk a crick in the neck talking to him."

"Ah, just the man I was hoping to see," said the Secretary approaching Willoughby.

"Oh goodie. Well I am delighted to make your hopes come true, dear boy," replied Willoughby graciously, recovering his poise. "Especially as it seems to have involved no effort on my part. All part of the service. Is it my decorative features you wish to enjoy, the noble profile, the natty tailoring, or...."

"Hallo Reverend, hallo Harry," said the Secretary, belatedly acknowledging their presence. "No I wanted to speak to you."

"I am all ears dear Secretary. Well not in a literal sense you understand, I am also arms legs, head, stomach and things. Indeed, if Mrs C is to be believed, I am rather too much stomach. But you get the gist."

"As I said, I was hoping to have a word with you."

"Your hopes can be granted. Indeed, have two, have a whole load. Have sentences of them if you wish. Perhaps not paragraphs though, eh? We do not want to do overdo things and get you over excited and put you off your afternoon tasks of going through the petty cash or tidying the lost property boxes."

"I can assure you that I will not get overexcited."

"Your self-control is admirable."

"It is about the Competitions Committee."

"A fine body of men, sterling fellows one and all, no doubt. I get down on my knees every night before bed and include them in my prayers that they may be delivered from evil and be aided in their deliverance of wise judgments. Well when I say every night, I probably only mean alternate Tuesdays on balance, as I have lots of things to pray about – world peace and all that, and whether I will be able to get up from my knees at my advanced years at the end of it all and make it into bed."

"Yes indeed, quite. No it was about you and your involvement with the committee."

"Not guilty, m'lud, I have had no involvement with the committee other than total, undiluted veneration from a distance. They have not been harassed or inconvenienced by me in any way in the course of carrying out their vital work. You have collared the wrong man. I'm innocent guv."

"No, I want you to be involved."

"You mean you do wish me to harass and inconvenience them? You are a surprising man Mr Secretary. Well, if you really think so, I suppose I could put whoopy cushions on their chairs before meetings – though it would be a bit unnecessary with old Orr – and pull faces at them through the windows during their earnest deliberations, but if you don't mind me saying so, dear Secretary, such behaviour may seem a little off to we solemn, sober souls, though I can see why a carefree, whimsical fellow such as yourself may consider it jolly larks."

"No, I meant about you being a member of this committee."

"Oh, say no more old boy – I understand what you are trying to say. Or about to say."

"Oh good."

"Yes, if you are looking for someone to sit on this committee to add, dare I say it, a touch of tone and gravitas as a bulwark against the tide of the more frivolous element among our number who advocate putting whoopy cushions on people's chairs and pulling faces through windows, then I accept your kind entreaty…"

"No, no…."

"I cannot offer wisdom in the Solomon class, but I shall do my best in my own small humble way. You can have my solemn promise on that Mr Secretary."

"No, no, you are already on that committee."

"Am I? Then old boy I cannot join the committee can I, kind though your offer is. I would have to be schizofrenetic to do that, and anyway it would get terribly complicated. Where would I sit, would I have to keep changing seats to vote twice, what happened if I voted against myself? Could I second a motion that I had proposed? Or propose a motion I had seconded? Would you need two whoopy cushions for me, or just the one? Sorry, old boy, it just wouldn't work, ingenious though the idea of yours is – shows that thinking outside the box spirit we hear so much about. Er is schizofrenetic the right word?"

"I doubt it," said the vicar, "I feel on balance that any word including frenetic is unlikely to apply to you."

"You are probably right padre, I am more your calm,

considered sort of fellow. Steady under fire, such as when standing on the 1st fairway and Snoddy is raining down sliced drives on you from that silly new 2nd tee."

"Do you mind if I sit down," said the Secretary, realising that this conversation was likely to be a long one, just as he had feared.

"Pull up a pew old boy. Scone?"

"No thank you. What I was talking about was your continuing involvement with this committee. I, er that is to say we would very much hope that you would like to continue sitting on this committee."

"Then again old boy I am delighted to be able to bring happiness and joy into your life, for I shall. Who can reject someone with such sorrowful eyes," he added as a loud aside to Harry.

"But you cannot."

"Oh can't I? Then I regret dear Secretary I cannot accede to your request. It was wrong of you to put temptation in my midst. That is one of the other things I pray about, padre – not to be lead into temptation."

"Very wise," replied the vicar. "But God is faithful; he will not let you be tempted beyond what you can bear. But when you are tempted, he will also provide a way out so that you can endure it."

"That's dashed decent of him. Sterling fellow God, always said so."

"What I mean is that you cannot unless you play golf," explained the Secretary.

"What, resist temptation?" said Willoughby startled. "Are you sure? I don't think the scriptures have anything about golf in them. But if golf keeps me on the straight and narrow and in with God, then that makes all those missed putts have meaning."

"No, not temptation, a place on the Competitions Committee," said the Secretary, failing to keep a tone of exasperation out of his voice. "The Competitions Committee – you have to play golf to be on that committee."

"But I do play golf. Look around you Secretary old bean, this is a golf club. You have probably had one too many cooking sherries to ward off the chill of the summer's day, and that's made you confused and you think this is the unmarried mother's knitting circle or something. An easy mistake to make no doubt, but this is a golf club. And though I do not wish to boast, if you have another look around you, you will see some pieces of wood attached to the wall, not as decoration to hide blemishes in the plasterwork, but as informative notices of the winners of the various competitions and yonder there, below several layers of dust and a rather impressive spider's web, you will see that young Godders and I were the Junior Foursomes champions two years running. I put it to the jury of my peers," he said looking at Harry and the vicar, "that said exhibit in front of you is indeed one golfer."

"What I am endeavouring to explain is that you have not played any competitive golf recently."

"Well not in the Junior Foursomes, I grant you. But I think it would be unfair to hold that against me. I fear my youthful good looks have confused you, dear Secretary, for I am in fact several decades too old to qualify for it now – hard though that may be to credit."

"And to qualify to be elected a member of the Competitions Committee you have to have played in at least three silver competitions during the previous season. You do not appear to have played in any so far."

"Nonsense dear boy, Godders and me – or should that be Godders and I? – played in the whatsit thingamy only the other week, some foursomes nonsense. We didn't do very well. Old Godders had his usual difficulty with that bunker on the 8th. His ball is like one of those water-divining thingyabobs – though in his case I suppose it's sand-divining – for wherever he is on the course, his ball makes a beeline for the nearest bunker, and the one on the 8th in particular and once in there it settles down for the night and orders breakfast for the next morning, and nothing Godders does seems to make it shift its mind. Indeed, I have heard it on good authority that at one stage the Royal Mail was planning to automatically redirect all his post to the bunker on the 8th."

"Godfrey Flower?" said the Secretary

"None other. You've probably heard of him – he was junior foursomes champion two years' running back in the day. Fine fellow of a man – I have played with him boy and man, a constant and enjoyable companion throughout many a round."

"But he died several months ago…"

"Nonsense, old boy, you must be thinking of someone else. People are dying all the time these days. It's because they live so long. I don't think the Royal Mail ever carried out their redirection, but I know one of the parcel delivery firms when they needed Godders' signature for something would head for that bunker if they found him out. I can remember him signing for a set of outdoor furniture – a table with one of those overgrown cocktail-stick umbrellas in it and some chairs. Well obviously he couldn't carry the darned things round with him so he left them there. Anyway when he came to reclaim them after the round he found some wag had erected them, and – rumour has it, though I fear the annals of history may have got distorted – it was even said that a family was picnicking there. I suppose it is the nearest one can get to a picnic on the beach in these parts, but even so seems a bit unlikely to me. But then other people playing the course early one morning once found a traction engine in the bunker on the second, so who knows."

"A traction engine?" asked Harry incredulously.

"Yes, it was Lord Hankley's," explained Willoughby with the air of one who had made it all perfectly understandable. "Not the current Lord Hankley the previous one. Or was it the one before that – they do seem to get through Lord Hankleys rather quickly."

"Membership of the Competitions Committee is restricted to active golfers who have participated in the minimum number of silver competitions in the preceding season," explained the Secretary.

"Active golfers?"

"Yes."

"Well I am a golfer – see exhibit A, one honours board yonder. It is a well-established fact that I with the noble, if admittedly often futile, assistance of old Godders – well young Godders as he then was – am a two-time junior champion of the foursomes. And active – well do not let my current reposed state confuse you, for I can still be active when the call comes. I can demonstrate if you like," and with that he waved his arms about; also one leg.

"Ouch!" The Secretary yelped in pain.

"Oh sorry," said Willoughby for he had accidentally kicked the Secretary on the knee. "Awfully sorry old boy."

"Don't mention it," said the Secretary, rubbing his knee.

"Well I wasn't planning to include it in my memoirs, I confess. It can remain our secret. If you like, I could do a little dance at the AGM to prove that I am still active? I could do a rum baba – no I don't mean that, a rumba –

with Mrs Cornwallis if you like. Mind you, she is not a member, thank God. Perhaps Anun would be prepared to dance with me. She is a social member and finds a great joy in physical expression."

"It is not your physical state which is the issue but whether you have been playing golf recently."

"I played only the other week with Godders. Well perhaps only the other month, I should say, for matron has put me off games at present because of my ankle."

"Your ankle?"

"Yes," said Willoughby, waving his left foot to demonstrate, "Oh sorry," he said, as he had caught the secretary another glancing blow on his knee, causing the latter to emit another sharp cry of pain. "Yes, my ankle."

"How long have you had your ankle?"

"All my life. I left mother well provided for. She was good to me."

"I mean how long have you had this injury to your ankle?"

"Oh some weeks or so," Willoughby replied airily.

"Some weeks?"

"Yes."

"But you don't appear to have played golf here for around nine months now."

"Nah, not me. I fear you are confusing me with another. The Archbishop of Canterbury perhaps – I understand he hasn't played here all year. Maybe you are confusing me with him?"

"Is the Archbishop of Canterbury a member?" asked Harry excitedly.

"No," replied the Secretary promptly, keen not to have the conversation side tracked.

"Oh. I didn't even know that he played golf," said Harry.

"I don't know he does," said Willoughby Cornwallis.

"Well not the current one – they change Archbishops quite often I understand, bit like Lord Hankleys, so who knows. If the padre gets a well-merited promotion… You won't forsake us would you padre, if you get made Archbishop of Canterbury?"

"No," replied the vicar chuckling with delight at this piece of whimsy, "I think the good Lord would still wish me to keep up my golf."

"No, the result sheets show you have not played golf," persevered the Secretary, "well not in a silver competition."

"Nonsense, I was playing just the other week with old Godders. I remember it well, as he got into the bunker on the 8th and spent a fair chunk of the afternoon – well I think he would like us to believe he was trying to chip out, but it was suggested he was trying to tunnel to Australia. Opinion was sharply divided on the matter."

"The bunker on the 8th?"

"That's the one. You can't miss it – it has lots of confused kangaroos and wallabies falling out of it upside down. Yes – it was always one of Godders' favourite haunts. Actually that's not true. I would like to retract that particular statement. 'One of his frequent haunts', I should say."

"But that bunker has been taken out."

"Taken out?"

"Yes."

"Oh, by a hitman you mean? Hmm, wonder if old Godders has finally flipped and hired an assassin to kill the bunker. Never mind, I am sure we can all club together and give him an alibi. Anyway the charge can only be justified manslaughter by anyone who knows Godders' history with that bunker. Er, can you even kill a bunker?"

"I mean the bunker has been taken out, removed, lost, it is no longer there, hasn't been there for half a year or more."

"Lost? You've lost a bunker? That's jolly careless. But I suppose it was just left lying around and things like that have tendency to go missing. Have you searched Benton's for it? Under his floorboards perhaps? It could have joined the Hanky Panky Cup there?"

"No, the Greens Committee had it filled in, turfed over. It was thought that bunker was a little too unfair."

"I think that was a very judicious move on that committee's behalf," interjected the vicar feeling the Secretary needed the respite of steering the conversation to calmer waters. "The land all rolled toward that bunker so it trapped a lot of only slightly off-target shots and it was quite demanding for some of us lesser players to extricate ourselves from without wrecking our card."

"Gone eh? I wonder what Godders is going to do with all the extra time he will have, now he doesn't have to devote hours of his time and those of his playing partners to the rearranging of the sand in that bunker. He'll have to take up bird watching or something."

"I regret it is too late for that," said the vicar sadly.

"Yes, his eyesight is a bit ropey these days: I noticed that last time we played. He can no longer really see where his decent hits go – often he just has to guess which bunker they have rolled into. But perhaps if he restricted himself to the larger birds he could manage it – kestrels, penguins and the like."

"There is a silver competition next weekend, perhaps you could sign up for that?" suggested the Secretary hopefully.

"Oh, yes I could sign up for that. No problem in doing that at all."

"Oh good."

"Trouble is, I couldn't actually make the starting grid.

My ankle you see. I wouldn't be able to get round 18 holes, not at present. If we had buggies here, I could maybe attempt it – it would still be excruciating agony of course, but I would do it for you Mr Secretary, such is the deep respect I hold you in. But we don't have any buggies."

"More that we cannot, you can't access many parts of the course by buggy. Some of our steep, narrow paths are buggy impassable, as you well know. You just can't get a buggy round here."

"Nor can a chap with a dodgy ankle get round. You forget, as you still probably see me as that callow fresh-faced youth who vanquished all in the Junior Foursomes all those years ago, that we aged crocks need to be in tip-top shape to take in the parts of the course that even the local mountain goats and rock climbers tend to give a miss in bulk to."

Turning to Harry, Willoughby confided: "You probably don't know this young Gary, being new to the club, but when Hillary Tensing and Sherpa Shetty were looking for financial backers for their clamber up Everest, there was a group of potential investors who were uncertain if they could achieve the summit or whether it would just be a gigantic waste of their money – so they invited them down here for a game of golf and having seen how they managed to get up to the 4th tee box with no bother they decided Everest would be a piece of cake for them after that. Which reminds me – is it 4pm yet? Barry would you be a pal and ask yonder steward fellow if he is finally prepared to disgorge some fruit cake as someone seems to have wolfed all the scones and cream. Would you like a slice Secretary? No? Quite sure? It might help mop up some of the cooking sherry?"

"About the matter of the Competitions Committee, it

would be advantageous in several ways if you were in a position to continue serving on it…"

Harry approached the Steward with slight trepidation. "I believe some fruit cake has been ordered for Mr Cornwallis and the vicar?"

"No-one has ordered any fruit cake, Sir."

"Oh, I thought Mr Cornwallis had."

"No-one has ordered any fruit cake and fruit cake is not served until 4pm in the afternoon."

"Oh, can I order three slices of fruit cake then please, for that table over there," he said pointing to where the Secretary was rubbing his knee and Willoughby was again apologising.

"Cake is not served until 4pm in the afternoon, Sir."

"But can I please order it now. To be served at 4. In three minutes."

"Cake is not served until 4pm in the afternoon, Sir. If you wish to order fruit cake you will have to come back at four o'clock and order it."

Harry returned feeling defeated, to find Willoughby in full flow: "Benton wants to get on the committee? Why? Does the committee look after the silver cups or something? Or is it just that he has failed to get elected to every other committee?"

"I am not sure of his motivation, but if we have the same number of people standing as there are vacancies then there is no election. If we have more candidates than places, then we will have to have an election and then the membership can make their selection as to which candidates they consider the most suitable."

"In other words, no blasted Benton."

"It is not for me to judge the suitability of any candidate," said the Secretary piously. "But I am sure that in certain circumstances the membership would welcome the chance of making a choice for themselves via the ballot box."

"Harry here was wondering whether to put himself forward for a committee," said the vicar. "Perhaps he could be persuaded if you are looking for what might be termed suitable candidates? His would be a fresh voice, and there might be felt to be some attraction in that?"

"Sadly he is not eligible – not long enough."

"Long enough?" snorted Willoughby. "What, there is a height restriction now on committee membership is there. Cor this club doesn't half have some darn silly rules."

"Harry hasn't been a member for long enough. Never mind, it's not your fault," he said addressing Harry. "You have got to have been a member for at least a year before one is eligible to stand for committee. That has always been the case."

"In which case how did they form the first committee?" asked Harry.

"Good point young Larry," said Willoughby approvingly. "See what a nimble young mind we are depriving ourselves of on our committees Mr Secretary?"

"Only for a year. And I do not make the rules."

"Ah well, perhaps a few hefty slices of fruit cake through the year and he will grow tall enough to join the committee."

"What about you vicar?" suggested Harry.

"Alas, I do not think it wise to be on a committee here. Some people confuse the dog collar with the man and think I speak for the church."

"But God is everywhere in heaven and on earth so why not be on golf committee?" argued Harry, feeling strangely and briefly emboldened.

"God may be everywhere in heaven and on earth," Willoughby remarked, "but most golf club committees inhabit a special part of hell – and God traditionally leaves that place to the other chap."

"It would be easiest all round, Willoughby, if you were able to stand again," said the Secretary. "Perhaps if I could coax you into playing a little more golf? Perhaps you might like to join the Doctor's Orders?"

"You forget my doctor's orders are that I don't play, not until my ankle improves."

The Secretary automatically flinched, but unnecessarily so. "No the Doctor's Orders, they are a group that play a nine-hole roll up on Tuesday mornings."

"All their doctors are telling them to play golf? Sounds like their quacks are disciples of Dr Alastair Mackenzie," Willoughby remarked.

"Is he the local GP?" Harry butted in, "would you recommend him, I have to…"

"No," cut in Willoughby. "He is a golf-course architect, well was – designed Augusta National and whatnot. He had been a GP but decided to give up medicine for golf course design as he reckoned he would make more of a contribution to the nation's health that way. He was quoted as saying how frequently he had, albeit with great difficulty, persuaded patients who were never off his doorstep to take up golf, and how rarely, if ever, he ever saw them in his consulting rooms thereafter. Fellow was an Army surgeon before he was a GP and used ideas he had learnt in the Boer War about camouflage in his designs. He reckoned the key to great course construction was to make artificial features indistinguishable from natural ones. He's quite right. Interesting fellow. It was fortunate, of course, that his patients didn't have bad ankles."

"The Doctor's Orders take their name from bingo and play a nine-hole roll up most weeks – maybe that would be a way to ease you back into the swing of things?" suggested the Secretary.

"I would love to join these medical fellows but..."

"... I know – your ankle. But when your ankle is better?"

"Tuesday mornings you say?"

"Yes."

"I regret that is when myself and Mrs Cornwallis subject ourselves to the ministrations of a Mata Hari. Mrs C is very keen on me reducing my stomach," he added by way of explanation. "She is rather disappointed that all this golf I have been doing has not reduced my waistline."

"She employs a Mata Hari to do this?" asked a bewildered Harry. "That seems very um, modern."

"Well, Mrs C likes to be modern and up with all the trends, and she thought this would be a fun way for me to do it. But she does it herself too."

"What? She is a Mata Hari?" asked Harry.

"No, no, I don't think she would be any good as a Mata Hari – she uses one. The same one obviously – we all do it together."

"I don't think you mean Mata Hari," suggested the vicar.

"Don't I? She puts me in lots of positions she gets out of some Indian book – last week we were doing dogging."

"My god, I think you do mean a Mata Hari," said the Secretary.

"What sort of positions?" asked the vicar.

"Yoga positions. Last week we were doing downward dogging."

"I think you mean yogi then, not Mata Hari," decided the vicar.

"Yogi – isn't that a bear?" queried Willoughby.

"Yes, but that was a different yogi. Yogis are also yoga instructors and I suspect that is what the good lady Mrs C has hired, not a Mata Hari."

"Oh yes that sounds like what we have. Every Tuesday morning."

"Downward dogging you say? That sounds intriguing."

"Yes you have to get down on all fours and..."

"Bark?"

"No, as far as I can tell you then shove your backside into the air as far as it can go."

"Is that what dogs do?" asked the vicar. "I have not noticed it myself."

"Perhaps only dogs that do yoga do it? Have you ever seen a dog doing yoga? I can't say I have myself. All the poses seem to be named after animals."

"Is there also an upward dog?"

"I suppose there must be. We haven't come to that part of the curriculum yet. I imagine an upwards dog is when you lie on your back with your hands and feet in the air and the Mata... the yogi bear tickles your tummy and says good boy and gives you a biscuit. I think I might like that exercise."

"I think it might be more in your line," said the vicar with a gentle smile.

"I think it might. Though – and please forgive a wee boast – the downward dog is something at which I mildly excel. Do you wish me to demonstrate?"

Harry, who had been watching the clock, got up and approached the Steward. "Please can I order three slices of fruit cake?"

"Sorry, no Sir."

"What do you mean?"

"Sorry, no, you cannot order three slices of fruit cake. I am sorry if I had not made my meaning clear, Sir."

"But it is now four o'clock. Indeed it is two minutes past by my watch."

"We go by the clock on the wall, Sir, not by your watch." Harry turned round to look at the clock. "But that says two minutes past four as well!"

"I did not say that it did not, Sir. I was merely informing you that we go by the clock on the wall, not your watch. I was merely trying to be helpful, Sir, knowing that you are a new member."

"So why can't I order some fruit cake then?"

"We don't have any fruit cake."

What Harry said in reply to this was drowned out by a sudden crashing noise. Turning to see its cause, he saw lying on the floor in a state of disarray, two tea cups, two plates, a tea pot, a milk jug and one Golf Club Secretary.

Chapter 7

"Have you been branching out into Greek weddings, vicar, or has Mr Ramsbotham upped his campaign of assault on the club crockery?" asked the newly arrived Anun, surveying the debris scattered around the, now righted, table.

"Hullo," said Willoughby, "I didn't hear you come in – Wilko and his good lady obviously aren't here. No, the Secretary has been running amok."

"Why?"

"Who can say? An unhappy childhood? A lost ball at the 17th? Too much cooking sherry after lunch? Too much cooking sherry before lunch? A lunch that consists solely of cooking sherry? His great sadness that Harry is not tall enough?"

"The Secretary became unbalanced, shall we say, and this is the result," explained the vicar.

"Unbalanced? Oh dear. Will he end up on the roof waiting for high tide, too, do you think?"

"No, he tripped backwards making an unwisely attempted hasty retreat. I think he was worried he was in danger of being kicked again," explained the vicar.

"Again?" queried Anun. "Who on earth had been kicking him?"

"Hullo all. Oh gosh, what's happened here," interrupted Rikki, who had just bounced in with a large tin under her arm. "Willoughby what have you been up to now?" she demanded.

"Why do you presume it was something to do with me?" he responded, putting on the most innocent, wronged face that he could manage.

"Experience and geography – I know you and you are sitting surrounded by upturned tea cups and broken crockery on the floor. Normally such items are kept upright, unbroken and on a table. Oh, sorry, has Mr Ramsbotham just been here?"

"It is true I was a witness," Willoughby said stressing the last word, "but it had nothing to do with me, other than it was the pot of tea that I had ordered that you see in fragments about the place. The Secretary... ah here he is, you can ask him yourself if you like."

"Apologies, apologies, again," said the Secretary rushing up after an absence while he had retreated to the locker room to restore his dignity and to check whether, as his feeling told him, some cream had become attached to his face in the upheaval. It had. "Now, let me get the mess cleared up and please let me order you some more afternoon tea – on me. Ah Steward," he said, noticing the club servant had arrived on the scene, "where do you keep the clearing stuff – dustpan and brush and so on?"

"I do not."

"What?"

"I do not keep any cleaning stuff."

"Why not?"

"I am catering, not cleaning. The cleaner keeps the cleaning stuff."

"Well, where does the cleaner keep them?"

"In her cupboard I would imagine."

"What cupboard is this?"

"The cleaning cupboard."

"Tcch! Where is that?" The Steward told him and the Secretary went off to get a brush and pan.

"You see, young Rikki," said Willoughby, "that the Secretary has just apologised for his savage, unprovoked attack on the club's crockery and our pot of tea. It pains me, as one entrusted with your moral welfare, to see you make false accusations against a pillar of the community."

"Sorry, I am not sure I quite caught the last bit – was that word 'pillar'?" Willoughby stuck his tongue out at Rikki, who replied in the same way.

"I will let you off this time, but don't let me catch you getting up to mischief, Willoughby," she admonished.

"I won't."

"Good."

"I don't let you catch me. You two ladies joining us for tea I hope?"

"We'd be charmed to," replied Anun.

"Rather!" said Rikki.

"Scones?" asked Willoughby.

"Rather!" said Rikki. "I'm feeling a trifle peckish."

"Yes please," said Anun.

"Steward, please could we have a pot of tea for five, and two helpings of scones with lashings of cream and jam for my delightful young friend here," he said indicating Anun, "and her sister." Rikki stuck her tongue out again at Willoughby. "And charge it all to the Secretary."

"With pleasure, Sir."

The Secretary came bustling back. "The cupboard is locked," he complained to the Steward.

"The cleaner keeps it locked," replied the Steward.

"I have gathered that, I want to unlock it."

"You will need the key then."

"Where is it?"

"The key?"

"Yes, the key."

"That will be where she keeps it."

"And where is that?"

"On a hook above the door."

"That's a daft place to keep it, anyone could see it there

and just unlock the door," he admonished the Steward as he hurried off.

"So sorry, we were rudely interrupted," the Steward said turning back to the table. "To confirm: that is a pot of tea for five, and scones with cream and jam for the two ladies?"

"Spot on!" replied Rikki.

"Would you like some nice crisps with it as well?"

Willoughby laughed: "No thank you."

"I will go and get your order." He turned and almost bumped in the onrushing Secretary who complained: "There isn't a dustpan and brush in that cupboard."

"No. She uses a hoover. Brooms do not work that well on carpet."

Rikki interrupted: "Do you have some carpet cleaner in there? You need to get something into it to stop the stain settling."

"Er, um," replied the Secretary.

"Show me where the cupboard is. And Steward, can't you just pick up the bits of broken crockery please?"

"Yes, Steward – pick up those pieces," ordered the Secretary feeling that he ought to be taking charge and wasn't.

"Where is this here cupboard then?" demanded Rikki of the Secretary. Shortly afterwards, having armed herself with some selected contents of the cleaner's cupboard, and having delighted Willoughby with the foam that came out of the aerosol, and having refused Willoughby's request that he too could 'have a jolly play with it', Rikki had cleared up the mess. When her ministrations were finished she got the approval of Willoughby, despite his continuing disappointment that he had not been allowed to use the foam canister. "Splendid work young Rikki, you have earned yourself some refreshment. Find yourself a cup; the teapot is behind you. Now tell us about hundreds of things."

"Hundreds? That's a lot."

"Well start with one and work your way up if you feel up to it. How about starting with what is in your intriguing tin."

"Cake."

"Cake!"

"Yes, cake."

"How splendid. Well dosh it out then young Half Pint."

"It's not for you."

"You have bought a cake to a tea party and are not prepared to share? Even a greedy guzzleguts like yourself cannot eat a whole cake at one sitting."

"I am not having any of the cake either. It's for the Steward."

"The Steward!"

"Yes, the Steward. It is part of a plan."

"Sounds a perfectly rotten plan to me. Why are you giving away cake to such an undeserving person as the Steward, when there are far more deserving persons present. Like me. Or young Barry – the Secretary has just been in here saying he needs feeding up. Or me. Or the padre here. Or, for instance, me. Or does it have ground glass in it? Weedkiller?"

"My plan was that, as Mumsie's getting rather bored being confined to quarters since her accident and she loves baking, she could make the cakes for the club. The members get the chance to eat delicious cake and Mumsie gets some welcome pin money. Clever eh?"

"Yes, sir?" said the Steward.

"Sorry?" said Willoughby

"You called me, Sir."

"Did I? Oh yes, I did," said Willoughby remembering he

had recently exploded 'Steward' rather too loudly. "Er do you have any Swiss roll today?"

"No, Sir."

"Oh never mind, thanks – that was all. Sorry to have troubled you."

"Ah Steward," said Rikki rushing after him clasping her cake tin. "Can I have a word please?"

"So your mother is getting a wee bit stir crazy is she while recuperating from her accident?" said the vicar to Anun.

"Just a bit. But she has now got back into painting in a big way."

"Painting?"

"Still lives, scenes around the farmhouse, me – I have become a model, as has everything else that moves or doesn't move around the farmhouse. Mum used to paint a bit when we were younger, but had given up. Now she has turned one of the outbuildings into her artist's studio. Very drafty it is for us skimpily clad models, too. Be great if she could be diverted into baking instead."

"I believe your mother has a fine reputation as a baker," said the vicar. "Well please do send your mother my regards. Do you think it would be helpful if I dropped in to see her sometime?"

"I am sure she would love that."

"Would one afternoon around four perhaps be suitable?"

"Anytime, vicar, anytime. Mum is confined to barracks so you will always find her in. If she is not at the main farmhouse look in the artist's studio, further down and to the right. You can't miss it – just follow the sound of chattering teeth."

"I will, thank you. Well I regret duty calls so I must be away. Please say goodbye to your sister from me. Goodbye Willoughby, goodbye Harry."

"Toodle pip padre."

"Yes, nice to meet you, vicar."

"Oh yes, and good luck with your yoga, Willoughby, I must say I wonder if I should do something like that to ease my increasingly creaking joints."

"Join us if you like, padre, next Tuesday morning. Be delighted to have you along."

"I regret I am not free then, I chair a diocesan meeting on Tuesdays."

"Oh, never mind. Some other time maybe."

"See you all soon," said the vicar, bowing slightly to the group and leaving.

"Anun, I am glad you are here," said Willoughby.

"Of course you are, me and Rik-pig add a bit of tone to your humble gathering, as well as wit, charm, elegance and sophistication."

"Why do you call your sister Rik-pig?" interrupted Harry eagerly.

"It's the name of our pig, well her pig as she sees it. That's why the pig is called Rik-pig. We got this piglet when we were little and little Rikki was fascinated by it – she always has been a sucker for anything involving animals – and she would drag any visitors down to see it and tell them it was her pig, or 'Rik-pig', as her attempts to say 'this is Rikki's piglet' came out as. So the name Rik-pig stuck and our pig is always called Rik-pig. But you were saying, Willoughby, how enchanting it was to have my company."

"That goes without saying," said Willoughby, "it is always a delight, but what makes it doubly so now is that you are lady of vast knowledge and experience in certain matters."

"I deny it all. Rumours only."

"Of bingo I mean."

"Well maybe of Bingo, perhaps."

"So tell me all you know."

"Of Bingo? Well you've met him."

"What?"

"Bingo – you've met him, at Easter."

"Who's Bingo?"

"Who you just asked me about."

"We appear to talking at cross purposes. I am endeavouring to improve my education in matters of the popular pastime of bingo, referenced in a recent conversation with the Secretary of this club and what is I understand is popular with ladies of a certain age and owners of disused cinemas. I am in particular keen to know what Doctor's Orders have to do with anything. Now what on earth is it that you are gibbering about my dear?"

"Oh I thought you were asking me about my chap Bingo."

"You have a chap called Bingo?"

"Yes. You know that."

"Called Bingo?"

"Yes."

"That's a very odd thing to be called."

"Not when your name is Bingo. Then it is a very sensible thing to be called."

"Is Bingo short for something?"

"What on earth could Bingo be short for?"

"I don't know, er Bingo Bango Bongo?"

"There's no such name, you're just making things up. As Rik-pig would say, you do fib so."

"No, it's a golf game," said Harry excitedly, "I played it yesterday with a couple of the members. It's all to do with side bets," he said addressing Anun. "A Bingo is awarded to the player who first gets their ball onto the green, a

Bango to the ball closest to the pin after each player has played onto the green. A Bongo goes to the player who first holes out."

"So Bingo gets his balls in the right place soonest? Well that might be said to be encouraging. Bingo's brother is called Marquan by the way, so his parents obviously liked odd names."

Harry started laughing.

"What amuses you?" asked Willoughby

"Someone called Annunciata having a conversation with someone called Willoughby about people having funny names."

"Do you know this chap?" asked Anun of Willoughby, "is he a friend of yours?"

"No, never seen him before in my life," said Willoughby. "Bing Crosby was called Bingo, now I come to think of it, but it got shortened to Bing. Though his name wasn't actually Bingo, it was Harry."

"Just imagine – someone called Harry getting called by another name," laughed Harry.

"Do you know this chap?" asked Willoughby of Anun, "is he a friend of yours?"

"No, never seen him before in my life," replied Anun. "My name was certainly a hindrance to excelling at school."

"How so?" asked Willoughby.

"Well when you have a name like Annunciata Saithe-Winsor, by the time you have written your name on the exam paper the exam is already half over and you haven't had the chance to earn a mark yet. Mummy says my education improved when she moved me from a mixed school to an all-girls one. But it was nothing to do with sex, it was because I started the new school as Anun Winsor – gave me a better chance in exams."

"So I have met this Bingo fellow then?" asked Willoughby.

"Yes, Mummy invited you to tea in the Easter hols. I think the idea was you were to give him the once over to see if he was suitable. Mags Murtle came too. Remember?"

"Oh yes, I remember him well – small, weedy-looking fellow with spots and halitosis."

"No!" said Anun slapping him on the leg, "he is tall, muscular, blue eyed, good in..." and at that she stopped.

"Good in what?" asked Willoughby mischievously.

"A crisis. Good in a crisis."

"Do you encounter many crisis?"

"Enough to know he is good in one."

Willoughby looked around to see who was about and, as there was no-one else in the bar other than two old ladies also taking tea, remarked: "Someone once told Rambo he was just the man for a crisis. He took it as a great compliment; very chuffed he was. What the chap had meant was that Rambo was good at causing them."

"Remember Bingo now?" asked Anun.

"No. He doesn't ring a bell. What he did we have for tea?"

"I don't know, oh I think we probably had cherry cake and some macaroons and..."

"Oh yes I remember, and we had those lovely light cherry biscuits your mother makes so wonderfully. Oh yes, I remember him – your chap Banjo wolfed all the macaroons."

"No he didn't, Bingo only had one, the last one, and that was only cos Mummy had urged him to, after you had already scoffed about half a dozen of them. Yes," continued Anun taking up her theme again, "I have become an artist's model. You hear these romantic notions about models being an artist's muse, what they don't say is it involves sitting around in next to no clothing and getting told off for moving when all one is doing is shivering. That is why I have escaped here. I was sitting there in just a tiny bikini, trying to look like a mermaid. She leant forward slightly: "Can you imagine that, Harry, me sitting there in just a skimpy bikini?"

But Harry was not paying attention, for Rikki was returning, clearly angrily disappointed with the world.

"What's up?" Harry asked.

"Silly Steward turned down Mumsie's cake."

"You mean he wouldn't taste a slice?" asked Willoughby. "Did he say it would have been very rude of him to do so when you hadn't offered any to your friends and host? You could always remedy that."

"Oh no, he had a slice alright, said it was jolly nice cake – which it is – just that he said he could not take Mumsie on as a designated supplier."

"Why not?"

"Oh lots of mumbo jumbo about hygiene regulations and committee approval and general guff, flapdoodle and hooey."

"Can't you appeal to some committee or other?" suggested Anun. "This club must have a committee for the choosing of cakes or something – I could see you being the ideal chairman, Willoughby – it seems to have one for almost everything else."

"Yes, that would be a committee worth serving on," agreed Willoughby. "We did have a wine committee at one juncture."

"Oh did you serve on that? I'd like to serve on the wine committee. Do you get to go to tastings? How does one get on it?"

"No, I wasn't on it. Tricky things wine tastings. Can have unintended consequences. But I don't think it exists any more – it was an ad hoc arrangement as I recollect.

Catering comes under the auspices of the House Committee, but I regret their powers have been curtailed following the incident of the Great Crisp Ordering Fiasco," replied Willoughby.

"Go on, you interest me strangely, Cornwallis," urged Rikki.

"Well the Chairman of the House Committee saw a good deal to be had in cornering the market in cheese-and-onion crisps as packets of same were going at bargain-basement prices. So said chairman decided to buy 50 packets. Unfortunately he did not understand the ordering system and instead ordered 50 boxes. Hence why the club is stuffed to the gunnels with cheese-and-onion crisps. The Steward has been trying to find ways of getting rid of them. Since then the committee's powers have been suspended and it is all down to the Steward. So on this one I regret that we cannot appeal over his head."

"He said cheese-and-onion crisps were good for hangovers!" complained Harry.

"I thought drinking too much the night before was best for that? Can't see how crisps will make you hungover," reasoned Willoughby.

"No, for curing them – cheese-and-onion crisps. He said it was the ruffleine."

"The rustling? Of the bag you mean? How does that help?"

"I'm not sure. He said no doubt I had studied it at school and, not wishing to look stupid, I said I had."

"Chap I knew, a stone mason called Jim, swore by taking a load of vitamin tablets before you went to bed to avoid a hangover in the morning," advised Willoughby. "He recommended taking two Vitamin C tablets, two B complex and a couple of multi vitamins before turning in after a night on the sauce and he was always as right as rain in the morning. He swore by it. Mind you, he swore by, or at, most things. But to be fair to the chap, he always turned up for work on time all bright eyed and bushy tailed even after regularly imbibing a skinful the previous evening and was a damn fine worker."

"So it worked for him?"

"Up to a point. He died of liver failure."

"Pigs like potato crisps," remarked Rikki. "I sometimes give Rik-pig some as a bit of variety. Hers is a predominantly potato-based diet."

"We'd better get some pig members of the club – I will suggest it to Brian, that'll confuse him – then the Steward could sell them crisps," said Willoughby. "Well so long as they like cheese-and-onion ones. Is there a flavour they favour?"

"Don't think it matters much," replied Rikki.

"Smoky bacon ones might be a bit tactless," remarked Anun.

"I could always make your mother the official cake supplier to the Billiards Committee, I suppose," mused Willoughby. "Not that that would exactly bring her a lot of custom. We only meet once a year."

"The club has a billiards committee?" queried Harry.

"Yes, it is one of the longest-standing and most prestigious committees of the club. Been in operation since the club was founded. Lord Hankley himself was the first chairman."

"Why?"

"He was keen on billiards and he wanted to control the billiards action I suppose."

"No, why does the club have a billiards committee?"

"Well some body has to be in charge of the Billiards Room."

"I didn't know we had a billiards table."

"We don't."

"You just said we have a billiards room."

"We do. But we don't have a billiards table. It's the room

back there. Ever noticed that room without any windows, only some horizontal slots above head height, the idea being that no one is in danger of putting a cue through the window? That's the Billiards Room."

"No I've never seen it, or been in it."

"It's kept locked as no-one is allowed in there except for the playing or practising of billiards. It is in the club's rules. Part of the club's foundation in fact. Lord Hankley was very insistent on that. He didn't trust the members of the club – he thought that all they were interested in was golf. I don't know how much of the club history you have learnt from your Rambo ramblings?"

"Not a lot, all he has done mainly is tell me on four different occasions about the origins of the term service in tennis. Well, he has told me four times but it was only three separate occasions, to be fair."

"Well the founders of the club didn't own all the land they wanted for the course and clubhouse, and some of it was part of the Hankley estate. The estate has – or had I think as most have been sold by now – parcels of land dotted all around here, one of which was wanted by the club for the clubhouse and other bits. Lord Hankley wasn't a golfer, but he was keen on billiards, and so he agreed to make the land available to the club if the clubhouse included a billiards room. Cos he didn't trust the members not to take over the room for their own purposes it was written into the constitution that that room was exclusively for the use of 'billiards, whether practice, play or in the form of billiard table demonstrations and no other use of that room shall be permitted except for these purposes'. When the first Lord Hankley was here it was busy in there when he was down, so it's said. He had a sort of farm down here and he and his set used to come here. But the members never used it much I understand and, well, who plays billiards nowadays?"

"Is that why the club got rid of the table?" asked Harry.

"The club didn't get rid of the table. It just disappeared – no-one knows exactly when it went. Or how."

"Did the club try to get a new one?"

"I did look into it. In the local rag I found a small ad for a full-sized second-hand snooker table, so I phoned up, but when I explained who I was he said he already sold it. Found out later it was one of Benton's businesses that was selling it."

"So what does cake have to do with the committee?"

"Chairmen get an annual budget for modest refreshments for their committee meetings. As we only meet once a year, and the committee is kept small, we can spend all our budget on a dashed fine blow out."

"I suppose as plan B we could try and interest the Steward in Mummy's home-made wine; she has been making some," suggested Anun.

"Cripes no," exclaimed Willoughby.

"I beg your pardon?" said Anun.

"I was just meaning, I'm not sure that is a good idea. Flipping lethal stuff it is."

"Lethal, how do you know?"

"I have drunk it."

"You are still alive so it can't be lethal."

"Okay, Miss Pedantic, it is of a strength and ferocity that renders those who partake of it in a state of general befuddlement and incapacity that would disrupt the orderly life of the clubhouse – that better? Well orderly anyway when old Rambo does not spy a milk jug within 50 paces, or the Secretary is testing the clubhouse's suitability for Greek weddings."

"Is there a story behind this?" asked Anun.

"Would you like a scone?" asked Willoughby proffering her one.

"Not at the moment, I would like the story."

"I'll have a scone," said Rikki, thrusting out a hand to grab one.

"Sure I can't persuade you to partake of a scone Anun? The Secretary got them especially for you."

"The story," prompted Anun.

"Oh it's not very interesting, I wouldn't want to bore you."

"Don't worry, I'll take that risk. But I very much doubt I will be bored."

"We beg you therefore to tell us your story fully. Omit no detail that may be of importance," chimed in Rikki.

"Well if you must. Your mother invited me over one evening to sample her homemade wine. She had made some different varieties and she was thinking of serving it at a do, and wanted the opinion of a man, and your father was away. I dutifully came and sampled the wine and gave my opinion, as requested."

"And?"

"Then I left."

"And?"

"Well I was somewhat wobbly on my feet I must confess and rendered not as sure of my bearings as usual due to the force of your mother's fearsomely fermented grape juice."

"And?"

"Well if you really must know I took a tumble into the pig sty."

Anun shrieked with delight. "I knew there was a story. What happened next?"

"The pig didn't seem particularly pleased to have a guest that time of night, and well I don't know if you have ever been in a pig sty in the dark with an agitated pig butting you in places you would much rather not be butted and with large dollops of pig poo about the place just waiting to be fallen into, but it does nothing for a chap's look or fragrance. Your mother fortunately rescued me."

"Poor Rik-pig having your hulking great frame crash in on her," said Rikki, "disturbing her from sweet dreams about turnips and potato crisps or whatever she dreams about."

"Oh it wasn't Rik-pig. It was before her time."

"Can't have been," laughed Anun, "it's always been Rik-pig, every pig Rikki's had has been called Rik-pig."

"No, this predates Rik-pigs, both in human and porcine form."

"Who did you say is both in human and porcine form?" asked Rikki indignantly, through a mouthful of scone.

"Your pig, my dear, is in porcine form. Comes from the Latin porcus meaning pig."

"Porcus – now that would have been a good name for a pig," said Anun. "More distinguished than Rik-pig."

"Well if you and Bingle Bangle Bongle ever set up house together you can get a pet pig and called him Porcus. Or Porcus Horcus Dorcus or whatever his actual name would be."

"Ugh, you know that is never going to happen. I'm not having a smelly thing about the place."

"Told you he had halitosis."

"Not Bingo!" said Anun, slapping Willoughby on the leg, "a pig. Talking of smelly things people don't want about the place – I bet Mrs Cornwallis was pleased to see you roll in in the early hours of the morning drunk as a skunk and smelling much like one, too."

"Oh I didn't manage to get home that night. Your mother said both I and my clothes needed a wash and brush up before I could present myself again in civilised society.

She kindly washed my clothes and gave me a bed for the night, before I slunk home the next morning, not quite the dapper chipper fellow I usually am, but at least a little more presentable."

"And was Mrs Cornwallis any more pleased to see you in the morning than she would have been the previous night?"

"No, not really. But then she rarely gives the impression she is that keen to see me, so who can tell."

"You should have borrowed some of my father's clothes."

"Unfortunately your father was small and wiry whereas I am um…"

"Slightly less small and wiry."

"Well put, yes. Your mother did offer me one of her maternity gowns – I regret you girls have inherited your mother's cheek and impudence, she has passed on some bad genes – but even seriously sozzled I could see that turning up in the early hours of the morning wearing another women's dress was not the kind of thing Mrs C would take easily in her stride."

"You mean if it was one of her own dresses she would have?" suggested Anun.

"No; no, I think she would have looked askance at that, too."

"So Mummy was pregnant at the time? When was this?"

"No, she wasn't. Well, actually technically she was."

"You can't be a little bit pregnant; you either are or you are not. Just like you can't say something is totally unique, it's either unique or it isn't. I remember people getting in trouble for that in English lessons."

"For getting pregnant? I'm not surprised. No wonder your mother moved you from that school. No, what I mean was your mother was indeed pregnant at the time, but no-one knew that she was, including herself. The maternity gown was one she had from when she was carrying you."

"I wish I had known father," sighed Rikki, "and I wished he at least knew of me. At least he knew Anun, even if you are too young to remember him. He didn't even know I was on the way, that I was going to be his daughter. But I always think it romantic that on his final night with Mumsie, well you know that he left her with me."

"I never knew him either, not at the age I was," pointed out Anun.

"No, but he knew you. You at least have that photograph of him holding you. You have that connection, and at least he knew of you."

"Well Rikki if your father was here," said Willoughby, "I am sure he would be very proud of you. In fact, I can absolutely guarantee it. Indeed both you girls would, I am sure, have been the continuing source of great paternal pride and quite justifiably so."

Anun squeezed Willoughby's knee just as Willoughby said softly to Harry by way of explanation: "Their father was lost at sea, and Rikki was born almost nine months to the day after he had left on that voyage. It was a difficult time for their mother, losing her husband and then finding she was to become a mother again."

"It wasn't actually nine months to the day was it," said Anun softly to Willoughby, "I found some old bits of family history the other day, when tidying up, and it was nearer ten."

"Oh that's right. So it was. I can remember your mother was keen for Rikki to pop out but she wasn't having any of it. She was snug in there and knew everything was being done for her, with catering laid on, and she wasn't shifting. Yes, nine months is a figurative term, bit like three score years and ten, not one to be taken literally. A full-term pregnancy is anything from 37 to 42 weeks, and 42 weeks takes you to almost ten months, whereas at 37 weeks you are nearer eight. And Rikki had obviously booked herself in for the full 42 weeks and she wasn't leaving until they were up. I remember your mother complaining she didn't have a baby human in there but a baby elephant."

"Who are you calling a baby elephant?" said Rikki, looking up from balancing a large dollop of cream on the last of the scones.

"Just remarking how the gestation period of an elephant is over a year and half. No-one is suggesting anyone here is like a baby elephant. Why don't you have another scone? Oh, I see you already have."

"When babies choose to pop out can be a bit random," continued Willoughby. "I remember going round a stately home with my ma when I was young, and there was a story in that family of a mother who gave birth to triplets and each was born on a successive Sunday. Lady Huntley her name was. No, Lady Palmer. I think. Or if that wasn't her name then it was something else. I was puzzled at how they could be triplets when they were born on different days, but my mother said don't be daft they're triplets if they come from the same batch. What's happened about that fruit cake?" asked Willoughby of Harry.

"Oh, sorry, yes – Steward said he doesn't have any cake."

"No cake?"

"No."

"I've got cake," said Rikki brightly.

"Yes, but you're not sharing are you, you old meanie when people around this table are half starved."

"You don't look like you are starving," said Rikki surveying his ample figure.

"I am putting a brave face on it."

"And a brave body, it seems."

"I am multi-faceted. Anyway why do you think I was talking about me? Young Harry here has been told by the Secretary only a few minutes ago that he needs feeding up as he is all the wrong shape."

"What wrong with Harry's shape? I think he is a lovely shape," replied Rikki, smiling at Harry as she said this. "But would you like a slice of this cake, Harry?"

"Having heard so much about your mother's baking prowess from excellent authority, rather. Thank you."

"Anun would you like a slice?"

"Not for me, thanks."

Then Rikki asked her Godfather with elaborate formality: "Willoughby could I possibly interest you in a slice of Mumsie's cake?"

"Well if you insist. Be rude not to."

"What was it you wanted to know about bingo," asked Anun, "the popular pastime I mean, not the hunky fella?"

"I am not surprised he is a chunky fellow the amount he eats. Tell him to lay off the macaroons in future, it's for his own good – perhaps just restrict himself merely to a half dozen not the full dozen. It was something cryptic the Secretary said. There is a group here of somewhat derelict and dilapidated members who totter out and play nine holes once a week. They go under the name of the Doctor's Orders, and I was wondering why."

"And you think with my wide knowledge of golf I would know?"

"No, but with your wide knowledge of bingo you might. Apparently this name has something to do with bingo and I know you and your mother's Mrs Mopp take in the local bingo scene."

"Well, only in that I've had to collect her from bingo; I don't play myself. So my knowledge is limited to that which I have picked up hanging around waiting for it to finish. The main thing, incidentally, that I have learned is that it doesn't finish nearly quickly enough."

"Oh. So you don't know what doctor's orders has to do with it?"

"No."

"Well you're a fat lot of good."

"You mean a willowy lot of good."

"If it's doctor's orders," suggested Rikki, "perhaps it's just that their doctors are worried that they are getting a trifle portly and occasionally they should venture out on the golf field and have a little waddle about while trying to hit things with those silly stick things?"

"Like Dr Mackenzie," chimed in Harry.

"No, we don't have members like that, Half Pint. We are all finely tuned athletes."

"You just said that they were derelict and dilapidated," pointed out Anun.

"They are derelict and dilapidated finely tuned athletes," replied Willoughby.

"There isn't any subtlety to bingo," explained Anun. "It's just a game of chance. A chap at the front draws out a ball and shouts out its number and name and if you have that number on your card you cross it off, and if you cross off your numbers first you win."

"How can numbers have names?"

"Nicknames I suppose is a better word. For example if the bingo caller pulls out three he shouts 'cup of tea'."

"Why?"

"Yes, please," said Rikki.

"What?"

"I thought you were offering me a cup of tea?"

"Help yourself," invited Willoughby.

"But why do they say cup of tea?" he asked of Anun.

"Rhymes with three, I suppose. A lot of them are rhymes. Do you know what 42 is?"

"Not a Scooby Doo."

"Close – Winnie the Pooh."

"Okay, so what rhymes with doctor's orders? Nope," said Willoughby after a bit of reflection, "that doesn't help."

"Oh, some nicknames are based on what the number looks like."

"Oh yes, like two fat ladies."

"Who are you calling fat ladies?" said Rikki through a mouthful of cake.

"No-one is calling anyone a fat lady, it's a bingo term," said Willoughby. "Cut yourself another slice of cake – oh I see you already have." Then to Anun he continued: "It's like in golf if you score eight, we call it a snowman cos it looks a bit like a snowman. What looks like a doctor's order? For that matter, what does a doctor's order look like?"

"You need to speak to Mags Murtle," advised Anun "she is keen on bingo – she'll know more than me."

"What's a pair of fat ladies – 33? What they look like in silhouette," asked Harry.

"I think it's 88."

"Oh, two snowmen," said Willoughby.

"Hallo," said a voice at Willoughby's shoulder, "I am looking for the Secretary, have you seen him?" It was Miss Murtle.

"Ah, Magnolia, how good to see you, you are just the lady we were hoping to see," said Willoughby rising from his chair to greet her.

"Oh, were you?" she said surprised.

"Yes, we were. I have a question for you. But to answer your question – he was in here recently throwing our tea things about the place. Young Half Pint has had to have four slices of cake just to calm her nerves."

"No, I'm looking for Mr Pirbright, not Mr Ramsbotham. Have you seen him? He said he was coming to speak to you."

"He was here recently. He's floating about somewhere. Can I proffer you a piece of cake? Rikki is doing the honours – it's her mother's cake. Most scrumptious."

"Well I really need to find the Secretary…"

"I have a question for you about bingo."

"Anun's young man? The one partial to macaroons? He really loves them doesn't he?"

"Hah!" said Willoughby triumphantly, looking at Anun. "No I mean the game. I understand you are an expert on its inner workings?"

"Well I play, but I am not sure you could call me an expert as such."

"I am sure you are too modest. To the logician all things should be seen exactly as they are, and to underestimate one's self is as much a departure from truth as to exaggerate one's own powers. Pull up a pew, Miss Murtle, and have a slice of cake and educate us."

"Well I really need to catch the Secretary."

"What would you do with him when you've caught him? You'd only have to throw him back. Might as well have a bit of cake and help us with our problem. Consider it a one-slice-of-cake problem we are presenting you with."

"Well I am supposed to be working."

"Ah but this is work. It is an important question about the workings of the club put to you by some of its most distinguished members and one that only someone of your knowledge and experience can answer."

"Oh in that case, if it's work, yes please I would love a

piece of your mother's cake then Rikki, thank you very much, very kind of you."

As Rikki did the honours Willoughby continued: "It is to do with the Doctor's Orders."

"The group that meets on Tuesday mornings?"

"Them's the fellows. Now their name has something to do with bingo I am told."

"Does it?"

"So the Secretary says. So we were wondering what is a doctor's order in bingo."

"Oh that's easy. Doctor's orders is what the caller calls out for number nine."

"Why?"

"Well, all the bingo calls have a name as well, to help you hear what was said. Some of them are rather clever – for instance eighty is Gandhi's breakfast – as in ate nothing. Some are, I regret, rather vulgar, such as 81 which is 'fat lady with a walking stick', or 'is she worth it', which is 56 as the marriage licence used to cost 5 and 6. I always hope I don't get those numbers on my card and they don't get drawn."

"Oh, in golf when you lose 7 and 6 we refer to it as a dog licence because that is what that used to cost."

"So to get a dog cost more than getting a wife?" asked Anun.

"Makes sense. A dog can be relied upon to give you love and devotion throughout their life; wives less so I have found," reasoned Willoughby.

"And number nine is doctor's orders," explained Miss Murtle.

"Why is number nine doctor's orders?"

"I don't know I'm afraid. One you might like is 83 – time for tea."

"Would you like a number 3, Magnolia?"

140

"A...? Oh, a cup of tea! Yes, please. Thank you, very kind."

"Hallo, hallo, hallo, what is going on here?"

"Oh hallo Mr Secretary," said Willoughby looking up. "Well you appear to be doing a comedy policeman's routine, and we are partaking of what I have every expectation will be a culinary delight of afternoon tea. Would you care to join us – cup of tea perhaps or a slice of Rikki and Anun's mother's most excellent cake?"

"No I cannot have a slice of cake."

"Well I wouldn't be so pessimistic, it's quite hard to get the greedy guzzleguts over there to disgorge some but with your winning ways you can persuade her. Some of us have more difficulty," continued Willoughby, ignoring the face Rikki was pulling at him.

"And you Miss Murtle, I am surprised at you being a party to such a thing."

"Oh blame me, Secretary, it is all my fault," said Willoughby.

"That does not surprise me."

"For I waylaid her when she was hot on the trail of you in the manner of the most assiduous bloodhound – I stress in manner only for she looked nothing like one. She especially lacked the long droopy ears, for I have always considered Miss Murtle's ears very perky and most elegant, set off wonderfully always by her splendid taste in earrings." As he said this he could not help but look at Miss Murtle's ears, which were blushing red as she murmured "Oh Willoughby you do say the nicest and daftest things," and then when he looked back at the Secretary he saw that his ears too were turning red, although of a darker shade.

"No, I cannot have a piece of cake," said the Secretary.

"Oh you can," Willoughby assured him. "I know it is

quite hard to get Half Pint to disgorge some, but with perseverance it will happen. If you like, I can put in a good word for you, for I know she looks up to me and lets me guide her in important matters. I also used to read Sherlock Holmes stories to her, and that forms a bond."

"Would you like a slice of Mumsie's delicious cake, Secretary?" asked Rikki.

"There you are, Secretary," said Willoughby, "I said it was not impossible – you just have to know the right contacts and how to pull strings. Which, incidentally, is also how one gets on as a self-employed puppeteer I believe."

"Thank you, but no Miss Winsor. Steward!" he bellowed signalling to him to come over. "This is all most irregular."

"Is it?" said Willoughby peering at the remains of the cake. "I don't think cakes are supposed be regular. But it is round; well, it was."

"I'm not talking about the cake, well I am, but I am not."

"You confuse me, Mr Secretary, I think you are either are or you are not. It's a bit like being pregnant for, as Anun so wisely put it only a few minutes ago, you are either pregnant or you are not – in your case I would hazard at 'not' being the answer – and so you either are talking about cake, a fascinating subject on which I am always happy to listen to a talk about, especially from such a gifted orator as yourself – or you are not."

"I am talking about club rules, and propriety."

"There are elements of the club," said Willoughby, "who, I regret to say, advocate putting whoopy cushions on the chairs or pulling faces at committee members through the window or even – and I know this will shock you Secretary, so you may wish to take a seat hurriedly – try to eat cake at one minute to four. But against this tide of hooliganism and debauchery your Steward, our Steward, stays firm, he rules over us with a rod of iron, upholding the rules of the club in all their glory and idiocy without fear or favour. Indeed, I understand that the Amalgamated Association of Traffic Wardens have twice tried to pinch him from us for that very reason, although they might use some fancy term as 'head hunted', but we all know what was afoot there."

"What was afoot?" said the Secretary, who Willoughby had by now thoroughly addled.

"Twelve inches. Well it still is I believe. Though, as we are getting bigger, if it is really supposed to be as long as a foot maybe they will have to add an extra inch at some stage, so maybe one day a foot will have to be 13 inches."

"And we all know what big feet in a man signifies don't we?" said Anun. "Big shoes," she tittered.

"Ah, Steward what is the meaning of this?" demanded the Secretary after the Steward had arrived having deliberately taken his time to arrive.

"These gentleman and these ladies have been partaking of afternoon tea. You may remember you were with some of the group earlier, when there was that regrettable incident with you smashing up the club crockery."

"No, what I mean is what are they eating? That cake?" The Steward realised for the first time that the group were eating cake.

"Do not worry Mr Secretary," advised Willoughby, "it is past the hour of four. You probably haven't noticed it, as you hadn't spotted the honours board of the Junior Foursomes champions, but if you look a few feet – twelve inch ones for the time being – to the left you will see a clock, and it clearly shows that 4pm today is but a memory for it, a part now of all our yesteryears."

"Yes, that cake. What do you think you lot are doing and what are you doing Steward in allowing it? This is not a picnic area, people can't just bring their own food in here. If they wish to eat here they must buy the food provided. How on earth do people expect us to run a financially solvent institution if people treat the bar and restaurant as a self-catering facility."

"Ah I see where the problem is," continued Willoughby, making sure that the Steward had no opportunity to speak. "You have come across a group partaking of some afternoon tea, just like those fine ladies from the church over there are, and you have identified this as illegal contraband smuggled into the club, and the Steward is complicit in allowing such a gross breach of club rules and trust, and by his negligence and dereliction of duty in not in this case ruling the bar with the rod of iron for which he is so famous, he is guilty of an action which would undoubtedly lead to disciplinary measures being taken against him; indeed, even possibly the sack."

"Yes, indeed disciplinary measures look to be in order and I could not even at this stage rule out a termination of employment," said the Secretary, seizing on what Willoughby said as a way to try to get in control of the situation. He was still smarting at his earlier encounter with the Steward and saw this as a chance to put the blighter firmly in his place. "Yes very serious business, would have to make a recommendation to the committee. This is undoubtedly a breach of trust and terms of employment," said the Secretary firmly.

"Ah, it would be if what you thought you saw was indeed what you saw. But what in fact you see is young Rikki doshing out the club's own produce."

"You just said it was her mother's cake!"

"Those possessive pronouns can be awfully confusing can't they," said Willoughby sympathetically. "It is their mother's cake in that she baked it; it is the club's cake in that they owned it, having bought it from their mother. So you see it is both their mother's cake and the club's cake, but that does not mean of course that their mother is the club, or indeed, is in the club, despite still owning maternity wear."

"The club has bought the cake?" enquired the Secretary.

"As the Steward will attest, Rikki has just had a discussion with the Steward about her mother, a fine baker by the way, becoming an official supplier to the club for baked goods, isn't that so, Steward?"

"Yes, but..."

"And so you wrong the Steward by presuming that he is allowing illicit eating on the premises." The Steward tried to say something else, but Willoughby quickly cut across him: "I think, Mr Secretary that an apology from you may be in order to this wronged man."

The Steward no longer tried to interrupt, seeing that matters had fallen his way and that the Secretary was being invited to apologise to him in front of several witnesses. This was going to be one of his more enjoyable days at work. Well less unenjoyable ones anyway.

"Well is this true Steward that you have you taken on Mrs Winsor as an official supplier to the club?"

"Yes Sir, but only on a trial basis of one month."

"One month was what Rikki had suggested, but the Steward, quite rightly in my humble opinion, said it should be longer to give it a fair trial, so he suggested three months, and Rikki agreed to his suggestion and furthermore," Willoughby continued talking over what he sensed was going to be another attempted interruption from the Steward, "at the Steward's firm insistence, Mrs Winsor has agreed to take part of her fee in packets of cheese-and-onion crisps at cost price."

"Crisps," said both the Secretary and the Steward at the same time. The former by way of a question; the latter by way of an involuntary cry of delight.

"Yes crisps. She occasionally gives her pig a packet of crisps by way of a treat – apparently the pig goes to bed dreaming of crisps."

"Is that so, Steward?" demanded the Secretary.

"I regret that I cannot confirm or deny this, Sir, for I do not have sufficient data about what Miss Winsor's pig may dream of."

"Not about the blasted pig, I mean about taking on Mrs Winsor as an official supplier."

"Yes, Sir, that is true. She has offered, so I have been reliably informed, to take some of her fee in cheese-and-onion crisps," said the Steward looking at Willoughby.

"That is indeed what Mrs Winsor has agreed," said Willoughby, "at cost price."

"You seem to know a lot about it," said the Secretary sourly to Willoughby, "considering this doesn't seem to have involved you at all."

"I am merely reporting what Rikki has told me, and indeed the whole table. You can check with her if this is an accurate report."

"Yes, Willoughby does tell the truth so," replied Rikki.

The Steward said: "On the basis outlined I have agreed to buy baked goods from Paddock's Farm and Mrs Winsor for the club to serve in the clubhouse for a trial period."

"Of at least three months," Willoughby reminded him.

"Of three months, yes," agreed the Steward reluctantly.

"So you see Mr Secretary," summed up Willoughby, "what you see before you on Rikki's plate can be said to be Mrs Winsor's cake in that she made it; Miss Winsor's cake as she is eating it; the club's cake in that it was supplied by the club, and your cake."

"My cake?"

"Yes, for you have paid for it – remember you said this afternoon tea was on you after you had kicked the last one about the room?" The Secretary let out a small groan. "Are you quite sure I can't interest you in a slice of cake, Mr Secretary? It is very good."

"No, thank you," he groaned, "I don't want any cake."

"Perhaps you would prefer some cheese-and-onion crisps, Sir?" ventured the Steward.

The Secretary, knowing when he was defeated, retreated.

"Well this has all been most jolly, I have enjoyed it," said Miss Murtle. "But I regret I must leave you to go back to work," and with that she left with a parting "and tell your Mother how much I enjoyed her cake, please Rikki."

"I will," replied Rikki cheerfully. "I better tie down the deal with the Steward," she said getting up.

"Negotiate hard, Half Pint."

"I will," she said leaving.

"She will, too," Willoughby said to Harry.

"Why do you call her Half Pint?" asked Harry, eager to absorb as much about Rikki as he possibly could.

"When she was younger – me too as a matter of fact – we used to go for nature rambles. She had got the Boys Bumper Book of British Trees for her birthday, or perhaps it was the Girls Ginormous Guide to Great Trees in her case and we used to go for these long walks, well route marches really – oh they were so long – trying to spot and tick off the trees in her book."

"On one of these route marches on a baking hot day, we off saddled for a drink at a wayside tavern with a shady garden and I went in and ordered our drinks and the barmaid said she'd bring them out to us. When she did she said 'I have a pint here and a half pint', and up squeaked Rikki, 'I'm Half Pint', and the barmaid said 'hallo Half Pint' and the name stuck."

Rikki returned to the table looking triumphant. "All successfully arranged?" asked Anun.

"Most definitely," beamed Rikki.

Harry told her. "We have just been learning how you got the name Half Pint."

"Oh yes from our afternoons at that pub. Willoughby would take me to this nice pub, and we'd sit in the garden and play silly, fun games, and eventually he'd say 'let's go for a walk and see one of those trees of yours', and we'd tootle down to the foot of the garden and look at the trees there and then he'd retreat back up the garden saying he was absolutely exhausted and needed another drink and the barmaid would bring him a pint of beer and me a half pint of ginger beer."

"Oh how you malign me Half Pint. What would happen is we would walk for miles and miles and miles and by the time I was about to pass out from dehydration and exhaustion and my blisters were themselves getting blisters – and it was no good hoping a St Bernard would come and rescue me as they had long since handed in the towel, and were having to be rescued by other St Bernards driving ambulances – she finally allowed me a couple of quick gulps of barley water before she route marched me several more furlongs in quest of the lesser spotted Black Poplar or somesuch. Only to find when we got there that it had given us the slip and gone to the cinema or something. One day, I remember, she marched us all the way up to John O'Groats to find the Wentworth Elm, and when we got there Half Pint found she had had the book upside down and we should have gone to Land End's instead and so she turned us around and marched us straight down there instead."

"Oh Willoughby, you do fib so," laughed Rikki. "But those days of ours tree-hunting were great fun," she added firmly. "Remember the song we used to sing?"

"Oh that's right, you thought it so funny."

"It was," said Rikki, and as she said so she put her middle finger on her nose, palm facing towards her and giggled. As this was exactly how, as a young child, she used to laugh at something she knew was coming. Willoughby was transported happily to those days and the childish glee involved. Almost involuntarily he began to sing the verse, and Rikki soon joined in:

Paddy wrote a letter
To his Irish Molly O',
Saying, "Should you not receive it,
Write and let me know!
If I make mistakes in spelling,
Molly dear", said he,
"Remember it's the pen, that's bad,
Don't lay the blame on me.

The Steward had come over: "I must ask you Miss not to sing in this room please, it is not allowed. And Sir," he said addressing Willoughby, "whatever it was you were doing I would respectfully ask that you desist from that, too."

Rikki again put her finger on her nose and giggled, and Harry said when the Steward had walked away: "Doesn't he know you are chairman of one of the most distinguished committees of the club?"

"I think he knows exactly that, and that is why he said it," remarked Willoughby.

"Why do the members put up with him?" asked Harry. "He is obnoxious to everyone."

"Our stinker of a skinker? Well one is that he is actually good at his job in marked contrast to some of his trandled predecessors, and he was once so rude to Benton that Benton has refused to set foot in the bar until the Steward is dismissed. For that alone he has a job for life. For the length of Benton's life that is."

"Well I better be off to tell Mumsie the good news," said Rikki. "She will be thrilled," and she bounced around the table and said: "Willoughby you were marvellous, thank you," and planted a kiss on his cheek.

"All part of the service spreading sweetness and light. Oh, what about the cake," said Willoughby as Rikki was leaving.

"Oh yes, I better leave that shouldn't I?"

"Yes, leave it here in case some people might want some more. Someone might perhaps."

"Yes, I will leave it with the Steward in case anyone else wants to buy some cake this afternoon."

This was not what Willoughby had intended and his dejected face made Anun laugh. "Poor Willoughby," she said. "Still, on the positive side it will help you keep in Mrs C's good books."

"I like your optimistic use of the word 'keep'. How?"

"She was telling me of her desire to see a slimmed down you, and of her regret that all this golf you do has not exercised off what she sees as an excess amount of Willoughby."

"You have been talking to her?"

"Yes, I bumped into her in the street t'other day and we had a long chat. She told me she had you doing yoga."

"She has indeed, every Tuesday morning. We both do it

– she and I have a yogi bear getting us to bend ourselves into positions most entertaining if somewhat perplexing."

"That I would like to see."

"Come along and join in the fun if you wish, the more the merrier – any Tuesday morning, just follow the sound of creaking joints. But I can demonstrate now if you like. Though I say so myself, my downward dog is something of a work of art."

"Oh go on then," said Anun, "let's see it."

Willoughby got up and with great glee proceeded to demonstrate under the amused eye of Anun, the curious one of Harry, and the bewildered ones of the two ladies who were taking tea nearby, his somewhat idiosyncratic interpretation of the downward dog.

"I am not entirely sure you are doing it quite right," advised Anun.

"Ah well you must understand," retorted Willoughby, "that I am doing it under the handicap of this bad ankle which so troubled the poor Secretary." With this comment his waved one of his feet out by way of amplification of his point, which had the unfortunate effect of making it look like he was imitating a dog doing his business alongside a tree. It also caught the passing Mr Ramsbotham, causing him to trip and throw out a hand to steady himself as he stumbled towards the table where the ladies were taking tea, and his flailing hand knocked their milk jug onto the floor.

Chapter 8

Willoughby rose to his feet quickly: "I am most terribly sorry ladies," he said addressing the two ladies who had been taking tea and who were now minus some crockery, "this gentleman gets rather agitated around milk jugs. I am sure he means them no real harm. You must forgive him if you can find it in your heart, for he is probably more to be pitied than censured."

Mr Ramsbotham had struggled to his feet in a state of indignation. "It was you who did that," he said crossly to Willoughby, ignoring the ladies. "It was your leg!"

The Steward had by now arrived on the scene and was surveying the wreckage. "Has there been an accident?" he asked somewhat redundantly and to no-one in particular.

"I am afraid Rambo spotted a milk jug," Willoughby replied, "and you know how that can end."

"Oh dear yes," said the Steward to Willoughby, then to the ladies: "I am sorry for that."

"It's quite alright really," replied one of the ladies, "there is no real harm. It's just that this gentleman tripped and had a slight accident and knocked our milk jug off the table. Could be cracked, I fear."

"I have indeed heard it suggested of him. Do you require some more milk?" asked the Steward.

"If you would be so kind, thank you. There is still some tea left in our pot."

"I will get it straight away for you, madam – and apologies for the inconvenience."

"It was you who did that. It was your leg!" Rambo was saying over again, getting ever more cross that everyone was ignoring him.

"No, my dear Rambo," said Willoughby, "it was your

hand that dashed the jug to the floor. My foot was nowhere near the jug – what do you think I am, a go-go dancer, one of the chorus of the Hippodrome? But don't worry, we all know of your antipathy towards milk jugs."

"I don't have anything against milk jugs," shouted Mr Ramsbotham, "that's a lie!"

"No doubt it started it. I am sure it behaved very badly whatever it did. Did it attack you – in which case you can always plead self-defence? Did it come at you with a knife? Or a teaspoon?"

What Mr Ramsbotham had been saying during this speech was hard to decipher in his spluttering fury. "It was your foot that did it!" shouted Mr Ramsbotham again, having recovered the power of coherent speech.

"Cheer up old bean," said Willoughby, "look on the positive side, you may have rid the world of one more of those china milk jugs you hate so, although the fact will not been known for certain until the Steward has carried out an autopsy. Do you want to stamp up and down on it just to make sure?"

"It was your foot that did it!" shouted Mr Ramsbotham again.

"I feel you are a little overwrought," advised Willoughby. "As I have said, my foot was nowhere near the milk jug. Don't forget there are witnesses," he said waving towards Anun and Harry.

"I saw it all your honour," said Anun "and I cannot tell a lie, it was definitely Mr Ramsbotham in the bar with the milk jug," before adding as an aside to Harry: "I am only glad it missed me this time and I wasn't drenched."

"No," shouted Mr Ramsbotham increasingly furiously, "it was you that caused it, waving your foot about like that!"

"No need to shout, old bean," said Willoughby.

"I am not shouting," shouted Mr Ramsbotham.

"I think you are shouting a bit," suggested one of the ladies quietly, leaning towards him.

"I am not shouting," he shouted at her.

"Now, now, my dear chap," said Willoughby in a soothing voice, "you can't go round shouting that I kicked the jug off the table. For one thing I would have to be some sort of karate kid to do that, and I am no longer a kid, nor indeed am I one of those whatyamacallits like that chap in those films, whatsisname, Bruce Springsteen," the last two words said with a touch of hesitancy.

"Lee," corrected Harry.

"Thank you, Larry. Lee Springsteen," said Willoughby.

"No," said Mr Ramsbotham stamping his foot. "It was your leg."

"If you are indeed trying to stamp on the milk jug, you need to step back a touch for it is behind you," said Willoughby affably.

"I was not stamping my foot," shouted Mr Ramsbotham stamping his foot again, "it was you waving your foot about what tripped me up and in trying to regain my balance I had to go," and at this point he demonstrated what he remembered of the incident by flailing his arms about. Unfortunately this was at the point, both geographical and temporal, that the Steward was returning with a replacement jug of milk which Mr Ramsbotham's flailing arms dashed from his hand.

"Mr Ramsbotham!" shrieked Anun as most of the contents of the milk jug had landed in her lap.

Mr Ramsbotham spluttered something incoherent in his agitation as he looked round for someone to blame.

"I beg your pardon," said Anun, "do you have something to say to me?"

"He was apologising to you, weren't you Rambo," said Willoughby firmly, seeing how annoyed Anun was.

By now Mr Ramsbotham had regained the power of intelligible speech and said crossly: "Sorry Anun but it was not my fault."

"Whose fault is it then," she replied icily. "The Archbishop of Canterbury's, the cat's, Denis Compton's?"

"I didn't know the Steward was there."

"You ought also to apologise to the Steward," suggested Willoughby, "for hitting him."

The Steward was at that moment apologising to the ladies and assuring them that he would bring them some more milk, but that it would be best done when Mr Ramsbotham had left the room "as he can be quite excitable around milk jugs, as you can see."

"Come on Rambo, it's probably better if you left these ladies to get on with their tea in peace," said Willoughby calmly ushering him to the door. "You can apologise to the Steward later when everything has calmed down."

"I am perfectly calm," shouted Mr Ramsbotham, "it is everyone else who is not."

"You have had plenty of fun already today and you don't want to overdo it and I am sure you have something terribly important to be getting on with," soothed Willoughby.

"Yes I have, I have been organising the agenda for tomorrow's Heads of Committee meeting," replied Rambo then, feeling he was being deliberately diverted from the main issue, asked angrily, as Willoughby held the door open for him: "What were you doing down there waving your leg about?"

"Yoga."

"But why you were doing it there?"

"Well I could hardly do it somewhere where I wasn't could I?" reasoned Willoughby, closing the door on him.

The door opened again promptly and the Secretary burst through it. "I heard shouting, what has been going on?" Then the Secretary spotted debris on the floor, and stopped and said to the Steward: "I thought I had told you to clear up all that mess ages ago."

"Oh this is not that mess," intervened Willoughby, "this is a new one."

"A new one?" queried the Secretary.

"Is Mr Ramsbotham safely outside the room now?" asked the Steward approaching Mr Cornwallis and ignoring the Secretary.

"Yes, I have secured the area. You should be safe to make a milk delivery now," replied Willoughby.

"What has been going on?" asked the Secretary. As the Steward simply walked away ignoring both question and Secretary, Willoughby took it upon himself to answer. "Rambo spotted a milk jug and, well, you know how that tends to work out."

"Yes, indeed. But there are two jugs on the floor?"

"The Steward unwisely tried to deliver another jug to the ladies when Rambo was still in the room, which showed a determination to carry out his duty without thought to his own wellbeing which one can only grudgingly admire; however his judgement, I regret, one cannot laud. Rather predictably, Rambo, presumably with the adrenaline rushing through his veins from having recently taken out another of those pesky milk jugs he hates so... well I am sure I do not need me to paint you a picture. If it was any consolation, it was over in a flash and I doubt the milk jug suffered any pain."

"Yes, quite. Odd fellow. I wonder why he does it – to milk jugs I mean."

"Who can say? It is probably some deep-seated neurosis caused by an incident in his past. Maybe his wife left him for the milkman?"

"No. It can't be that," replied the Secretary, "he still lives with his wife. Well in a manner of speaking: she keeps him in a shed at the bottom of her garden I am told."

"I am sorry ladies, I hear you have had an unfortunate interruption to your afternoon tea," said the Secretary turning to them, "I do so apologise – is there anything we can get you?"

"No, thank you, the Steward is kindly already getting us some more milk."

The Secretary stalked off to find the Steward to order him to clean up the mess.

"We were just wondering," said one of the ladies to Willoughby "what it was that you were doing on the floor that caused that other gentleman to trip over you?"

"Oh that – yes I was showing the young lady here my dogging technique. Me and my wife have recently got into it – a bear lady comes once a week and my wife and I do this and other things with her. I have just been discussing it with the vicar actually and he said it all sounded great fun and he was thinking of joining us. Would you like me to demonstrate?" asked Willoughby eagerly.

"No, I do not think that would be at all appropriate."

"Sure?" said Willoughby disappointed.

"Yes, quite sure. Come on Ursula," she said to her companion, "I think it is time we left."

"Is it?" said the other vacantly.

"Yes it is, come on."

"But you said there was still some tea left in your pot?" said Willoughby shocked at the waste.

The lady who wasn't called Ursula, blanked him. After

they had left, Willoughby checked their teapot. "Ah well: waste not, want not," he said swapping it with the empty one on his table.

"Now where were we?" said Willoughby sitting back down with Anun and Harry.

"If you gentlemen will excuse me," said Anun, "I will just pop to the ladies and see if I can dry my dress with the hand-drier. Dumbo isn't half a menace."

"I have been thinking" said Harry to Willoughby as Anun was leaving, "of something you were saying about... oh heck I always get it confused, what's the difference between foursomes and fourballs?"

"Fourballs involves four balls being played, teams of two, each member playing his or her own ball. Foursomes also involves teams of two but each team only has one ball, and the team members play alternate shots with it. Americans, displaying their more literal interpretation of the world, call the format alternate shot."

"Thank you, foursomes it is – why if each player has to take half the tee shots does it have to be alternate tee shots?"

"Good question – dunno."

"Why can't they just agree to play half the tee shots over the course of the round?"

"Well you could, it just wouldn't be traditional foursomes but some other format."

"Oh have the ladies left?" said the Steward who had just brought the replacement milk jug.

"Yes, they hurried off for some reason," replied Willoughby.

"They had ordered some more milk," grumbled the Steward while picking up the debris from the floor. "They said there was more tea in their pot."

"Oh, if you have some milk there might as well bung it over here please," said Willoughby, "as we have run out."

"Were those ladies members?" asked Harry.

"Must be I suppose," replied Willoughby. "I have seen them in church, but not in here before. Guess they must have become social members. Quite a few people use this as a restaurant-cum-pub as there isn't anywhere else in the village these days. We used to have the Castro pub, but that's gone so this is the nearest we have to a pub nowadays."

"I think the term you were looking for is gastro pub," said Harry, feeling he was now friendly enough with Willoughby to correct him.

"No, it was known as the Castro pub because it was owned by a communist fellow. Keen fan of jazz he was. Never been my thing I confess – jazz that is, as I was fond of the occasional visit to a pub in my younger, freer days. What was the chap's name? He was a member here, quite a good golfer actually, when he talked he used to wave his hands about like an octopus semaphoring a speed-reading exercise – when he and Rambo were together in passionate discussion you had to batten down all the pint glasses in the local postcode as well as all the milk jugs otherwise carnage would ensue – loved an argument and you could tell he knew when he was losing as he started overusing the word 'ludicrous', ludicrously so. But stimulating company always; intelligent, learned fellow. Oh what was his name? Was the same as one of the big department stores funnily enough for someone dedicated to the overthrow of the capitalist system."

"Ah, Brian," Willoughby called to the passing Membership Committee chairman, "you might be able to help us. I have a question for you."

"Oh hallo Willoughby are you here for the Head Committee meeting too?" asked Brian.

"No, that is tomorrow."

"Is it? I thought it was um."

"Nope, you will just have to contain your excitement for another 24 hours. But I have a question for you."

"Do you?"

"The chap who owned that Castro pub, jazz chap, member of the club – remember him?"

"Yes I do," replied Brian and walked on.

"No, Brian come back," called out Willoughby after him, "that wasn't the question."

"Oh wasn't it? What would you like to um."

"Know? What was the fellow's name?"

"What fellow?"

"The chap who used to have the Castro pub."

"Oh him. I was just talking about him to someone."

"Were you? That's a co-incidence. Can you remember his name?"

"Who I was talking to? It was um..."

"No, not that chap, the Castro pub fellow, what was the name of the Castro pub fellow? All I can remember is that it was it was the same as some department store or other."

"Oh yes, that's right. It was a shop my wife used to..."

"Excellent, now what's the name?" prompted Willoughby as the conversation seemed to have stalled.

"My wife's? It's um, it's um, it's...."

"No, the Castro pub chap's name."

"Oh him. Dorothy Perkins."

"Dorothy Perkins?"

"Yes."

"I don't think that was the chap's name."

"Wasn't it?"

"No, I think I would have remembered if he was called Dorothy."

"Oh yes, see what you mean. Unusual name these days. Memorable. You don't find many Dorothys about now."

"Harvey Nichols!" exclaimed Willoughby triumphantly. "That was the fellow's name. Showed his contempt for the capitalist system by ignoring its principles and going bust. Pub got converted into flats. Thank you, Brian," said Willoughby as the other wandered off.

"So you see young Larry, you slur me by saying I got the name wrong – that was why it was known as the Castro pub."

"Okaydoke, I will give you that one, but your reputation for getting names wrong is perhaps still deserved – you just called me Larry."

"That was just to tease you, you young pup," he said, his eyes twinkling, "I am well aware, young Gary, that your name is actually Barry. I know Old Whatshisname says that I am bad at remembering names but don't listen to him. He does fib so, as Half Pint would put it."

"Hallo, what are you talking about?" asked the returned, slightly less damp, Anun.

"I was just telling Larry about the Castro pub."

"Oh, Peter Jones' place? Shame that went. It means this is the only place to go of an evening now. Not, I hasten to add, that this is not of course a fine establishment with some delightful people in it. But it is, well, you know, a golf club."

"Of which you are a member don't forget," pointed out Willoughby.

"I know – I said it has some delightful people in it."

"Talking of impudent pups, as we just were, what were you saying about my most excellent rendition of the downward dog?"

"Oh yes. I just think that particular dog is more mongrel than pedigree."

"Paddington said it was very good. I mean Yogi."

"Show me again and I'll show you," said Anun.

"Should I be exercising on a full stomach?" queried Willoughby, not keen to be criticised, for he was rather proprietorial of his artistic interpretation of the downward dog.

"If you can't exercise on a full stomach, then you won't ever be able to exercise," said Anun teasingly.

"What was I was just saying about impudent young pups," remarked Willoughby as he levered himself onto the floor in readiness to give a reprise performance of his much-talked about, albeit only by himself, downward dog.

"Hey," called out the Steward, "you can't do that here. This is a golf club bar not the local gymnasium. That sort of thing has already caused enough trouble today."

"I suppose the bar is beginning to fill up with the old soaks coming in for their evening snifter," said Willoughby levering himself back up again. "Come on Anun we'll go to the billiards room, we can do it in there without any danger of being pelted by milk jugs."

"I regret that I cannot allow that Sir," said the Steward. "The billiards room is only for billiards. Also that room is locked, and I have the key. That room is for billiards only, Sir," he repeated to ram home the point.

"That room is for, to quote the constitution of the club 'billiards, whether practice, play or in the form of billiard table demonstrations and no other use of that room is permitted except for these purposes'," replied Willoughby affably.

"Precisely, Sir."

"And that is what we are going to do."

"If you will pardon the observation, Sir, you appear to be planning to do some sort of geriatric gymnastics in there rather than a game of billiards. Also, as that room does not have a billiards table you cannot play billiards there," he added with a triumphant flourish.

"I see where your confusion lies oh faithful Steward, we are not going to be playing billiards. What we are going to do is the aforementioned billiard table demonstration. A billiard table is, I am sure I do not have to tell someone of your intelligence and wide knowledge, a well-known yoga position, so-called because – well it will be easier if I get Anun to demonstrate it to you if you don't mind fulfilling the role of my glamorous assistant my dear?"

"I am at your service," smiled Anun. "It doesn't involve being sawn in half does it?"

"No, no, you will remain undiminished throughout the whole process, it is all based upon billiards."

"So, people will be putting their balls in my pockets?"

"No, not that either. It's, oh we'll show the Steward," said he turning towards the club servant. "Oh hang on a mo, you won't allow us to do yoga here so I am afraid we cannot. But I will describe it to you. It is so called because you make your body into what is whimsically called, by the strange people who tag such things, as looking like a billiard table. You put your arms and legs out so as to make the four legs of the table and then you have to make the rest of your body as flat as you can, thus replicating and completing, so the myopic inventors of the position believe, the green baize tabletop of a billiards table which, as you no doubt appreciate, relies upon being flat for its usefulness."

"Come on you two," he said victoriously to Anun and Harry, "let's go into the billiards room and practise our billiard tables." Then adding, to crown his victory: "I have a key as I am Chairman of the Billiards Committee."

"I am not sure I can do the move in this tight dress. I think I may have to take it off – you won't mind if I take my dress off Harry?" Anun purred. "Don't worry, I still have my skimpy bikini on underneath it."

Chapter 9

Brian walked into the bar and looked around him. He was seeing who was there and hoping that this would jog his memory as to why he had come to the club that evening. He knew there was a reason. He was vaguely aware that he was wanted for something, or had to do something at the club, but as to what it was he had no idea. He must have known when he left home, leaving two clues of The Times crossword still to do, he rationalised, as otherwise he would not have left home.

"Hallo Brian," said Martin Cowmeadow, Chairman of the Competitions Committee, who was standing at the bar. "You been playing golf?"

"Golf? Um, yes, well no. Well yes. Well no, I have, but um not today. Playing golf I mean."

"Can I get you a drink, Brian?"

"Oh. A drink? Oh yes, a drink. Yes, a drink. Yes please, that's very good of you."

"What would you like?"

"A drink please."

"But what particular drink?"

"Oh, ah, I will like um..."

"Would you like your usual Sir?" suggested the Steward.

"Is that what I normally have?"

"Yes, Sir"

"Um, yes please."

"Certainly, Sir."

"Did you hear about Rambo last night?" asked Martin as the Steward went to get Brian his drink. "Rushed across the bar and rugby tackled the Steward I heard."

"Did he? Why?" asked Brian.

"Caught him holding a milk jug."

"Oh. Right. He gets pottier doesn't he?"

"Yes."

"No wonder his wife keeps him locked in a shed."

"Yes."

"Rugby tackling people, eh? At least Pike didn't um."

"Oh, that reminds me, have you heard about Pike? Making good progress apparently and they reckon he may be released this week. The hospital that is."

"That doesn't um."

"Doesn't what?" the other prompted when it became clear that yet another of Brian's sentences had ground to a premature halt.

"Oh, yes, um doesn't surprise me. I visited him a few um and he seemed quite alright to me. But the um staff seemed concerned that he wasn't um really aware of what was going on, they said he could often be a vague about um."

"Vague about what?"

"Um, you know – things."

"It's great that he will be coming out, he's been in there a heck of a time. Perhaps the club should ask if they will take Rambo in part exchange."

"Does it work like that?"

"No, I don't think so," said Martin laughing.

"At least Pike didn't rugby tackle people."

"Nope Pike didn't do that. But then saying you are a pike and sitting on the roof waiting for the tide to come in was probably potty enough on its own."

"Inconvenient, too – I had to clamber onto the roof to give him my cheque for um."

"I gave mine to Mags Murtle."

"Did you?"

"Seemed easier one way and another."

"Oh, I didn't think of that. Always struck me as a bit odd

what he did, you know that business of saying he was waiting for the tide to come in."

"I think it struck everyone as a bit odd. Well apart from Pike himself presumably."

"Made no sense. Pikes aren't seawater fishes; they are freshwater ones."

"You can have tidal rivers which are freshwater."

"Oh, I hadn't thought of that. Oh yes, it makes perfect sense now."

"Does it?"

"Um, well no, I suppose not."

The room was beginning to fill up with other people, several of whom were arriving for the committee meeting. One of the new arrivals was Willoughby who saw an old friend sitting alone at the end of the bar. "Hallo padre," he greeted him. "This is not your usual time to be here, you've not been roped into this darned committee meeting too?

"No, I avoid committees at the golf club."

"Very wise," said Willoughby.

"I came I here because I've just had an odd experience."

"And you wanted another one?" enquired Willoughby.

"No. It was all most puzzling. You know those ladies who were in here yesterday? Stalwarts of the local church."

"The pair whose milk jugs Rambo kept confiscating and hurling around the room while performing war dances?"

"Yes, I heard about that. He gets pottier doesn't he? Those ladies, Abitha Tatsby and Ursula Gibbs their names are. Well one of them, Abitha, has just come to the vicarage and well it was all most odd. Most odd indeed."

"Was it?" asked Willoughby.

"Yes, it was all most odd."

"Was it?"

"Yes it was. Very curious. Can't really explain it."

"So I am noticing."

"Yes. Very odd indeed."

"How many whiskies have you had padre?"

"Erm, only two. I thought they would help calm my nerves. I was feeling well a bit unsettled, especially after my meeting with the Rural Dean earlier, which was also most disturbing. Very disturbing. Quite worrying."

"Your meeting with the Rural Dean?"

"Yes."

"Oh dear."

"Yes, you could well say 'Oh dear'."

"I know and I did."

"And well might you. It was also most odd. Abitha seemed, well she seemed a bit odd really. She said to me that, well that she and Ursula will no longer be coming to my church."

"But the pair of them must have been in the second pew since the dawn of time. Well it can't have been that long of course unless they were particularly visionary. But probably since Jesus' time anyway. Well perhaps a little before that, as they always like to get there early to reserve their seat."

"Yes, they have always been most conscientious attenders of church since I have been parish priest here. But now they say they would feel uncomfortable going to my church."

"Well those pews can get a touch uncomfortable if the sermon goes on too long, especially as we old folk get bonier. Perhaps if you popped some cushions about their pew? Women like cushions. Or had shorter sermons?"

"It's nothing to do with the seats. It's me apparently. They said they would feel uncomfortable in a service taken by me, considering the things I seem to find acceptable."

"Oh dear, have you been stirring up trouble from the pulpit with your firebrand speeches?"

"Hardly. You know me, my sermons are always boringly uncontroversial."

"Yes they are. I mean they are uncontroversial, but jolly interesting and thought-provoking at the same time. Perhaps it is your beliefs that have upset them?"

"So it seems. But I cannot believe my beliefs are controversial. Anyway they haven't changed, so if they have taken agin them now, why not at the beginning, or 10 years ago, or five years? It's not that my views have changed – I have been saying exactly the same things for years now."

"Indeed. What do you believe has caused it?"

"No idea."

"You must have some inkling?"

"Well I know what I believe, but not what they believe I believe, believe you me."

"Perhaps if you were to talk to her?"

"Well I did try, but she seemed very embarrassed and insistent. It was a very awkward conversation. Would you like a whisky Willoughby? If I am going to be accused of being a whisky priest I might as well enjoy a glass of whisky."

"Well I shouldn't let you drink alone."

"She was going on about dogs and car parks."

"Who was?"

"Abitha."

"Why?"

"I don't know."

"Dogs?"

"Yes. Dogs in car parks as far as I could make out. In public."

"In public car parks?"

"No I don't just think public car parks why?"

"I don't know really."

"Do you think it makes a difference if it is a public car park not a private one?"

"Could do. Depends what it is about."

"What what's about?"

"Whatever it is."

"But I don't know what it is."

"No, neither do I."

"It wasn't just car parks," said the vicar remembering, "It was public spaces."

"Dogs in public spaces?"

"Yes."

"Well that's it. She was probably upset about dogs being in public spaces not being on their lead or something, or owners not clearing up after their dogs have been using it as a public inconvenience. But you don't have a dog do you?"

"No."

"Well it can't be that. Unless she thought you did and blamed you for someone else's dog. Or perhaps they keep stepping in the puddles in your potholed car park when they come to services and so have decided they can't come to any more services?"

"The car park is being resurfaced next month. Do you think that is it?"

"Could be. I don't know. What did the Rural Dean say?"

"He didn't say anything about dogs. That was Abitha."

"No, you said you also had an unpleasant meeting with the Rural Dean today."

"And then there is what the Rural Dean said: 'The diocese is reviewing your church's function'."

"Don't they know what the church does – you'd have thought the Dean would have got the hang of it by now, tell him it is all about God and things. They must have heard of him, he's well spoken of round those parts I understand."

"It's also about bums on seats, well in pews, and we don't have enough."

"Pews?"

"No, bums. They have some management consultants in to look at rationalising the operation with these forms and their boxes to tick and well churches are being closed all over the country, so I suppose why should I expect mine to be any different? Some property developer would no doubt love to get their mitts on yet another one and turn it into luxury apartments for the tilly tosser brigade."

"They're going to close our church? They can't do that."

"Who says?"

"I do."

"Well that is very kind of you, but with respect I don't think the decision is yours."

"With respect, padre, I will make the decision mine. I have decided that they will not close your church, so it will not happen. What would happen to you if they shut your church?"

"Oh I won't get made redundant, don't worry. They'll send me somewhere else."

"No, no, they can't do that. You are far too valued around here. You'd be a huge loss."

"Oh thank you, Willoughby. Nice of you to say so."

"Yes, who I am going to have afternoon tea with on Thursdays if you are sent away? No, it's not on. Who has proposed this watboddled idea?"

"It is what some overpaid management consultants will decide. The money that the deanery showers on those trandled strendelbarns could be used to keep the church open instead."

"Are they definitely bent on closing it down?"

"Oh no, not yet. They have an expensive rationalisation assessment process to go through first, so as to waste more of the church's money and line their own pockets. The diocese has set out its strategic plan and these bods then decide whether each church in the area fits into it."

"We can't have your church lost padre. There is damn all in Tangents already what with the Castro pub gone and if the church were to go as well, well we'd be left with just the club. We need the church."

"But no-one goes to it Willoughby. Well not enough people anyway."

"That's immaterial. That's not what the church is there for. It's there to be there."

"They also want me to demonstrate outreach work."

"You mean home visits and whatnot?"

"They want a clearly defined role – it's all about box ticking. They want me to have a chaplaincy, you know be a hospital chaplain or prison visitor or something. But how? We don't have a hospital here. We don't have a prison here."

"There's Rambo's shed?"

"Oh cripes I don't want to visit him."

"No, quite."

"That is a role for those of a more senior position in the church: I am only a vicar not a saint."

"Anyway the church would have to pay you danger money in case he starts throwing milk jugs at you. And from what you say the deanery is trying to save money not spend it. Okay, park that one for a bit. What else do they want?"

"Bums on seats."

"They want you to perform to packed houses?"

"Well certainly a few more than the half dozen regulars at present. You could come along more often Willoughby, that would help a bit."

"Would it? Oh, um, er, no there must be a better way. You just need to build up the crowds slowly over time. How long have you got?"

"Two weeks."

"Ah. What, they want to close you in two weeks?"

"No, the watboddled dumpelrumps of the management consultants are coming in two weeks' time. Oh and then the week after as well as they say they can't just take a snapshot – they have to have an average. It's all about processes and consultations and efficiency and rationalisation and other mumbo jumbo. They do this through some independent body, for which read someone with no prior experience or knowledge so knows sod all squared, no cubed, about the subject is brought in to judge what sort of role each individual church plays in the community. It's a way of passing on the blame. But it's all tick boxes and things."

"I will pray for you and your church padre."

"Ooof, I need something better than that."

"And I will also do something even better than that."

"What?"

"Just leave it with me. I am sure there is something that can be done. You have called upon me in your day of trouble and I will deliver for thee. Just give me time." Then, as welcome way to change the subject, having seen the Chairman of the Membership Committee ambling towards them: "Hallo Brian, you here for this confounded Heads of Committee meeting?"

"Erm, what, um, no, I um went to that yesterday."

"Can't have old bean. The meeting wasn't yesterday, it is tonight."

"Are you sure? I could have sworn I went to it yesterday. You were there, too. Don't you remember?"

"No, well, yes, it's true you came here to go to it yesterday, but it didn't actually happen."

"Didn't it? Oh got postponed did it? They might have postponed it before it had happened, not after. Been more considerate."

"Well it didn't actually happen at all, Brian."

"Oh, didn't it? I could have sworn I attended it. Are you sure I didn't?"

"Yes. Wouldn't you remember if you had been to the committee meeting?"

"Oh I doubt it. I can never remember what meetings I go to or what happened at them. No-one does. That's why committee meetings have minutes, as otherwise no-one would know what happened in them. I normally write the um minutes of my committee meetings before they happen. Much easier that way."

"But what happens if what the minutes say happened doesn't then happen?"

"No-one remembers anyway, certainly not six months later when we um and approve the minutes of the last um. It was a little trick I learnt. First time I chaired a committee I forgot to ask anyone to take the minutes and um I didn't know this until next committee when you know the agenda thing had to be um and so I cobbled together some stuff that sounded like it was the sort of thing we could have said and um everyone passed it as being a true and accurate account or whatever the guff is and um, that is what I have done since."

"Ingenious."

"Anyway every committee meeting is the same. We all agree we need more members, no-one has any ideas how we might actually achieve this. We all agree to go away and think about it and bring back ideas to the next meeting, and we all don't. Oh, and we review the categories of membership to ensure we are making a suitable and attractive offering to the time-sensitive consumer in the modern leisure market."

"I beg your pardon, what was that last bit?"

"It's a phrase. I borrowed it from some management consultant bore I got stuck next to at some dinner," Brian replied proudly. "It shows our committee is keeping up to date and on the um."

"Ball?" suggested Willoughby after a period.

"Button. A ball? You think a ball would do it? It might. A big grand ball. We could call it the Golf Ball," he said brightly.

"Do what?"

"What?"

"What would this big grand ball do?"

"Well, um I don't know dancing, and um things."

"No, I mean what's its purpose."

"Dancing? I don't know, people seem to like it. Exercise?"

"No, how does a ball bring in new members?"

"Well um, you know, it could be a way of interacting with the wider community."

"True. But how would that work in converting them into members?"

"We could invite people to the ball and um. I don't know. Do you think it would work Willoughby? We've been told to find ways of connecting with the outside world, haven't we?"

"Have we?"

"Hasn't your committee?"

"I don't know. No-one worries much about the Billiards Committee. Has your committee discussed it?"

"It might have, I can't remember – I'll have to look back through the minutes and see. Are you sure the meeting was not yesterday?" said Brian, looking around the room. "I am just seeing if other members of the membership committee are about."

"Who is on your committee Brian?"

"My committee? My committee, well it's um George Mason, Ernie Goldthorpe, and um Robert Thompson."

"Bob can't be on it, he died some time ago," pointed out Willoughby.

"They don't do what one might term by-elections here," the vicar reminded Willoughby, "so the deceased remain in office, as it were, until the next AGM. Or rather, are not replaced until then."

"But he must have died over a year and a half ago," replied Willoughby to the vicar, "so we will have had an AGM since then. At least it is to be hoped he died over a year and half ago, as you buried him padre. Otherwise you'd have buried a chap alive."

"No, no," agreed the vicar. "We don't do that. That would be naughty," he slurred. "Abitha would give me a strong ticking off for that. In the car park."

"I remember, it well," said Willoughby. "I went to the service. His widow put on a lovely spread afterwards including some especially fine brandy snaps and a jolly nice apricot and vanilla Swiss roll."

"Two years ago, actually," said Brian, sadly.

"Was it? Doesn't time – and indeed life – pass? I am sorry. Well then he can't still be on your committee as his term of office would have expired at the next AGM."

"Oh it did. But the AGM re-elected him. Twice."

"Even though he's dead?"

"Yes, that doesn't matter."

"Doesn't it?"

"No. Not so long as he's still a member."

"Is he? Surely one's membership expires when you do."

"Yes, a lot of people seem to think that. Well um almost everyone in fact. But I um don't."

"Don't you?" prompted Willoughby.

"No."

"Tell us, Brian," asked the vicar "how are you still a member when you are dead."

"I am not dead!" exclaimed Brian in surprise. He looked around as though checking all was in order and the vicar was not privy to some important information that had been kept from him.

"No, no, I mean how does one remain a member of the club after one is dead?" said the vicar.

"Oh, that's easy. Well technically I reckon your membership expires not when you die, but at the end of the subscription year as you have bought membership for the whole year. Otherwise we would have to give refunds for people moving away or dying, and we don't."

"Even so, that means he was no longer a member at the end of that subscription year, so cannot be elected onto a committee. The club has strict rules about that," said Willoughby. "Only club members can serve on club committees."

"Remember those 10-year memberships that were sold a few years ago when the Finance Committee needed to raise funds to rebuild the greenkeeping shed?"

"Wasn't a great success if I remember," said Willoughby. "Not many sold, then Benton found a builder he knew who built the hut cheaply for us, so we hadn't really needed that fundraiser anyway."

"Well only one membership was sold actually. Um to

Bob. So his membership still has several more years before it expires."

"Are you sure that's how it works?" queried Willoughby.

"The club meant a lot to Bob and he was a damn decent chap all told and it seems a bit, well, brutal really to expel him from the club just because he has died. I know he would not want that. The club meant a lot to him as did the chaps in it."

"But are you sure this is above board?"

"Oh yes we agreed it at the Membership Committee."

"Your committee all agreed with this?"

"Well um actually the other two disagreed and said that he should not remain a member."

"But you just ignored them?"

"Oh no, no. Can't do that. We had um we had a vote on the matter."

"But you would have lost that 2-1," pointed out Willoughby.

"No, I won it 3-2."

"How come?"

"I voted three times," Brian explained.

"Is that allowed?" asked Willoughby dubiously.

"Oh yes."

"Didn't the other two object?"

"Oh, have I told you this story before?" said Brian.

"No, I was just guessing wildly," replied Willoughby.

"Oh. Well they did in fact. The other two said it wasn't, but it is."

"Are you quite sure?" asked the vicar.

"Oh yes. We had a vote to determine whether it was and the committee agreed I could. By um 3 votes to 2."

"You must have a word with young Harry," said Willoughby admiringly. "He has plans to marry Half Pint and become a dictator chappy of some country so as to flog his books to his downtrodden masses. Sounds like he could take lessons from you in how to achieve it as all these dictators have to subvert democratic practices in the first place."

"Oh it was perfectly democratic."

"Are you sure?"

"Yes. At the end of his life Bob was rather poorly."

"Well technically at the end of his life he was dead," pointed out Willoughby.

"Yes, well um you can't get more poorly than that really," reasoned Brian.

"True, true," Willoughby conceded.

"Bob had given over his vote to me as his proxy as he was too poorly to get to meetings. So I cast his vote for him as his proxy. This meant the vote was tied at 2-2, so I as chairman had the casting vote."

"Ingenious," laughed Willoughby. "This seems the perfect way to run a committee. You can never lose a vote."

"I can. The last vote we had I lost. Shame really as it was something I had been rather keen on, but the committee voted against it."

"How come? Did Bob forget to vote?" enquired Willoughby.

"Oh no, he voted. He voted against me."

"I thought you cast his vote?"

"I do. But he didn't agree with me. So he voted against me. We had um discussed it before so I knew his view."

"So, the other two also voted against you?"

"Yes, though they really agreed with me I think. Just that they were fed up of always being outvoted by me, so they voted with him to outvote me just to cheer themselves up,

I think," and at that Brian wandered off in quest of the members of his committee.

"There is a strange nobility and decency about Brian, you know," remarked Willoughby to the vicar.

"A very strange one," laughed the vicar. "But, as it so happens, I was thinking the same thing. I was also thinking that I have had perhaps too much to drink."

"Oh I wouldn't worry about that: talking to Brian tends to leave one with that feeling."

"Even so perhaps I should have a coffee. You want one Willoughby?"

"No thanks. I still have my whisky, and I am shortly off to this trandled Heads of Committee thing where there will be hospitality provided no doubt. Well I hope so. Depends who the chairman is as to what we get. Some get us a couple of decent bottles of wine; others are tea-and-biscuit merchants."

"Steward, may I have a coffee?" commanded the vicar.

"Certainly Sir, what sort of coffee would you like? Americano, latte, cappuccino, espresso, macchiato, mochaccino, Vienna, Antoccino, Breve, Cafe au lait, Espressino, Caffe Gommosa, Espresso Romano, con panna, Guillermo, Ristretto, Lungo, flat white, long black, thick grey, Cafe Zorro, Cafe Fox, Eiskaffee, Galao, bulletproof, Cortado, Gibraltar, Affogato, Cascara, Geisha, Kopi Luwak, Doppio, Turkish, Irish or instant?"

Willoughby slipped away as he wanted a word with the Chairman of the Competitions Committee, who he had just seen was at the bar talking to Jerry Best and Brian. "Ah, Martin and Jerry, just the very chaps I wanted to see," he greeted them, "as I have had this idea for a new competition..." But what he said next got drowned out by an outbreak of cheering from the room.

"What's happened?" asked Willoughby pivoting round to see what the cause of the commotion was.

"Oh, Rambo has just pulled down his trousers and tried to rugby tackle the Steward," explained Martin. "He missed. It was a rather feeble effort in truth."

"Why?" asked Willoughby.

"His technique was all wrong. He went too low, but then he started from too far away. Mind you, the Steward swerved nicely so shouldn't just blame Rambo."

"I meant why did he try to tackle him?"

"Goodness knows. He gets pottier by the day."

"The Steward was carrying a tray with a tea pot on it, so Rambo probably sensed there was a milk jug on it," said Brian.

"I'd heard that he does things like that," remarked Jerry. "But didn't believe it – but now I have seen it with my own eyes."

The commotion over, Willoughby went back to telling his fellow members of the Competition Committee his idea for a new competition. Over on the other side of the room, disappointed that her entrance had not attracted attention, but then she had entered at the same time that Rambo was putting on his floor show, Anun had walked across to where the vicar was.

"Oh hallo, Anun," he greeted her, "I have just ordered a coffee – would you like one too?"

"Oh that's kind of you. Yes please. I'll have a latte."

"Oh well done," said the vicar. "I didn't know what to have, and the Steward recited a list of 57 varieties at me."

"What did you pick?"

"Well I couldn't remember most of them bar the last two, and the last one was instant coffee and that was a bit dull. So I picked the other one I could remember."

"Oh what was it?"

"I can't remember. But it had one of the simpler names – that was another of its advantages," he chuckled.

"Ah Steward," the vicar said when the Steward returned with his coffee, "please can I also have a – sorry, what was it again my dear?"

"A latte please."

"Yes, a latte for this young lady here."

"I regret, Miss, that you cannot come into the bar looking like that," the Steward said.

"Oh dear, do you really consider me that ugly? I am sorry. But I might point out that some of the other members are hardly an oil painting themselves, though there is a Picasso or two maybe."

"I beg your pardon Miss, what I meant to say is that you cannot come in here dressed like that."

"But I have just come in," pointed out Anun, eyes blazing.

"But you should not have done. Denim is not allowed to be worn in the bar," he told the jeans-clad Anun.

"So if I was not wearing jeans I would look alright by your standards?" said Anun, her eyes flashing bright.

"By the standards set by the club members, yes. They are not my standards Miss, I am merely a humble servant of the members."

"OK then," said Anun standing up and taking off her jeans and wrapping them around her neck in a defiant gesture. "That suit you?"

"No, Miss, you cannot dress like that."

"But I am not wearing denim," she shot back.

"No, Miss you appear now to be wearing a denim scarf. As I have already said Miss: no denim is allowed to be worn in the clubhouse."

"Is that okay now!" blazed Anun, whipping the jeans from around her neck and hurling them to the floor.

"That is most acceptable, Miss."

"No it is not!" exclaimed the vicar. "We cannot make young girls stand in their knickers for the sake of some daft club rule. There are moments, Steward, when one asks oneself, do trousers matter?"

"The feeling will pass Sir."

"No it will not. If this young lady is to sit here without her trousers then so shall I," and at this the vicar defiantly got up and removed his own trousers. "It is not right we should treat a young lady like that."

"My, vicar," said Anun surveying a brightly multi-coloured pair of boxer shorts, "who would have known?"

"Ah yes, they are a present from my sister. She thinks it sad that I am always forced to dress in black, so she always gives me a garish pair of boxer shorts for Christmas. She used to give me brightly coloured socks instead but some of the parishioners complained that it was not seemly for me to wear such items."

"They are most splendid vicar," said Anun approvingly.

"Ah Reverend Smith." He looked up and it was Ursula Gibbs. "Please excuse me for interrupting but I just had to have a word with you as it was weighing badly on my conscience. But I feel bad about what happened and I would just wish to say that I do not agree with Abitha and I certainly know that you are not a moral degenerate as she put it..."

What else she was to say will never been known for at that moment she noticed that the vicar was sitting with a girl dressed only in fancy underwear from her waist down; next moment she noticed that the vicar was also not wearing trousers. The moment after that she was rushing from the room shrieking.

"Oh dear, should I go after her?" said the vicar more aloud to himself than to Anun.

"Best not," said Anun, "I am not sure chasing old ladies when not wearing your strides will persuade her or anyone else that you are not a moral degenerate."

"Oh dear, oh dear," said the vicar.

"It's okay, I shall go and see her tomorrow and say in fact you were defending a lady's honour and behaving like the chivalrous upright gentleman you are."

"Oh dear," said the vicar. "They already think I am morally reprehensible and this will put the tin hat on it."

"Why? I mean why do they think you are morally reprehensible?" asked Anun, interested.

"Willoughby thinks it is because I let dogs in the church car park. But I am not sure that is the reason."

"I am almost certain that it isn't. How about you tell me all about it over our coffees?" invited Anun. "Tell me your story fully. Omit no detail that may be of importance, as Rikki would say."

Chapter 10

"No, no, Martin," Rambo was saying peevishly, "I do not require rugby lessons. I played at a school. I was prop forward for the 3rd XV. I was captain of the side for the final 10 minutes of our last game. Well it was probably nearer 15 minutes in fact."

"Ah yes, props do not tackle that much. That explains your right bog of an attempt to take down the Steward."

"I was not trying to take down the Steward. It was my trousers."

"You were trying to take down your trousers? In the middle of a crowded bar?" said Martin, only slightly surprised at this further example of Rambo's eccentricity. "You shouldn't do that old boy, there might be ladies present."

"No. I didn't want to."

"Well why you were trying to take down your trousers then? Is some kind of compulsive behaviour like with milk jugs?" he asked sympathetically.

"My button flew off when I was rushing to hand the Chairman of Estates the agenda and my trousers fell to the floor and this tripped me up. It just happened the Steward was nearby."

"Carrying a milk jug," Martin pointed out.

"I know nothing about that," said Rambo peevishly, adjusting the club tie which he had pressed into service as a makeshift belt. "Now, is everyone here?" he asked to those people who had been drifting in to the committee room during this conversation.

"Hands up all those who aren't here," joked Willoughby, taking his seat as the last to arrive.

Brian looked round the room. No hands were up. "I think we are all here," he reported.

"I am in the chair for this meeting of the Heads of Committee under the rotation basis established in... well it doesn't matter when, it doesn't matter when, as I am Head of the House Committee. I am chair of this meeting of the Heads of Committee as it is the turn of the chairman, or head if you will, of the House Committee to chair the Heads of Committee meeting."

"Oh get on with it do," said the Chairman of Estates.

"I would be able to get on with it if I wasn't having these constant interruptions," complained Mr Ramsbotham. "As I was saying, I am chair of this meeting of the Heads of Committee. As I am the chair I am also in the chair as it were," he paused and looked round the room, waiting for some laughter at his little joke. There wasn't any. "So it is my duty to organise the refreshment as that is the traditional duty of the chairman. So I have asked the Steward to bring us some bowls of cheese-and-onion crisps. Now who is taking the minutes?" demanded Rambo. "Who is taking the minutes?"

"Who did you ask to take the minutes?" asked someone laconically.

"I, I..." at that moment Rambo realised he had not asked anyone to take the minutes.

"Brian would be ideal to take the minutes," suggested Willoughby.

"Do you agree to that, Brian?" Rambo demanded. Brian, who had not been paying attention, looked up. He was dimly aware that he had heard his name and this meant he was probably being asked his view on something, or to agree to something, but he had no idea what it was. It seemed a bit early in a meeting, especially a Rambo-chaired one, to be making decisions. Normally there was lots of flaff and waffle to get through first. He looked around the room, Willoughby was gently nodding as a sign to him.

"Yes," Brian said as that seemed to be simplest thing.

"Oh good," said Mr Ramsbotham. "Right some parish notices, as it were, although of course they are not about the parish but about the golf club, so perhaps I should call them golf club notices but of course that does not mean that they are the same as the notices that go up on the golf club notice board because they aren't. Though some of them could be I suppose, but in this case they aren't. So perhaps it is best if I call them parish notices so as not to cause any confusion. First parish, or golf if you prefer, notice is that I went to see Mr Pike last week."

"I hear that he is much improved and is coming out soon," said Martin. "That is good news isn't it," he said looking around the room, to general murmurs of consent.

"Yes, I was told the same thing when I went to visit, for I went to visit him last week," said Mr Ramsbotham. "I went to visit him last week. And they told me that. Pike and I had a nice long chat actually. They had told me he was likely to be leaving in the next day or two, but I later heard that just after I left he had had a relapse and so he was going to have to stay in a while longer."

"The second parish notice, or golf notice if you prefer, is that Benton Snivelgate has given me the result of the raffle. I am not sure why he gave it to me, as I had not instigated this raffle, but he has. But perhaps he thought it easiest as I was playing him in the Shack at the time."

"Did you win?"

"No."

"Damn."

"As I was saying, I don't know why he gave it to me rather than the head of the Fundraising Committee who no doubt organised it..."

"We didn't organise that raffle," interrupted the head of that committee. "Had we done so we certainly wouldn't have put Bent Snivelgate in charge. I presumed the Finance Committee were running it," he said looking across at the Chairman of Finance.

"Nothing to do with us, we thought it was your doing. We would never let Benton have anything to do with the club's money. You would have to be mad to do that."

"True," said the Chairman of Estates. "Sure you didn't organise it, Rambo?"

"No, I didn't. He just reported in to me. Well someone must have organised the raffle? Who has?" Going round the room, it was clear no-one had.

"Well he can't just have organised it off his own bat," complained Rambo.

"Clearly he has," responded the Chair of Finance. "Anyway what were you going to tell us about it?"

"Oh yes, the raffle has finished now and the draw made. Benton said people had been reluctant to buy tickets. But he has made some money for the club from it."

"How much?" asked the Chairman of Fundraising eagerly.

"£10."

"£10!"

"Yes, £10."

"Who has won the first prize anyway? His wife?" asked Mr Wilkinson.

"I have the winner's name here, Wilko," said Rambo fossicking among a pile of papers he had in front of him. "I have it here, somewhere." Eventually he found it. "No his wife did not win first prize."

"Well that's something at least."

"She won second prize. I can tell you who won first prize if you like as I have that on another piece of paper.

Ah here it is – first prize was won by his daughter. Alright, on with the items on the printed agenda and the first item on this agenda is our outreach programme."

"Our what?"

"Our outreach programme."

"I didn't know we had one."

"We don't."

"Then why are we wasting time talking about it you fool?" harrumphed the Chairman of Estates.

"Because we have been asked to have one, to help market the club to the local community. As you know, the committee has been asked to think of ways we can, well, market the club to the wider community. We are short of members and this means we are short of funds. Well I have had an idea which will do the trick. I can give a lecture on the history of golf. That would attract people. People like an interesting talk and I could introduce people to the game and encourage them to join the golf club. I have some quite interesting stories to tell. For example..."

"No, no, Rambo we haven't got time for one of your stories," cut in another member hurriedly, to general murmured consensus and a couple of cries of 'Hear! Hear!'

"Brian and his Membership Committee have come up with an idea," remarked Willoughby "which Brian was telling me about, haven't you Brian?"

"Was I? Oh yes, we should make membership open to pigs."

"No, not that one. Perhaps I better explain Brian's idea as he is distracted with taking the minutes. What Brian was telling me about – and correct me if I am wrong Brian – what he was telling me the committee had suggested was that we have a golfers' service at the local church, to be held in one of the Sunday morning slots so you already have all the regular churchgoers involved. That would bring us to the attention of the good God-fearing folk of the parish. He got the idea from a cricket club he had read about which had done something similar and it had been a great success apparently."

Willoughby could see that he did not have the support of the room. "I don't know," said one committee member, "would the committee be expected to go to it, it's just that well I'm quite busy on Sundays and well, the vicar's sermons are not exactly riveting so I've heard."

"Oh yes," said Willoughby, "the committee would be expected to attend."

"Well I'm not really sure this is quite it, clever idea though it is," said Mr Wilkinson.

"Just as the committee would be expected," continued Willoughby, ignoring the interruption, "to attend Rambo's, no doubt very long, detailed and discursive lecture if this committee decided that that were the better option."

The mood of the room rapidly changed as people began to see, and express, the merit of the church service idea. "You know," whispered Willoughby to Wilko, who was seated next to him, "that Rikki and Anun would come to it?"

"Rambo's lecture? Why on earth?"

"No, not that. They have no interest in golf: Rikki is almost contemptuous of it, and Anun loathes Rambo. No the church service – they will be certs to attend that."

"Will they?"

"Yes of course they will."

"My wife is a firm atheist, she wouldn't come."

"I know," whispered Willoughby, "but you'd be free to go wouldn't you? You'd have to go as a committee member, three-line whip. She couldn't stop you."

"I think it's an excellent idea this church service thing,"

Wilko announced to the meeting. "Congratulations Brian, splendid notion. Well done."

"I'm not sure," said Rambo, "I still think my lecture would be more successful at attracting people to the club. As I said, I have lots of interesting stories that would draw people in for instance..."

"No, no, Rambo, no time for that," said Willoughby firmly. "Anyway as I've mentioned before, you don't want to give away stuff from your book before it's published. Surely the time to delight the locals with a talk on golf is when you have your book to sell – you know a-meet-the-author, get-a-personalised-signed-copy type of event."

"I could talk about things I wasn't going to include in the book," he said defiantly.

"If by that you mean things too dull even to be included in your no doubt terribly tedious tome," said the Chairman of Estates, "I'm not sure that will exactly draw the crowds."

"I still think the idea of a talk is a good one," said Rambo peevishly. "Perhaps it would help the committee if I gave an outline of the things I could mention in my talk. Well first of all..."

"No, no," cut in Willoughby, "don't give away milk when you have a horse."

"Pardon?" said Mr Ramsbotham.

"Granted. Perhaps before you do that we should outline what the church service would do," suggested Willoughby.

"Yes, I was wondering that how it would work," said another committee member.

"Well, after we have it up and running we can try and attract a big name from the world of golf down to give a talk, well the sermon I suppose it would be. Several of the leading pros are practising Christians and they have Bible study groups on tour and whatnot. I am sure we could attract one of them down here to talk about their faith once the word gets round that we have this popular annual golfers' service."

There was an excited stir at the prospect of getting someone famous to their club. "Shouldn't we try to do that at the start?" suggested someone.

"We won't get someone at the start, that's the point," explained Willoughby. "We have to get the idea up and running and make it popular. Then it will be an enticing prospect for a big name to come and talk about their faith."

"But until then?"

"Well we just need an excuse for a service."

"How about linking it to the saint's day of the patron saint of golfers? There must be one – there're patron saints of all sorts of daft things."

"Is it St Jude?"

"No, that's the chap for lost causes."

"Well isn't that appropriate if you look at some of the swings and scores here?"

"No, it's St Andrew, it is a quite an interesting story actually." This time Rambo was not to be put off and he was going to tell his story. "The remains of St Andrew were being cared for in Istanbul by a monk called Rule, or was he a bishop? Anyway it doesn't matter, it doesn't matter. But I think he was a bishop, or perhaps he was indeed a monk? Anyway an angel came to him and told him to move the remains to the West as they were in danger where they were, so he set out by boat to do this. His boat was shipwrecked during a storm off the east coast of Scotland. The place where the shipwreck took place is now called St Andrews, as St Andrew's remains were placed in a chapel there. So you see that's a bit of golf history – interesting story isn't it?"

"So the Rules of Golf are named after the chap who discovered St Andrews," said Brian.

"No, he's got nothing to do with the rules of golf," said Mr Ramsbotham irritably.

"It must be. The rules of golf are decided at St Andrews where this Rule chap landed up."

"You have to agree Rambo," contended Willoughby "it would be a bit of coincidence this chap being called Rule and golf deciding the regulations of golf should be named Rules. After all they could have called them anything – the laws of golf, the conduct of golf, the Smith of golf, the protocol of golf, the iggleboggle of golf even."

"No, no, that is why St Andrew is the patron saint of golf, because he gave his name to St Andrews," said Mr Ramsbotham crossly.

"Was this bloke Andrew a keen golfer then?" asked Brian.

"No, he didn't play the game, he died in 60AD – the game hadn't been invented by then," replied Rambo.

"Seems a lousy choice to be the patron saint of golf then, if the chap doesn't even know the game exists," said another committee member. "What's the point praying to him that you don't three putt when he doesn't even know what a putt is?"

"Yes he's a dead loss all round," declared Willoughby. "Plus if we do it on St Andrew's Day everyone will think it's about Scotland. Also St Andrew's Day is in November and we want it in the summer."

"Will we be able to move St Andrew's Day to summer?" asked Brian dubiously.

"Why does it have to be in summer?" queried another member.

"Well who the heck is going to be enthused by the idea of coming to play in no fun, no sun, November?" said

Willoughby. "We need the long lazy days of summer when people long for the outdoors and our course is in its mid-season form. I suggest we go for two weeks' time."

"Why?"

"I happen to know the vicar has a slot free then. Otherwise we are looking at the winter months which are out, for reasons we have agreed, or postponing it for a year, which seems a shame."

"But how is a church service, which has nothing to do with golf, rather than an interesting talk on golf, going to attract people into golf?" asked Mr Ramsbotham huffily.

"A church service will attract a wide cross section, whereas a talk on golf will be preaching to the converted, if that's not mixing a metaphor," reasoned Willoughby. "Plus after the church service we can have a reception in that ante room of the church with tea and buns, or wine and nibbles or whatever, and we can talk to them informally about the club and we can network and whatnot."

"The wine and nibbles. Who is providing these, what will they be, who's paying and if it's us, what's the likely cost?" asked the Chairman of Finance.

"We'll have to provide the grub," replied Willoughby, "as we can hardly rock up to the church and demand they put on a service and a party afterwards for us – the refreshments will be our contribution to the service. As to what: well nibbles and whatnot. I am sure we could buy some cake off Mrs Winsor, and as to other nibbles – well maybe nuts and things."

"I am allergic to nuts," said Rambo crossly.

"I know, I hear your wife said she had to take all the mirrors out of your shed," said the Chairman of Estates.

Rambo, replied earnestly and a little puzzled: "There weren't any mirrors in the shed. It didn't have any mirrors."

"Something I have always wondered," said Brian, "whenever you see pictures of vampires they are always clean shaven, but how do they see to shave perfectly when they have no reflection in their shaving mirror?"

"Well, okay we can have crisps instead," suggested Willoughby, whilst wondering how it was that vampires did shave. "We might be able to get our hands on some somewhere," he added drily.

"The House Committee can provide crisps," enthused Rambo. "It will, er help in case anyone has a nut allergy. Alright shall we vote on it – who is in favour of the idea?"

All hands went up.

"That is a decision then. Note in the minutes that we voted to have crisps."

"I thought we were voting on the church idea," said Martin.

"No, we were talking about crisps," Mr Ramsbotham said.

"Well we must have, de facto, accepted the idea of a church service if we are voting whether to serve crisps at it," pointed out Willoughby.

"Not necessarily," said Mr Ramsbotham sulkily. "We haven't decided what event the crisps are to be served at: my talk, my talk about golf; or this service, this church service not about golf."

"I think there is a clear majority for the church service idea," said Martin, "and I think we should vote on it now," he added to general murmurs of approval.

Reluctantly Mr Ramsbotham put it to a vote and everyone bar him voted in favour of the church service.

"Alright," said Mr Ramsbotham, "now we have decided to have this odd church service, we have got to decide how to market the club through it. One idea I have had is that I could give a talk at the service about the history of golf. I have some interesting stories, for instance..."

"No, no, Rambo," cut in Wilko. "We will have to let the vicar give the sermon."

"But he is so terribly boring," said Rambo. "Why would people want to hear a boring talk?"

"Well I have another suggestion as part of our outreach programme," said Willoughby. "I think it might be a good idea to appoint the vicar as chaplain to the club. Lots of sports clubs have chaplains and this would be a visible way to link ourselves to the wider life of the community. The padre would do it, I am sure, if we ask nicely and we all come along to his golfers' service to show our support for his new role. It would help to give the service a focus, and give the newshounds an angle."

"Newshounds?" queried Mr Ramsbotham.

"Yes young Harry, our newest member, he's a freelance writer chappie and we have that other chap, a country member who is a journo, old hoojamaflip, you know old twiddlytwonk, wears tweeds, parts his hair."

"Oh yes I know him, old whatsisname," chimed in Brian, "I know him."

"That's the fellow," said Willoughby. "I am sure he and Harry will write nice things about it and help spread the word about our golfers' service. After all why do we all know about this probably otherwise utterly unremarkable cricket club? It's because Brian read an article about its special annual church service which has made their club moderately famous."

"Are you sure the vicar would do it – we won't be able to pay him," said the Chairman of Finance firmly.

"I am good friends with him and I am sure I can twist his arm," said Willoughby. "It might be the done thing to offer him his membership free by way of a thank you. Would your Membership Committee consider that doable Brian?

Brian? Brian – I think your committee would agree to that wouldn't they?"

"Oh yes," said Brian. He hadn't been listening to what anyone had been saying, as he had been wondering if vampires just seemed clean shaven in comparison as they hung about with werewolves; but he knew agreeing was always the easier option in these circumstances.

"Excellent, and that's settled it – we can't make the chap our chaplain and then try to ban him from speaking in his own church," said Willoughby firmly to Rambo.

Rambo had to concede defeat. "Next item on the agenda and the main purpose of this meeting is to decide a design for the new flag, as you know and so I am sure you don't need reminding –"

"Then why are you telling us?" complained the Chairman of Estates.

"– the current Lord Hankley, or rather the business manager of his Lordship as you might term him, the adviser I mean not the peer of the realm. I am not sure of his exact title, but just let's say for the sake of argument it is business manager though I don't know that it is, I don't know that that is his official title, or – job title I mean not title as in lord, for he is not a lord, well I suppose he could also be a lord, but I don't think he is, but it doesn't really matter what his job is called, it doesn't really matter. But he has said that we can no longer use the Hankley crest on the flag..."

Several paragraphs later Mr Ramsbotham came to a halt and others had a chance to chip in. The flag design was a simple one, divided into quarters. In the bottom right corner was the Hankley crest, which the current lord had decided was no longer appropriate for a club that he had nothing to do with personally. In the top left of the flag was the symbol for the parish of Tangents, the church spire; to its right was a flagstick and bottom left were crossed golf clubs.

"How about another golf image?"

"Wouldn't that unbalance the design? Three golf images and the village symbol?"

"It would be a shame to lose the Hankley connection – it's part of the history of this club, the Lord Hankley Cup – wheresoever that may now be – the Billiards Room and so on. Could we not find a way to connect the club to the Hankley line without using their crest?"

"Terribly common man, the current Lord Hankley," said the Chairman of Estates. "It would be nice to stick it to him. Very rude feller too – and I can't abide rudeness." This suggestion proved popular, although no one could see how to carry it out.

"Perhaps it would be better to decide this with some actual designs to look at?" suggested someone.

"But who would do the designs?"

"Mrs Winsor," proposed Willoughby, "Rikki and Anun's mother is a talented artist and could be prevailed upon, I am sure."

"How much would it cost?" asked the Chairman of Finance.

"We might be able to persuade her to do it gratis on a quid-pro-quo basis," said Willoughby. "I hear she is planning an art show soon, on the Sunday after our golfers' service in fact, and if we all agreed to go along mob-handed to that – there will be tea and cake and things – then I am sure she could be persuaded as a favour for a favour. So long as people here don't mind putting in the effort to eat cake and socialise with one another whilst looking at some art, or pretending to."

Everyone agreed they were prepared to do so, and it was voted that Mrs Winsor would be asked to provide some suggestions for the design.

When Willoughby walked out of the committee meeting, he looked for the vicar, but he had gone.

"Good job Willoughby that you remembered me reading that article for I hadn't," said Brian. "What did it say?"

"No idea, I've not seen it."

"But I must have told you about it."

"Yes that's what they thought didn't they," said Willoughby happily.

Chapter 11

Willoughby was walking to see the vicar. Optimistic by nature, he was trusting that the vicar would focus on the good news more than on the bad news although, as Willoughby saw it, the bad news itself was good news in that it reversed some previous bad news. Anun had phoned him earlier that morning to explain that she had seen Abitha Tatsby and sorted things out between the ladies and the vicar.

In the distance he spied a familiar figure walking towards him. He raised his hat in greeting: "I was just thinking that this glorious summer morning could not be more perfect, but I am wrong for the sight of you in all your elegance, radiance and beauty has improved it even further."

"Oh Mr Cornwallis, you do say the daftest things," said Miss Murtle. "As it happens, I was hoping to see you. You were asking about the gentlemen who play on Tuesday mornings, well Mondays now it is, and why doctor's orders is the number nine call in bingo."

"Oh yes, indeed. Mondays you say? Oh dear, I will have the Secretary after me again."

"And I have an answer for you. I asked at our last meeting – number nine was a pill given out by army doctors in the war to pep people up or rather clear them out as it were."

"Clear them out? Oh, I see. Oh dear, better add that to the list of balls you don't want."

"Well I regret I won't be getting any balls for a while, they are closing the room we do bingo in for essential works and renovations. We will quite miss our weekly sessions, it's daft but it's fun and it's an excuse to get together."

"'We'?"

"Yes there is a group of us who meet up there. Those of

us who live alone, well it's nice to have some company about regularly."

"I imagine it is. I am a married man myself, and we often seek solitude for similar reasons."

"Yes, Mr Ramsbotham lives in a shed at the bottom of their garden."

"I have my study into which Mrs C never goes."

"Oh, talking of Mr Ramsbotham: I heard he got overexcited at the sight of a milk jug last night and took all his clothes off and ran around the bar."

"Something like that occurred."

"He gets pottier doesn't he?"

"Hard to say really, as he's always been fairly potty."

"Yes, he has hasn't he? Oh that is encouraging isn't it? Well hark at me, I can't stand here gabbing, Mr Pirbright will be wondering where I have got to, I must get on."

"I shall console myself," said Willoughby raising his hat as a farewell, "that the pain of parting will be nothing to the joy of meeting you again."

"Oh you are a daft one," said Miss Murtle, flattered.

Willoughby went on his way, turning over these new pieces of information, and wondering how they may be turned to advantage in his efforts at spreading sweetness and light. He went into the church and, after getting used to the light after the blazing sunlight, and to the coolness, he saw a familiar figure in the second pew, bent deep as if in prayer.

He walked as noisily as he could, trying to make his shoes click on the tiles so as to announce his presence, and sat down next to the vicar. After a while, as nothing had happened, he whispered: "You praying vicar?"

"What does it look like?"

"That you are praying. Did I get it right?"

"I am not feeling that chipper this morning, I think the

powers of coffee are over-rated. I do not feel up to much, so I am hoping if I kneel here people will view me as in prayer and leave me in peace."

"Is it working?" asked Willoughby amiably.

"It appears not."

"Oh dear. Er, how many whiskies did you have after I left?"

"None. If you are going to remain talking to me – and please don't feel you need to – can I ask that you kneel down and whisper, to make it look like we are praying together. And whisper."

"Are you sure? About the whiskies I mean," whispered Willoughby clambering with some effort into a kneeling position.

"Yes, I drank several cups of coffee after you left. Very tasty it was but it didn't seem to sober me up. In fact quite the opposite I became more um how may I delicately term it?"

"Sozzled, squiffy, sloshed, stewed to the gills, tight, tipsy, woozy, tired and emotional, stinko, blotto, potted, plastered, three sheets to the wind, befuddled, soused, smashed, hinkdinked, inebriated, pickled, intoxicated, tanked, feeling no pain?" suggested Willoughby.

"Have you actually come about something?"

"Yes, to give you some good news and an apology."

"An apology?"

"Yes, Anun has been on the blower this morning and well she had worked out why Tabitha Whatsit is annoyed with you – and apparently it is my fault. She told me off – she has a different technique to Rikki, her manner is more amused than censorious. I think I prefer being told off by Anun than Rikki."

"Are you going to get to the point?"

"Oh yes, Anun has sorted it out so those two old ladies have been reassured of your moral propriety and all round sterling set of values and that you only view car parks for the purpose that nature, or town planners anyway, had intended."

"But why did they think I did not have these views?"

"Well it appears something I said may have been misconstrued."

"What was that?"

"I was telling them about yoga, and remember how you were thinking of joining Mrs C and I in doing it?"

"Was I?"

"Well you said you were, or were you just being nice?"

"I am always nice to people, you trandled twerp – I am a vicar, it goes with the territory. But why do they equate you doing yoga with my moral delinquency?"

"Well it appears, as far as I could make out, the double meaning of the term downward dogging. No, just dogging Anun said. It has more than one meaning."

"Yes it means to pester someone. You may care to think on that."

"Well it also means, well doing something Mrs C only indulges in on such occasions as state funerals and sightings of Hayley's Comet, and then only in the bedroom, after dark, with the curtains drawn and the lights off. Well some people take what might be termed an opposite view of this activity and see it as a chance to put on a show for invited spectators – like they were performance artists in one of these open-air theatres, except these shows seem to be put on in laybys – hmmm I wonder if that's how they got their name; probably not – and car parks, as apparently you have to do it in a car."

"Car parks!" exclaimed the vicar and then wished he hadn't as the words sliced through his head.

"Yes."

"Abitha and Ursula thought that I would do that!" he

said indignantly. "Well of all the trandled strendelbarns."

"If it's any consolation, I understand she feels very embarrassed and ashamed."

"So she should," whispered the vicar crossly. "Is that the good news? If so, I don't want to detain you."

"No. No, that was the apology. But it is good news also, isn't it? No get ready for a bit of good news: you have been appointed a chaplain."

"Of what?"

"The golf club."

"Of course why didn't I think of that! It was obvious wasn't it, it's the only thing around here."

"The world is full of obvious things which nobody by any chance ever observes," remarked Willoughby.

"Yes, of course, I should have thought of that. Obvious really, don't really have to have much of a brain to work that out. Silly me. Well, thank you for telling me."

"Oh there is more good news."

"Is there?"

"Yes, we are going to have a golfers' service."

"A what?"

"A golfers' service."

"What is one of these?"

"Well I rather hoped you would know. It's a service for golfers, well for the golf club, at the church."

"Here, at my church?"

"Yes, it's a church service. So a church seemed the best place for it."

"What does it involve?"

"I hoped you would know that, too."

"Well I don't."

"Oh."

"When have you set this for? I suppose this is your doing?"

"Two weeks' time, the Sunday morning service."

"I can't do it then! I haven't got time to flaff around with that, that's when the assessors come. I'll have far too much on my plate as it is."

"Precisely, they come and see a church bulging at the seams with people in chinos and polo shirts – why do people play golf in things called polo shirts not golf shirts, especially as polo is played in things like rugby shirts – and think wow we can't close down this church, look at the crowds, look at the outreach, look at the whatnot."

"Oh yes, yes, indeed," said the vicar, becoming enthused. "But what does it involve?"

"I don't know, just make it a normal service and bung in some golf bits, you know in the sermon and the prayers."

"But I don't have a sermon about golf. The Bible doesn't include golf you know."

"Yes, I have always considered it one of the book's deficiencies, but one which I have always overlooked in the spirit of Christian charity."

"But how do I give a sermon about golf?"

"You know, bung in a few golf references, stick in a funny story or two, put in a witticism."

"But my sermons don't have funny stories or witticisms in them."

"Yes, I know. But you must know some funny stories about golf as you must have sat through enough golf dinners, captain's day speeches, Rambo Rambles and the like."

"Well funny stories have never really been my thing."

"Okay, I will supply them."

"But it has to be a sermon with a theological message not a second-rate stand-up routine."

"Well I will link it into something to do with God. After all as Harry said, God is everywhere in heaven and on earth, and golf courses are on earth, and to some are a little slice, or maybe a little hook of heaven. That's an idea – I'll get Barry to help me. He is a writer after all and he's keen to get more involved with the club but the Secretary won't allow him as he's too small."

"Oh dear, yes the Secretary sometimes needs to be a bigger man."

"Don't worry Larry and I will knock something up for you to have a decko at."

"Oh good, well perhaps you'd like to go and see him now – strike while the iron is hot?"

"Oh no, after this I am off to see Mrs Winsor. That brings me to the second piece of good news."

"There is more good news?" said the vicar sounding a trifle exasperated.

"Yes, you are holding an art show the week after that in the church."

"In the church? We are a place of worship not an art gallery."

"Well you already have pictures around the place," said Willoughby indicating the walls, "so what's a few more? I was thinking you could use that ante room to hang them in."

"You mean the side chapel," said the vicar haughtily.

"That's right, the room where you store the broken chairs."

"And what's the point of that?"

"I have wondered – but I presumed you intended getting them repaired one day."

"No, in turning my church into an art gallery?"

"Attendance figures. We have a showing after the Sunday service, everyone comes along to gawp at the art and have tea and buns and things, and the management consultants are trampled underfoot by the crowds for the second week running and go away convinced that this is one church they should not close."

"But why would people want to come to an art show? What is it of? Rare Van Goghs?"

"The works of Mrs Winsor. Which are even rarer."

"Are they religious pictures?"

"No idea, but I doubt it – I think they are scenes from around her smallholding. Oh, and there's one of Anun as a mermaid I happen to know."

"Is Mrs Winsor's work a big draw? Is she a famous artist?"

"Completely unknown. But that's good."

"Is it?"

"Yes, when she becomes famous you will be the one who has discovered her. Feather in your cap."

"I don't think the management consultants have a box on their form about the work of the church for discovering unknown artists. Even ones who do pictures of mermaids."

"A very blinkered approach. They should re-assess their priorities – I wonder if management consultants bring in management consultants to assess their work? But the Winsors have contacts, people will come and support the family, I am sure."

"Are you?"

"Yes well Anun seems to know lots of young men, and they no doubt will enjoy the chance to see paintings of her as a mermaid."

"I admire your gallant belief that the men she knows will consider seeing her without clothes on as a novel experience. I hear, incidentally, she was spotted in the golf club bar last night in just her knickers, and with a man who was without his trousers."

"How much did you have to drink last night?"

"Oh no, this morning I heard that. I can't actually remember much about last night."

"And the golf club will turn out in force. Well the committee anyway, that'll boost the congregation – oh yes, we will be having tea and buns afterwards – Mrs Winsor can provide the cakes, can we rely upon the church ladies for the tea?"

"Yes, we can do that. Miss Murtle is looking after that side of things at the moment, have a word with her."

"Oh, I thought church catering was done by Mrs Haddock."

"Salmon. Yes well it was. But if you cast your mind back to the last funeral we had here, we have had to change that arrangement."

"Oh dear, didn't it go well, did she let you down?"

"It was her funeral. But why will the club committee come to this art show?"

"Well it's a kind of quid pro quo – club needs a new flag designed and we will ask her to do it. We can't pay her as the club is perennially skint, so in return we support her art show."

"She has agreed to all this?"

"She will," said Willoughby confidently. "She doesn't know anything about it yet."

"All for a flag?"

"A flag!" exclaimed Willoughby triumphantly, causing the vicar to wince. "That's an idea. You bless things don't you vicar. You could bless our new flag – that would give a golf content to the golfers' service."

"I thought you hadn't got a new flag."

"We haven't. But we have two weeks. Plenty of time."

"Not with the golf club. Doesn't it have to go through seventeen different committees, some of which don't even currently exist, before it will be agreed?"

"Oh no, it was all agreed at the last committee meeting."

"Are you sure? That sounds a bit dynamic for the club.

But yes," said the vicar enthusiastically, "blessing a flag would be a good way to get a bit of golf into the service."

"Yes, it was all agreed at committee," said Willoughby. "Which reminds me, I must see Brian."

"Oh, you off to see him now?" said the vicar hopefully. "Well don't let me keep you."

"No, no, Paddock's Farm awaits me. Well I must be off."

"Thank you."

"Not at all padre, always happy to help you out," and with that Willoughby tootled on his way, leaving the vicar to his prayers. The vicar set to them with renewed zeal. Now he had even more to pray about.

Outside, Willoughby saw Anun walking down the lane. "Hallo," he greeted her cheerfully, "you look like you have been dragged through a hedge backwards. I wonder why they say backwards not forwards, or just dragged through a hedge?"

"Hallo, how sweet of you to notice. It is a bit blowy today and I rushed off this morning to see Miss Tatsby so I didn't do my usual meticulous toilette it seems."

"Oh I thought you saw her ages ago."

"I did, but I bumped into a chap I knew afterwards."

"Here, let me," he said, "a twig has obviously blown into your hair at some stage," he said removing it, "oh and another one," he said spying another intruder. "I'm sure you mother would prefer to see you returning sans twigs."

"You been praying for our souls, Willoughby?"

"No, I have been arranging things. Are you on your way home?"

"Yes."

"I will walk with you them, if I may, for I have something I need to tell your mother."

"What about?" Anun said nervously.

"An art show. I am planning a show for your mother's paintings as you said you were always tripping over them as she had nothing useful to do with them."

"What a splendid idea. Where?"

"In the church's chair store, I mean side chapel."

"Oh? Is that a good place for an art show?"

"Yes. I have arranged for lots of people to come already – and no doubt you can get your extensive fan club along as well. We'll see if we can knock out some pictures to aid the family finances and the decluttering of the corridors of Paddock's Farm."

"Is 'knock out' how the Bond Street dealers refer to it?"

"Undoubtedly in private. It's all money with them, not art."

"Oh Mummy will be so pleased. Er how is the vicar this morning?"

"Rather hilariously grumpy due to getting hideously hinkdinked last night and so being horrendously hungover."

"Oh dear."

"Oh yes, about bingo."

"He doesn't need to know what's happened," said Anun starting.

"Eh?"

"Pardon?"

"Bingo cards, you know those cards they cross their winning numbers off on – do you happen to know how many numbers they have on them?"

"Er, hang on, yes it's five across and three down I think, so fifteen. Why?"

"Cripes that is a lot. No, reason, just wondering if I could arrange a game of bingo."

"Your timing is off, they've just closed the bingo hall. They are rather fed up about it, the bingoists I mean."

"Are you sure bingoists is the right term?"

"What else would they be – bingoers?"

"Hmm, don't know. Bingo players?"

"That's far too dull."

"Well bingo always struck me as a bit dull."

"Then why do you want to be involved?"

"Oh I don't want to play. It's just that, well I might as well tell you now." After he had done so, Anun laughed and said: "It's a good job you are on the side of the angels, for if you acted for the other side none of us would have a chance."

Chapter 12

"Ah Harry, just the fellow that I was hoping to meet," said Willoughby, when Harry walked into the bar. "Have you time for a chat? Perhaps a spot of afternoon tea?"

Willoughby had earlier had a splendid lunch at Paddock's Farm where his idea of an art show had been received rapturously by Mrs Winsor. She had been just as keen on the idea of doing a design for the flag. Willoughby had been made to sing for his lunch by posing, with an umbrella, as that was the best thing to hand, for a painting of a golfer in action, or rather for a quick sketch to be used later as the basis of a painting. She had felt she needed a golf picture for her show if the golf club were to be supporting it.

"Excellent, excellent," said Willoughby when Harry said yes. "Now I have a favour to ask. I am hoping you can help me out, well me and the club. You may have heard that we are having a golfers' service at the church in a couple of weeks, and the padre has to give a sermon about golf and well, let us just say that his strengths and popularity as our local vicar stems from the pastoral side of his duties rather than unbridled eloquence from the pulpit. His sermons have never exactly been ones to put you off your Sunday lunch or distract you from whatever you might have been thinking about."

"So you want me to help pep it up a bit?" asked Harry dubiously.

"Well I really want some professional expertise in helping me write something for the vicar to deliver. He's a bit worried about having to include golf in his sermon as he rarely strays beyond the Bible in his talks and there isn't any golf in the Bible. So we need to get creative on his behalf. Any ideas?"

"A sermon about golf?"

"Yes. I wonder if we should bung in a golf story or two. Preferably one that Rambo has not told a thousand times to the same people – often during the same evening. Here's a good one I've not heard Rambo tell that we could use: the old joke of a player just about to start his round who asks his caddie 'you any good at finding golf balls?' And when informed yes, the player replies: 'Good – well go and find one then so I can start my round'."

"Ah Willoughby – sorry to interrupt Harry – but I was wondering if I could have a word about the Doctor's Orders?"

"Oh yes, Secretary good news: my yoga sessions with Baloo, no the er well anyway they have been moved from Tuesday mornings to Monday mornings so now I am free to join up with the Doctor's Orders."

"Oh, Mondays you say."

"Yes, that's good isn't it, so now I am free on Tuesday mornings."

"Oh, the Doctor's Orders have been moved to Mondays – as the course is emptier then it was thought that was a better time. Oh, so you are still not available?"

"Alas Mr Secretary, it appears not. Dashed shame. Never mind, canna be helped."

"No, no," said the Secretary retiring defeated.

"I like the joke," said Harry, "but if the fellow's so tight how come he is employing a caddy?"

"Ah, when I said it is an old joke, it is an extremely old joke. Centuries old. Dates back to when golf balls cost a small fortune and no-one could easily afford to lose one, whereas labour was cheap. Golfers often had not only a caddy, as in the chap who carries your bag of clubs, but forecaddies who were sent on ahead to spot where the ball had been hit to."

"I haven't heard of forecaddies before."

"They have all but gone from the game, except in top professional tournaments that is. Those events played by multi-millionaires who don't even pay for their balls."

"Should we include a bit of explanation of the history behind the joke?" asked Harry.

"Isn't that making it a bit like a Rambo Ramble?"

"Well I was thinking it might interest people, and we could link it into something. I know, how about something along the lines of forecaddies help show you the way, a bit like the Bible does, but ultimately it is up to you to use this help."

"Good thinking – a bit tenuous, but the vicar would approve of us lugging the Bible into it straight away. He's a big fan of the Bible. Oh yes, and we need to get lots of numbers into the talk, I mean sermon."

'Do we, why?"

"Can you keep a secret?"

"Yes," said Harry eagerly.

"So can I," said Willoughby. "So you will just have to trust me on this one. Right, should you write this up or shall I?" he said producing a writing pad and pen from a satchel below the table. "Okay – we'll open with that joke, explain what a forecaddie is – hmmm that is a rather ambiguous word isn't it, some people might think that is a number, okay, just need to make sure we get the number four into the talk later so it doesn't matter. Then link that into how everyone needs a bit of guidance in life and you need to know the right way to seek it, and we can lug the Bible into it there."

"These forecaddies, weren't they most useful on those holes where the player can't see where his ball has ended up? That could get some numbers into it?"

"Yes of course, blind holes – once popular with course

designers, but now rather out of fashion, thank goodness. Okay, we can bung in examples of famous blind holes. Know any good ones Harry?"

"Sorry no, I was doing concept on this one, I was leaving you to do the facts."

"Right, I must know of some. Yes of course the 17th at St Andrews, the Road Hole, is blind for the pros as they hit over that wall thing, and then there's the 9th at Royal County Down, oh and the 16th at Royal Lytham & St Annes. Great – that's got us three numbers in there straight away."

"But do we know if the vicar will use these examples?" asked Harry.

"You haven't been to one of the vicar's services have you?"

"Well, no, it's just that well..."

"No need to apologise, old boy. Very sensible of you, some might say. They are not exactly rip-roaring occasions. Great bloke, lousy orator. He is not a confident public speaker. He reads his sermon religiously – sorry, no pun intended – and he starts at the beginning and ploughs on taking no prisoners until he reaches the end. If it is on the page, it gets read. So don't go putting 'turn over' or anything like that at the foot of the page either."

"A tip I learnt from Winston Churchill..."

"Oh, didn't know you knew him."

"I don't, didn't," said Harry momentarily thrown off track, "but I read that he had a technique when reading speeches that he would divide them up into phrases, a phrase a line, and so he just read it aloud line by line, as that way it sounded naturalistic when delivered."

"Really? That's jolly clever. Churchill was a golfer, by the way. He and Lloyd George were members of Walton Heath, and both sat on its committee, and continued to do so during the Great War. The saying at the time was the war was being conducted from Walton Heath's 19th hole. On the eve of war, Walton Heath had four future or past Prime Ministers, 24 MPs and 21 members of the House of Lords among its membership. Littlestone at one stage had the prime minister, Herbert Asquith, as its captain and the leader of the opposition, Arthur Balfour, as its President. But I digress."

"Splendid notion of yours," Willoughby continued, "of laying out the speech that way – when we write it up for the padre we'll do it like that. That'll improve his delivery no end. A lot of what he says is quite good, well some of it anyway, but the way he delivers it – well no-one could ever accuse him of being dithyrambic. Right, we have a bit of golf now we need a bit of God – how are you on that?"

"No too hot I confess – you?"

"Well I have heard a lot about him over the years. Right, let's think laterally – we want something about leading the way. Let me see, the padre is always quoting the Bible at us, so we'll bung in a few quotes." Willoughby reached into the satchel and brought out a battered Bible. "Hmm there is something at the beginning of Proverbs about lighting the way or summat – ah, here it is, possibly, or possibly not, but it will do anyway – 'Trust in the Lord with all your heart and lean not on your own understanding; in all your ways submit to him, and he will make your paths straight.' Proverbs 3 verses 5 and 6 – magic that's three more numbers. Hey, I think this might be easier than I had thought."

"Oh yes, another one we could bung in is from Timmy," said Willoughby flicking through his Bible – something about 'if a chap competes as an athlete, he does not receive the victor's crown unless he competes according to the rules.' Complete tosh of course as Benton walked off with the Hanky Panky Cup. But never mind, it sounds good. Mark that down and I'll find the exact quote later," he said flicking through the pages of his Bible.

Two pots of tea, and four slices of cake – which ended up being divided three to one in Willoughby's favour – "to each according to his greed," as he explained to Harry when Harry declined his extra slice – and they had a sermon.

The next day, when they went to present it to the vicar, it was received well. The vicar suggested some minor rewrites, "but you can leave that with me, you have both done a splendid job," he said. "I really am most grateful, this is a lovely sermon."

"Ah well, we do need a final version of your text so when you have rewritten it, would you mind giving us a copy?" explained Willoughby.

"Why?"

"Well, we thought it would be a good idea if we had a few copies to give out afterwards at the tea-and-bun stage to impress the assessors in case someone asks for a copy of your sermon."

"No-one has ever asked for the text of one of my sermons before so I think you are being a tad optimistic."

"But you have never given a talk, I mean a sermon, about golf before to a congregation full of eager golfers. Also don't forget, this is a news item – young Harry here, and old Twiddlytwonk, you know the chap who parts his hair, are going to write about it in the press, so they will both need a copy of the sermon for starters so they can quote you accurately."

"You think I might be quoted in the press?" said the vicar excitedly.

"Well not if they don't have the text of the sermon. But yes, Harry here has arranged to write it for one of the golf mags haven't you?"

"Indeed – Golf Fortnightly."

"Golf Fortnightly, padre – the best of the lot. That'll make it harder for the Dean to boot you out."

"Yes, indeed I will certainly make sure you have a copy of the final text well in advance."

"Splendid, splendid. Oh yes, do you happen to know what hymns we will be singing?"

"No, I leave that to the organist, I used to choose the hymns, but our current organist knows so few tunes – fortunately hymns tend to recycle them – we kept on having to change them all the time, so now I leave it to her to choose with the only stipulation that we can't have the same hymn reappearing within three weeks. Even so, that only means hymns come round in a four-week cycle I regret. She is trying to learn a new tune, one which we selected as it works for eight different hymns – well slightly different anyway, the words are different at least – as that will extend her repertoire no end. But so far it has been eluding her."

"And who is the organist these days?"

"Mrs Alysson."

"Does she still live in that cottage down by the stream?"

"Yes, why?"

"Oh I just thought it would be nice to pop round and thank her in advance for taking part in the golfers' service. You know, as part of the club's outreach programme – I could outreach to her, er reach out to her."

"That's very kind, but I don't think it's strictly necessary."

"Oh, a little courtesy and consideration never goes amiss however unnecessary it may seem," replied Willoughby.

Chapter 13

"You know what you have to do?"

"Yes," replied Anun, "I give out the hymn books to everyone except those who Mags Murtle tells me not to, as she will be giving them a hymn book from her secret stash."

"Splendid. Where is your sister? She will tell me off if she finds out."

"She is sorting out the crockery as Mags Murtle can't as she's front of house with me."

"Excellent. That will keep her out of mischief. Ah here is our first customer."

"Good morning, Captain," Willoughby greeted him, "now when you give your reading make sure you say loudly where it is from, and oh and might as well repeat it just to be sure."

"Yes you have told me, I have no idea why I need to do that though."

"Good. Best that way. Thank you."

"Oh, and what do I have to do with the flag?"

"Oh yes, the blessing bit, better talk to the padre about that. I think you just walk up and present it to the vicar. He's around somewhere. He's a bit nervous."

"Why?"

"Oh, er, well he doesn't want to let the club down I suppose in his first official outing as our chaplain."

"Where's the flag? I haven't seen it."

"No, no-one has yet, but Rikki has it. She's in the kitchen I'm told. Telling off the crockery or something."

"Ah hallo, Brian," Willoughby greeted the next person in through the church doors.

"Ah, Willoughby, you here for the committee meeting, too?"

"No, Brian. This is the golfers' service."

"Oh that's right. Thought it odd having a committee meeting in the church."

"Oh yes, Brian, I have got the copy of the minutes for you."

"For a church service? Does it need them?"

"No, the committee meeting."

"I thought you said this was the golfers' service?"

"It is. But this is the minutes of the committee meeting when we agreed we would have the golfers' service. You agreed to take them, remember?"

"Take them where?" said Brian looking round as if seeing where might be a likely destination.

"No. You agreed to write them."

"Oh write them, um."

"And so I have written them for you."

"Have you? That's very decent of you."

"I thought it would save you the effort."

"That's very decent of you. Was I um at that meeting?"

"Yes."

"Oh. Um. I can't remember it."

"There you are," said Willoughby handing him a piece of paper, "pop that it your jacket pocket."

"No, not from Miss Murtle, Anun has your hymn book," said Willoughby as Brian tried to take a hymn book from the Secretary's PA.

"Oh. Why can't I take one from Miss Murtle?"

"The hymns are better in Anun's book."

"Oh, are they? Then I will have one of your books please Anun. Thank you for the tip Willoughby."

"Hey Willoughby, what's all this about the flag?" said Rambo bustling up in a state of agitation. "I hear a new flag has been made – but my committee has not approved the design."

"Oh the Heads of Committee agreed that Mrs Winsor

would do the design according to our instructions. Don't you remember?"

"No, that is not what the committee agreed, I should know I was the chairman. I was the chairman."

"Well I was there, and I remember clearly that we did agree to that. Who was taking the minutes?"

"It was, er..."

"Brian. I think it was Brian wasn't it?" said Willoughby. "Oh look, he's over there let's have a word with him."

"Brian, Rambo was wondering if you had written up the minutes of the last Heads of Committee meeting?"

"Um."

"You said, you would try to bring them today to hand to Rambo," Willoughby prompted him as Brian was looking blank. "Perhaps you have them in your pocket?"

Brian stood up so as to check his trouser pocket. "Nope nothing there, oh apart from my hanky. That wasn't what you wanted was it?" he said proffering it to Rambo in an unconvinced way.

"No, Brian, it is the minutes," said Willoughby, as Rambo chaffed beside him. "Perhaps it is in your jacket pocket?"

"Oh yes," said Brian delving into a pocket, "is this what you want?" he said producing something out of his pocket with the air of a magician surprised that his trick had come off.

"No, that's a hymn book. It is a sheet of paper we are looking for. Perhaps in your inside pocket?" suggested Willoughby.

"No," said Brian delving into the pocket, "all I have is my wallet and a piece of paper."

"The paper – what is that?"

"I don't know," said Brian unfolding it. "Oh, this is nothing important – looks like the minutes of some meeting or something."

"Excellent just what we want – now Rambo we can see for sure what was decided at the meeting," said Willoughby taking the paper from Brian.

"Ah here we are: 'The committee agreed that the design of the replacement quarter would be up to Mrs Winsor, who is to be instructed that the design should reflect the club's association with the Hankley family but cannot include that family's crest. Mrs Winsor is also to be instructed that the flag needs to have been completed in time for the golfers' service, where it is to be blessed as the centrepiece of that service'."

"Oh," said Rambo deflated. "That is not how I remembered it."

"Isn't it? Well it is exactly how I remembered it," replied Willoughby.

"Me too," said Brian.

"Well what is this design? I as the head of the Heads of Committee should have been informed what the design is."

"Well I understand it is a big secret, part of the great reveal – you know add a bit of excitement and drama to the service. Otherwise, well," and Willoughby lowered his voice to a conspiratorial whisper "I needn't spell it out to someone of your intelligence and awareness, but otherwise, well, the service could be a trifle dull, and we want our inaugural golfers' service to be a great success don't we, especially as you were so keen on it. Well I was as well, I thought it was an excellent notion of yours to push it through the committee. Showed real leadership. As did your attitude to the flag – many a chairman would have flaffed around and insisted we had another meeting to approve the design and lost the chance to have the blessing, but you didn't fall into that trap. Very wise."

"What's the design?" asked Rambo getting more agitated.

"Why do you think I know?"

"Well haven't you been organising this service?"

"I don't know. What do the minutes say?"

"But you must know surely?"

"Well I am aware of this rumour," and Willoughby moved himself and Rambo away from the rest of those who were gathering for the service and dropped his voice again, "that as it was agreed that the design had to reflect the Hankley family's connection with the club..."

"Yes, yes, I know that," interrupted Rambo impatiently.

"Well as you know only too well. Their crest used to be on the crockery we had, sadly only a few jugs of which are now left. So, and I don't know this for sure, but I believe it may be an upturned milk jug."

"It didn't happen, it didn't happen," he said crossly.

"What didn't?"

"I didn't turn a full milk jug upside down to see if there was a crest on its bottom. And anyway you weren't there."

"I wasn't there when it didn't happen?"

"Yes. No. We can't have a milk jug!"

"Perhaps it was thought that it also serves to underline one of the club's functions as not just a place to play golf but as a meeting place for the local community to come and have afternoon tea and socialise. It is part of our outreach programme."

"An upturned milk jug!"

"People would think it is a jug being poured. You know the milk pouring out of it, like when you poured it all over Anun searching for that crest."

"I didn't – you'd have to be a cretin to turn a full milk jug upside down like that."

"An absolute cretin," agreed Willoughby solemnly. "I have heard Anun say the very same thing."

"No, no, that's not right," said Rambo getting more agitated, "we can't have that. Who is in charge of the service? Who do I speak to?"

"At a wild guess – maybe the vicar?"

"The vicar! Of course. He will know who is in charge. Where is he, I must stop this, it's all wrong," said Rambo rushing off.

"Oh, look out," said Willoughby softly to Brian, "something wicked this way comes."

"Ah Willoughby," the newcomer greeted him.

"Hallo Benton, didn't know you were coming."

"I thought I better, as one of the most senior members of the club. I wondered if I could help out, perhaps I could ah, ahem take the collection plate around?"

"No, no that's all right, the sidesmen do that every week."

"I was ah, ahem thinking as it was a larger congregation than usual and they may want some assistance to get it all done. Thought, you know, the club ought to be showing willing."

"No it's fine, all sorted. What's done is done. Kind of you to offer though."

A thought occurred to Willoughby and he excused himself from Benton's company to go to see Rikki. His way to the kitchen was barred by a young man who would not let him past. "Sorry, Sir, no-one is allowed in here."

"I just wanted a word with Half Pint, I mean Rikki."

Rikki looked round from the sink she was standing at: "Oh it's all right he can pass, he's my Godfather and quite respectable. Well he's my Godfather anyway. Chap you are looking out for is fat," and then, realising what she had said, she added, "and also has a silly moustache and a comb over. And may be naked."

"What's all that about, Half Pint, do you have a personal bodyguard now?"

"No, I am a bit worried about Mr Ramsbotham getting in here. There are a lot of milk jugs about."

"Very wise. What will happen afterwards? We are serving tea and coffee. There will be milk jugs about then."

"I had thought of that," said Rikki. "The ladies who are serving have been told not to let him near a jug. But we hope he can be confined to the other end of the church after the service."

"How? And why are you washing up before the cups have been used? Isn't it more traditional to wash them up after they have been used? Or are you practising?"

"Some of these cups don't look like they've been used in yonks; they are full of dust and all sorts. They should have put them upside down when they are stored on open shelves," explained Rikki. "Well after the service the flag is going to be laid out at the other end of the church, so as to keep it far away from the foodstuffs. Perhaps you could persuade Rambo to guard it or something."

"Guard it? I know, we could tell him to stand by it to tell anyone interested in the history of it, bit like those room stewards at the stately homes my mother used to take me to. That's a wheeze. That'll keep him away from any milk jugs."

"Oh hallo vicar, all set for the off?" said Willoughby cheerfully to the new arrival.

"Why are we having a bouncer on the kitchen door?" asked the vicar.

"Rikki's personal bodyguard. All the big stars have them these days I understand padre."

Rikki threw a wet cloth at Willoughby, scoring a direct hit to the face. "Stop standing around looking like a wind sock in a gale and do something useful – grab that tea towel and start drying. Ignore him vicar, he's just being naughty. It's in case Mr Ramsbotham gets in here. There are a lot of milk jugs about."

"Oh dear, yes, I had overlooked that. Oh dear, yes, I have just heard him talking about milk jugs in a most agitated fashion. He was telling the Golf Club Secretary that he didn't want a milk jug anywhere. Oh dear, yes. Oh dear."

"Don't worry, padre," said Willoughby. "Lurch over there won't let him in here, and Rikki has a plan for the rest of the day. The ladies on teas are being told not to let him near a milk jug, and the idea is to keep him down the other end of the church, looking after the flag which will be displayed there."

"Does a flag need looking after?"

"It does in this case. Worry not padre."

"What happens if he takes all his clothes off? He does that I am told."

"Well I doubt the assessors have a tick box for 'did the congregation remain clothed throughout', so you will be alright," said Willoughby. "Got a good crowd in and the cry is still, 'They come!'"

"Yes, yes, it has been filling up nicely hasn't it? Haven't had a congregation for a normal Sunday service this large since, well, since my first year here. We used to get quite large congregations then, but they have tailed off. Church going is not as popular as it once was, sadly."

"Do you know what this chap who is coming for the Dean looks like?" asked Willoughby.

"No, but I thought by a process of elimination I might, as he won't be a member of the club or a regular communicant. But there are many people here I don't recognise. Mags Murtle seems to know a lot of those who I don't," he said with an air of slight puzzlement.

"Well obviously she'd invite her friends and acquaintances to the club sandwich, I mean club service."

"Yes, yes, oh that is good of her."

"Can you talk and dry Willoughby, not just talk," chided Rikki.

"Oh dear, I better leave you to it," said the vicar, "I must have a word with the sidesmen. Benton Snivelgate was asking to take round an extra collection plate and I must tell them on no account to let him near them."

"Don't worry padre, it's all going to be a great success," reassured Willoughby.

Chapter 14

Rambo had been steered down to the end of the church away from the teas where he was telling someone all about the flag: "It's not a milk jug at all, it's a traction engine, it's a traction engine, not a milk jug."

"Yes, I can see that. Why would it be a milk jug?" asked the puzzled parishioner, who was not a member of the golf club – all those members who hadn't already left knew better than to fall within Rambo's orbit and were at the other end of the building.

"It's a depiction of one of Lord Hankley's traction engines falling into a bunker, not the current one, the current Lord I mean, not the bunker, but the one before the one before this one, or was it the one before that? Anyway it doesn't matter, it doesn't matter, it was one of the earlier Lord Hankleys. It's quite an interesting story actually..."

At the other end of the church, Mags Murtle slipped out from behind the trestle table, behind which she was helping to serve teas, with a box in which was one of Mrs Winsor's cakes. A small group of ladies gathered around while she made a presentation to one of the ladies.

"What's going on over there?" asked the vicar of Willoughby. "Looks like some sort of presentation?"

"What to Miss Daisy Hawkins? Perhaps it's her birthday or something. Anyway probably none of our business. Well this has all gone well hasn't it?"

"Oh yes, it looks like you guessed right – it's a cake they have given her. Yes, yes, it went well didn't it, your sermon especially."

"Harry's sermon, he did all the heavy lifting."

"Yes Harry's sermon, that went down well. I have never before felt that some of the congregation were hanging on my every word. That group sitting with Mags Murtle especially, they were really into it. I have seldom felt that with my sermons, but Harry's clever way of phrasing things obviously hit the mark, a couple of them I think I saw even taking notes – they seemed to be writing something anyway."

"Well Harry's a professional writer – sounds like he has chosen his profession wisely."

"One thing puzzled me, why did that lady shout during the sermon what sounded like 'house', and then what sounded like 'full house'? That lady over there whose birthday it is."

"I wondered that. It sounded like 'house' didn't it but in fact she shouted 'mouse' as she thought she had seen a mouse."

"Oh dear. Had she? I didn't know we had mice. Oh dear."

"No, she was mistaken. The lady next to her – well apparently what had happened is her brown purse fell out of her handbag and catching the movement of a brown thing out of the corner of her eye caused her neighbour to shriek 'mouse'. Then when she realised she had been fooled, she said "fool – mouse!""

"Oh. I did wonder at some stage if I was going to be heckled by the congregation," the vicar laughed happily. "I must thank you Willoughby for a most excellent sermon – it went down far better than I could have hoped."

"Not me you need to thank. Harry wrote it."

"Even that joke about the caddy? That went down well."

"Yes, I laughed when Harry told it to me. It was a good one wasn't it? One I hadn't heard before."

"And I must thank you for having the idea of the golfers' service, most ingenious, and most successful."

"Again, you are thanking the wrong person padre – that was Brian's idea."

"Brian?"

"Yes."

"He is a deceptive fellow isn't he?"

"Apparently he read it somewhere about it being done by a cricket club and thought it'd be a good idea for us. He was right, too, wasn't he?"

"Indeed he was," said the vicar happily.

"Er, any idea as to who that fellow is over there on his own, seemingly watching everyone like a second-rate spy?"

"No idea. Never seen him before."

"Me neither. Guess that might be our man. I'll just go and have a word with him."

Willoughby went over to the stranger. "Hallo, haven't seen you here before. You a golfer?"

"Er, no. I was just in the area and er so came along to this service."

"Oh, have you been here before?"

"No."

"Oh, we normally have a few more than this, I think it being a service about golf put some people off. Plus of course quite a few people are away on their summer hols."

"More? There were 63 here."

"Actually it was 71 – pardon me, one of my little quirks, counting people at events."

"Odd habit."

"Must be one I share with you if you also counted them."

"Touché."

"Yes, it's an odd quirk isn't I. Don't know how it started with me, but I've always been interested in numbers, even as child."

"No, nor with me. I was a bit surprised though, I had heard that this particular church didn't have that large a congregation," said the stranger.

"Oh, you shouldn't believe everything you hear round here. Believe me. Is mid 70s large? I suppose it's all comparative."

"Well I do seem to have been misinformed if you say this is a slightly smaller congregation than usual."

"Did you enjoy the sermon?"

"Yes, I did actually. I loved that joke about the caddy."

"Yes it was good wasn't it? Typical of the vicar, that."

"I was a bit surprised as I'd heard his sermons were, well, not that good."

"Well you have seen for yourself that isn't the case; well heard for yourself, I suppose that should be. What you probably heard is that he is admired even more for his pastoral work than for his fine sermons. He is very well thought of in the village by everyone."

"I'd heard he just spends his time going around dropping in on people for afternoon tea; that or playing golf."

"Yes poor dear. It's part of his pastoral work in the parish and all these old biddies insist on giving him tea and cake and things. Poor lad has to plough through tons of cake in a year all the name of his ministry. Would you want to have to eats tons of cake every year?"

"Well no, I prefer savoury food myself."

"Me, too. So does the vicar. Just imagine having to plough your way through all those types of cake: chocolate ones, Madeira, Victoria sponges, lemon drizzles, red velvet, Dundee, angel cakes, or perhaps a slice of Battenberg, maybe some jam tarts, or a rock cake or two, who'd want any of that – yuck! But he can't really insult them by turning it down can he?"

"I suppose not. I'd also heard he has afternoon tea every Thursday with some old bore at the golf club."

"Really? Oh, him. Yes, terrible bore he is. Again what

the fellow puts up with for his ministry is much to be admired. But then I suppose he has to as he is chaplain of the golf club."

"Chaplain? I didn't know he was a chaplain anywhere."

"Oh yes, and that means he has to put in appearances there. He always takes afternoon tea there on Thursdays, I understand, so everyone knows where and when to find him. As I'm sure you'll appreciate, some people might feel a bit intimidated coming to the church to talk to a vicar, but when he is with them in a casual setting, it's much easier for them to slip into conversation whatever is troubling them. Helps break down barriers."

"Yes of course."

"And obviously he has to play golf, as part of, well I wouldn't say subterfuge, but you know, for people to see him there in a natural setting, to blend into that society, to be considered one of their own as it were. Very noble of him as a game of golf can take a long time, but he puts in the hours for his ministry does our vicar. We are very lucky to have him. Mind you, good in a way that he does play golf, otherwise he would balloon, all that cake his grateful parishioners thrust down his throat. Very good for keeping the weight down, golf."

"I take it you're not a golfer, so you must be a regular worshipper here?"

"Yes, I am. Are you coming along next week?"

"No, someone else will, er, um no, I won't be around next week, I was just er um passing through today and you, know, it's Sunday so thought I'd better go to church. Well I must be going, lovely to meet you."

"And you," said Willoughby cordially. "Ah Mr Secretary, good turnout wasn't it, hopefully it will have done the club some good."

"Oh, it has, it has. I have spoken to two people who have said they are interested in taking up membership. I got their names and contact details. I had wondered if one of them might be Larry Keene. He has never turned up you know."

"And was he one of them?"

"No, two entirely different people. Yes, most pleasing as we need more members and Brian and his committee aren't much good at that side of things."

"This service was Brian's idea."

"Was it?"

"Yes, he'd read about a cricket club doing something similar and thought why shouldn't we. He thought it might attract some new members."

"Oh, hallo Mr Ramsbotham, I was just saying what a clever idea this church service was," said the Secretary.

"Thank you. Yes, I am very pleased that my idea has been such a success."

"Your idea?"

"Yes, it was decided at the Heads of Committee meeting, of which I am the chairman at the moment. I am the chairman."

"Oh I thought it was the Membership Committee chairman..."

"No, no – I have the minutes here in fact to prove it: 'The committee considered two ideas to promote the club to a wider audience: a talk on golf, or a dedicated church service. In the end the chairman's eloquence swayed the room and the committee voted to ask the vicar to host a service for the club at his church one Sunday morning this summer.' I was that chairman, that eloquent chairman."

"Oh, well then you are to be congratulated Mr Ramsbotham. It has been a great success. Lovely touch getting the flag blessed, I didn't even know the flag had been done – that was jolly quick."

"Yes, we had to move quickly on that. I was very keen on that, so I made sure that the Heads of Committee agreed to it. I was the chairman of that Heads of Committee meeting. I was the chairman."

Willoughby slipped away. He felt a bit mean leaving the Secretary in the firing line, but the Secretary was paid for that sort of thing; he was not. He made his way towards the back of the church where the ladies were clearing away. He hastily grabbed the last slice of cake before the plate was taken away. He noticed Lurch was back on the door, on guard.

"Here, grab some dirty crockery and bring it through," commanded Rikki. He joined Harry in collection duties, Harry doing so with great happiness, as he had been asked to do so by Rikki. "Oh and might as well bring all those bowls of crisps in, too. No-one's eating them," instructed Rikki.

Willoughby went through to collect some more bowls and saw Anun, perched on the edge of a table such that her dress had ridden up her thigh, talking to Mr Wilkinson. He overheard her say: "Yes there is one of me as a mermaid, there are several of Rikki. There is one of her topless with her teddy bear. There are a couple of beautiful paintings of Rikki's tits," Anun enjoying seeing the reaction this caused in Mr Wilkinson.

Willoughby went in to the kitchen carrying a pile of crockery. "Hallo Half Pint I hear we are going to see topless pictures of you next week with your bear – is that Squeak?" Squeak was the bear he had given her as her birthday present when he went to see her in the hospital.

"Yes, me and Squeak – I had him down the other day and do you know he still has his squeak even after all these years?"

"I am not surprised. He's probably never been able to get a word in edgeways."

Willoughby ducked as a wet cloth came flying his way, instead it caught Harry, who was coming in with the last of the bowls of crisps, behind the ear.

"Oh please forgive me" said Rikki apologetically. "That was Willoughby."

"Ignore her Harry, she threw it. She does fib so, I regret. I am afraid she is very badly behaved. As her Godfather, I have tried to ensure she has impeccable morals and behaviour but I regret the task proved too great for me."

"Sorry Harry, the cloth was meant for Willoughby. Yes, a very beautiful painting it is too."

"Yes, Squeak was always a most attractive bear."

Rikki looked around for another cloth to throw, but she couldn't see one and anyway Willoughby had hastily ducked behind Harry crying "watch out Harry, I think she wants to throw another cloth at you."

"Ah padre," said Willoughby, "I had a talk with that fellow. He obviously was the man."

"What did he think you think? Did he say anything?"

"Very impressed he was, very impressed, and quite rightly, too."

"Oh good. Oh good."

"Different bod is coming next week, it seems."

"Oh next week, oh dear, oh dear, we are going to have to do it again. Oh dear, oh dear."

"Don't worry, it's going to be another great success," reassured Willoughby.

Chapter 15

All set for the action replay?" asked Willoughby of Anun and Miss Murtle, who were poised inside the church door with their respective piles of hymn books. "Do you think all your ladies will come this week?"

"I should think so, we all enjoyed last week. Made a nice change."

"Oh hallo, Brian, you're early. No, remember, Anun's books have the best hymns," Willoughby said as Brian tried to take a hymn book from Miss Murtle.

"No, I wanted one with a bingo card in it. Looks rather fun, how does it work?"

"In total secrecy," replied Willoughby. "There's an explanation on the card – winning numbers are the hymns, the chapter and verse of the readings and any number that is said in the sermon. Put at least an extra £2 in the collection plate if you are playing, and not a word to the vicar. Prize this week is one of Mrs Winsor's splendid iced cherry cakes. Mum's the word."

"Yes, Anun and Rikki's Mum," he said nodding to Anun.

"You've been rumbled, Willoughby," laughed Anun. "Does Rikki know she was supposed to put lots of numbers in the sermon?"

"No flipping fear. But Harry edited it after her. Fortunately he said Rikki had mentioned lots of artists and pictures, so he just had to look up their dates and bung them in."

"Oh has Rikki written today's sermon?" asked Miss Murtle.

"Yes, we're getting a sermon about the paintings in the church and religious iconography. What it is in fact is a rehash of her school project on the paintings in the church, with some stuff from a uni lecture bunged in," laughed Anun. "Oh, with added dates by Harry."

"Oh, how interesting. I shall look forward to that. Is Mrs Cornwallis coming today?" asked Miss Murtle of Willoughby.

"No, no, this is, well it's not her kind of thing. Paintings I mean, not church."

"Oh, you're wrong there," remarked Anun. "She came over yesterday and asked to have a look at them."

"Good lord, did she? She didn't tell me. Are you sure?"

"Does she have an identical twin sister?"

"No."

"Then I am sure."

"Though she does have an identical twin brother who is a cross dresser."

"I was surprised, too. Can't ever remember your good lady coming round to ours before, even with you. She came to see the paintings. Oh dear – and you say she is not coming. Doesn't say much for her opinion of Mummy's work does it?"

"Is Bongo coming?"

"Bingo. No, he has to work. But a few of my friends are coming along. Three of them are going to play golf this afternoon, if you care to join them?"

"This afternoon? Sorry, can't make it as I have promised Mrs C that I would help her with something."

The vicar bustled up, flustered. "A coach had just drawn up outside, and the driver has just asked if this is where they are showing An Intimate Portrait Of The Winsors At Home."

"That's alright, you knew the answer," said Willoughby.

"Yes. But why has a coach arrived for my church service? Apparently it is full of Americans."

"Well you can't expect them to walk all the way from America. It's a long way," reasoned Brian.

"With respect padre, it seems they have arrived more for the art than the service," pointed out Willoughby.

"Yes, you are right to correct me, that was rather egotistical. But why has a coach load of Americans come to our art show?"

"Sorry padre, can't help you: the workings of the art world are a mystery to me. So, too, for that matter, Americans. But it sounds like a good thing, more bums on seats. I wouldn't worry about it if I were you. Perhaps Mrs Winsor is big in America? Or about to be."

"Do you know what is going on, Anun?" asked the vicar.

"No."

"Oh well, as you say it all adds to the congregation. The more the merrier," said the vicar bustling off.

Anun was giving Willoughby a meaningful look. "Not my fault Americans can't spell," he responded.

"So that's why you were so particular that the show should not be called Life at Paddock's Farm as Mummy had suggested. Hallo Mr Wilkinson, looking forward to the exhibition?"

"Very much so. We can buy the pictures can't we?"

"Yes indeed, that's the idea," said Anun, "with a percentage of sale income going to the church. Just speak to either me or my sister afterwards. Anything which has a red dot beside it means it's been sold; otherwise everything is for sale."

"Including you?"

"I beg your pardon?"

"I mean the intimate pictures of you?"

"Yes, all the pictures are for sale."

"Can I look at them now?"

"Sorry, show only opens after the service. Harry and Rikki are setting it up now."

"What are you doing afterwards about Mr Ramsbotham, in case he tries to get hold of the milk jugs?" asked Miss Murtle. "I see he's just arrived."

"We are not serving tea today," replied Anun. "There will be a choice of Mummy's home-made wine, or Mummy's pressed apple juice from our orchard. It's an all Paddock's Farm production – art, drinks and foodstuffs are all made by well, normally Mummy, but me and Rikki did the apple juices. Even the cakes are made with eggs from the farm."

After the service the side chapel was opened for the art exhibition, and the congregation filtered in. First in had been Mr Wilkinson, who had taken a seat in the pew nearest the side chapel in readiness. After having a look around the exhibits, he turned to Anun: "Er excuse me, can you show me where that topless picture of Rikki is?"

"It's there," said Anun pointing to a painting of Rikki as a toddler, in nappies and standing with her back to the viewer, holding her beloved bear Squeak by the paw. Squeak had swung round such that his face was looking out of the canvas. "If you want it, I'm afraid it has already been sold," said Anun noticing the red dot beside it. "Must have been snapped up straight away."

"You admiring that picture, Wilko?" asked Willoughby. "It is rather charming isn't it? I think it's my favourite of all the ones here. Very evocative."

"Er, yes," said Wilko. "I suppose it could be seen like that."

"You are right Willoughby," said Brian, surveying one of the other pictures, "pigs obviously do play golf." He was standing in front of a painting of a pig in plus fours standing on its hind trotters hitting a golf ball. "Mind you, the fellow looks to have a slice."

"Probably hard to grip a club properly with trotters," reasoned Willoughby. "Maybe that's where the phrase 'a slice of bacon' comes from? Pigs slice; fish hook."

"That pig's swing is a bit like yours. Fun game, by the way."

"Golf?"

"No um church bingo. Enjoyed it. Don't know why more churches don't do it. Makes you listen to the sermon. It was a rather good one wasn't it?"

"It was indeed. Excuse me Brian but I spy a spy," said Willoughby moving off.

"Oh hallo, good to see you again," said Willoughby to his quarry. "I didn't think you were coming this week?"

"Well I wasn't, but then someone fell sick and, as there was going to be an art element to this service, so I thought I would come along."

"Oh are you interested in art?"

"Why else would I be here," he replied nervously.

"For Sunday worship?"

"Oh yes. Of course. Well that goes without saying. But yes, I have always been interested in art. I collect it."

"Do you? What particular type of art do you collect?"

"Modern art, sculptures in particular, but I am interested in all artistic expression."

"Well everything here is for sale, so anything you fancy and is not red-dotted dive in there."

"Thank you, but this is all a bit literal and amateur, I prefer more sophisticated works which are not what they appear yet are what they are appear, if you see what I mean."

"I do," replied Willoughby. "Not everything is at it appears."

"I saw that you and that fellow there were having a discussion about the picture of the golfing pig. I take it he is a member of the golf club?"

"The pig? No."

"No, I mean the chap... oh I see you were making a joke."

"Yes indeed we have just discussing that work. Although he feels that painting does not really reverberate with him on an offset sentient level, he thought that the optical suggestions of the gesture making resonant the sublime signifier was neatly underlined in an abstract yet parmesan-like way. I had to agree with him up to a point but I have to say I do worry a tad that this piece threatens to overly penetrate the metaphorical exploration of discordant elements of the substrata thus clouding the essentially transitional quality of the action. What do you think?"

"Er, um, well I have to say you are indeed right," he replied, "when you had said that there would be more people this week and there are. Nice mix of ages, too."

"Oh, still doing the counting thing?"

"Yes, 'fraid so," he laughed nervously.

"How many did you make it here today?"

"You first, as you count too."

"Oh I didn't count the congregation today, I am trying to give it up for Lent."

"But it is not Lent."

"I am also trying to give up giving up things for Lent only in Lent. You like modern art do you? Well this is a piece you may like," said Willoughby ushering him away from where the American coach party had congregated and were getting a bit querulous.

Later, when almost everyone had drifted away, Willoughby, looking even more content with the world than usual, bumped into the vicar. "Hallo padre. I wondered where you had got to, haven't seen you around since the service."

"I got waylaid by some of that coach party. They were asking me all sorts of questions about the Royal Family. I have no idea why they thought I'd know."

"Well our monarch is head of the Church of England, so they're only asking you about your boss."

"Thank goodness, as that at least enabled me to waffle on in giving some sort of answer. Gosh, they are very literal Americans, aren't they? How has the sale gone?"

"Well, reasonably well, I suppose," said Rikki, looking disappointed. "The larger sunset has been bought by one of the Americans, Mr Wilkinson has bought the mermaid one, and Mrs Alysson the smaller one of my tits at the bird feeder. So that's three sales we've had, oh and that painting of Squeak and me, of course, so it's four in fact. Oh and we've also sold about a dozen bottles of wine, mainly to Anun's friends."

"Well that's none too shabby a result," said Willoughby. "I've sold a work of art, too, so that's five pieces sold. But that one was not one of your mother's though."

"Don't be daft," Rikki told him, "everything in this room is Mumsie's work."

"A management consultant fellow considered the pile of broken chairs in the corner a most interesting piece of modern art, so I flogged it to him for two hundred quid."

"What?" said the vicar.

"I thought you could use the money to buy some chairs that actually work. I hear golfing congratulations are due to you padre? Word on the street is that you're in the final of the Shack?"

"Yes, I won my semi-final yesterday. I think I'd got so nervous about today that I couldn't get nervous about the golf. I putted far better than usual. The same happened last Saturday in my quarter final on the eve of our golfer's service."

"Who have you got in the final, you do know yet?"

"Benton Snivelgate."

"Oh dear."

Chapter 16

"Oh. Willoughby. What are you doing here?"

"Representing the Competitions Committee, Benton."

"You ah, ahem just going to see us off?"

"I am going to go round with you."

"Me? Really? Ah, ahem, why?"

"You and the padre obviously. To watch the match, a chance to see two top golfers duelling for a prestigious trophy. Well, you and the padre trying to win the Shack anyway."

"You going all the way round?"

"Of course. Well so long as that storm they are forecasting does not break. They say it could be a big one. If so, I might leave you and the padre to become two old soaks while I beetle back to the dry bar."

"A storm forecast?" said Benton looking at the blameless blue sky dotted with occasional puffs of white cloud.

"So I am told. Sudden storm coming in reportedly. But don't worry, the Competitions Committee have taken action."

"To stop the storm? That is good of them."

"To make sure the match gets round in time. We have hired forecaddies so as to reduce the time looking for the ball and we have persuaded the padre to have a caddy – against his will – but that will stop him having to hump his bag around the hillier bits and speed things up. Do you want a caddy as well? You're also getting a bit derelict."

"I am fine thank you. I am perfectly capable of carrying my own bag. Will his caddy be allowed to read putts and give advice?"

"Of course, caddies can. And you'd better hope he does, for Harry has been a golfer for about five minutes whereas the padre has been playing these greens for years."

"Who are the forecaddies?"

"Well I had to rope in the younger fitter, sharper-eyed elements of the club, so I have persuaded Rikki and Anun to give up their time in return for a good lunch."

"I don't think that is necessary. They don't play golf – do they even know what to do? Kind of you to suggest it, but I don't ah, ahem think that is appropriate."

"Don't worry, all in order. The Competitions Committee run this competition and they have put it in place. It's not exactly rocket science, Benton, looking to see where a ball has gone. But don't worry, they will both be under supervision of a member of the Competitions Committee."

"You mean you?" said Benton sourly.

"Jerry and Martin are coming round, too."

"We are truly being graced. When I played in the final of the Lord Hankley Cup there was none of this," said Benton testily.

"Isn't it good?" said the just-arrived Jerry. "When I played in my Lord Hankley we didn't get any of this either. This is a much better way of doing things."

"It seems ah, ahem a lot of fuss, can't we just be left to get on with our match?"

"That's exactly what you can do now," said Jerry breezily. "You are being left to get on with your match without worrying about ball spotting and all the rest of it."

"Ah, here're the girls, and Harry. Now we just need your opponent," said Willoughby.

"If he is not here ready to start at 9am then he is disqualified. He has two minutes to get here or I have to be declared the winner," said Benton.

"It is only five minutes to nine, if you look at the clock on the clubhouse," remarked Willoughby.

"He's here," said Harry. "He's just changing his shoes in the locker room."

"Hallo, everyone ready?" asked Martin Cowmeadow, joining the group. "I will accompany the golfers as referee and Jerry and Willoughby will act as forecaddies with the assistance of Rikki and Anun, I believe? That should get us round it time – nasty storm coming I am told. Where's the vicar – ah here he is," he said spying him coming round the corner. "Okay forecaddies if you'd like to move on down the fairway please and I'll see the players off. Good to see forecaddies again – the old ways are the best."

"Here, you come with me, Anun," said Jerry. "I'll show you what you need to do."

"That means you're landed with me, Rikki," said Willoughby. "Come on."

The vicar drove off first and his drive found the middle of the fairway. Benton hooked his drive off into the rough on the left.

"I think those on the left will get more of the action as Benton's a hooker," Willoughby said to Rikki.

"Is he? What does that mean? In golf I mean," she added hurriedly.

"That his bad shots curve away to the left. The padre has always been steady from the tee. It's putting that lets him down. He has all the composure on the green of a man being tasered whilst disco dancing during an earthquake. Oh, Benton's blocked out by that bush whereas the vicar has a clear way in to the green. Advantage to the cloth on this one."

"What does that mean?"

"The cloth? The clergy."

"Oh, I thought it was another of your silly golf terms."

But the vicar, although getting on the green in a shot fewer than Benton, missed a short putt, bringing forth an annoyed exclamation of 'Fossilised Fishcakes!' and could only halve the hole.

On the second hole Benton hooked into the rough. The vicar had found the fairway, but again let slip the chance to win the hole by an atrocious piece of putting, causing him to yelp "Feta Cheese French Flipping Toast," as if in pain.

"Never noticed that the padre is obsessed with food, before," remarked Willoughby. "He cannot stop talking about it. Odd habit."

"Perhaps he is just thinking of his next sermon," suggested a smiling Anun. "Maybe it's on the loaves and the fishes?"

"I wonder what puddings we have on the menu today," mused Willoughby.

"There is strawberry pavlova," said Rikki with relish.

"Is there? How splendid, I'm fond of a good pavlova. How d'you know?"

"I checked before coming out. That's why we were a bit late. I thought we were a lot late as when we walked over we saw Benton playing and thought the game had already begun."

"What do you mean 'playing'?"

"He was over on that bit by the footpath from our place. He was hitting lots of balls from inside a white painted circle at that stick thing. But we thought it couldn't be the game against the vicar as we couldn't see the vicar and we thought they would be made to play together."

"No, Benton must have been practising. That hole is the 17th."

"The seventeenth what?" asked Rikki.

"The 17th hole."

"Oh," said Rikki.

The third hole was halved.

"No need to lug the bag up to the top of the 4th tee, Harry," said the vicar. "Just give me my driver, oh and perhaps a spare ball just in case." Harry was delighted to take the opportunity to go and stand by Rikki doing her duty as a forecaddie.

"Hallo, you come to join us?" said Willoughby. "Didn't fancy being a sherpa?"

"I didn't mind; the vicar told me not to."

"Swell. If you don't mind helping Rikki spot on this hole – we are not getting much of the action anyway – I'll just nip and have a word with the head greenkeeper. I think about now he has his elevenses in his hut."

"Elevenses? It's about half past nine," said Rikki.

"They get up early greenkeepers, so it is eleven o'clock in greenkeeper time."

As Willoughby ambled off, Harry asked Rikki: "How come Willoughby is your Godfather? Is he a good friend of your mother's?"

"No. Oh, I don't mean that they don't like one another. They do. But it's just that I have never divined that they had much of a friendship before I came along."

"So Willoughby was a friend of your father's?"

"Don't think so. Willoughby never talks of my father in a manner that suggests he knew him that well either. So, to answer your question, I am not sure why Mumsie chose Willoughby. But I am jolly glad she did for he has been absolutely ace and we did lots of fun things together when I was growing up."

"You, him and your Mum?"

"No, Mumsie never joined us. I can't remember going anywhere with Mumsie and him together. Oh, sometimes he would come to tea – but only when I badgered Mumsie to invite him. I remember overhearing him saying once to Mumsie that he and she shouldn't be seen out together with me as tongues might wag."

"How so?"

"I imagine he was thinking of Mumsie's reputation. That a young attractive widow shouldn't been seen going round with a married man. He was being chivalrous."

"Isn't that a rather old-fashioned attitude?"

"Willoughby is old fashioned! He has his code. He might seem a rapscallion at times, but he knows right from wrong. Well, sort of."

"What is Mrs Cornwallis like? I've never met her."

"Hardly ever met her myself. She never approved of me for some reason, so I was rather kept out of her society."

"Perhaps she is just one of those people who don't like children?"

"No, I don't think it was that. She was always fine with Anun; it was just me who had somehow got into her bad books when I must have been too young to remember whatever it was I'd done wrong."

"Here comes the vicar's ball," remarked Harry. "Nice and straight, as ever."

"How can you tell it is the vicar's? They look alike to me, especially from this range."

"The vicar played first as he has honour."

"Is it the honourable thing to play first?"

"No the person who won the previous hole has honour, so tees off first."

"But no-one won the last hole it was drawn."

"Halved."

"What?"

"In golf you say 'halved' not 'drawn' when you mean tied."

"Why?"

"Dunno, just do."

"Does anyone say anything sensible in golf? Why is the green called a green for example when everything is green on a golf course except those sand pit things."

"Bunkers."

"And bunkers to you too, Harry."

"I mean those sand pits are called bunkers."

"I rest my case m'lud."

"Oh, Benton has hooked into the woods. He did that when we played, too. Let's go and help find it." But by the time he and Rikki got over there, Jerry had located the ball. "Right behind a tree, impossible shot," he said trying to keep the glee out of his voice. The vicar won that hole, as Benton had to take a penalty drop and then all he could do was hack out sideways from the woods on to the fairway.

"Well I think you and I won that hole," said Jerry to Anun as they walked to the next fairway.

"How clever of us. Especially when we weren't playing. How did we do that?"

"Well if no-one was here to find the ball then Benton would have magically found it sitting up in a lovely clear spot with an unimpeded route to the hole."

"I had been wondering what was the point of Operation Forecaddie as all we seem to be doing is spotting Benton's ball as the vicar's is always in the middle of the fairway. I thought the idea was to help the vicar to win?"

"Well it's rather to make sure Benton does not walk off with the trophy. That is exactly what he did with the last one he won."

"Can't you just ask him to give it back?"

"He claims he did. Claims he gave it to the Secretary."

"Well can't you just ask Mr Pirbright if he did?"

"Wasn't during Pirbright's time, it was when Pike was here when he was in his er, well towards the end of his time as Secretary when he wasn't quite on top of things."

"You mean when the thing he was on top of was his roof?"

"Well, yes."

"Why would Benton Snivelgate keep the trophy?"

"The Lord Hankley and the Shack are our oldest trophies and are both solid silver. There is a strong body of opinion that believes that Benton has sold it to be melted down. The fear is if he gets his hands on the Shack that will go the same way. Hence why we don't want Benton to win. Careful, don't go too far back or you will end in the stream."

"Oh yes, I did one night in the dark."

"One night? What were you doing out here in the dark?"

"Falling in the stream. I just told you."

"Careful – incoming," said Jerry as a ball came towards them. "Cor that's a lousy shot by Benton. I think having an audience is putting him off. Good."

"What happens if the ball goes in the stream?" asked Anun.

"He won't be able to play it from there, so he will have to elect to take a penalty drop and drop the ball by the stream for a one-shot penalty."

"I've just noticed that ball has gone in the stream" said Anun who had just kicked it in. "What happens if a ball is lost?"

"Player has to go back to where he played the last shot and play again with a one-shot penalty. So if he loses his tee shot, for example, he has to go back and tee off again and that repeat tee shot counts as his third shot."

Benton lost that hole, to send the vicar two up after five holes.

Willoughby came back, looking even more content with the world than usual. "Enjoy your half past nines in the greenkeepers hut?" asked Rikki.

"You are like the padre, obsessed by food. I have had no refreshment, other than that of stimulating conversation with one of the unsung heroes of the club. Nor did I even go into the hut for that matter as it fell down during the night. The greenkeepers are most put out – in all senses. I merely wanted to arrange something with the head greenkeeper. I did a favour for him a while back and he said if he could ever do anything for me I only had to ask. I have just asked. Who's winning?"

"Er, it's either the vicar or the other chap," replied Rikki.

"Most helpful."

"Well it is in a way, it's not being drawn, er halved. Someone is winning by two goals."

"Holes," corrected Willoughby.

"It must be the vicar," said Rikki, "he looks happier."

That lead was reduced to one hole as Benton won the 7th easily, finding the centre of the fairway and then the centre of the green, before one-putting for a birdie.

"Are you enjoying it, Rikki?" Harry asked when he caught up with her as they left the green, Willoughby having ambled over to have a chat with Martin.

"I am looking forward to my lunch."

"But it's not even half ten."

"Is hitting a golf ball more interesting than watching someone hit a ball?"

"Yes."

"I thought it must be."

"Ah Godders' infamous 8th hole," said Willoughby rejoining Rikki as Harry went off to resume his caddying duties. "Oh that bunker has indeed gone. Shame."

"Why is it a shame?" asked Rikki, more to make conversation than because she was interested. But Willoughby did not answer. He was roused from his thoughts by a cry of "Fore left!" from the tee, Martin's voice carrying loudly.

"Why do golfers shout fore?" asked Rikki. "Why not 'heads' or 'watch out' or 'duck' or something sensible? Oh, I've probably answered my own question."

"The short answer is that no-one knows."

"I'm really glad I asked now."

"The long answer is it is probably a foreshortening of something. But then as fore means 'situated in front' it could have just have been a warning to the group ahead that someone has pinged a ball their way. One suggestion is it's an abbreviation of forecaddies, to warn them, as often they could not see the players hitting. Another is that it's a shortening of 'beware before!' the term used by artillerymen to warn the infantry ahead on the frontline that they were about to launch missiles over them. Come on, we better give Anun and George a hand as they don't seem to have found Benton's ball."

"Sorry Benton," Jerry was saying when Willoughby and Rikki approached, "we didn't pick it up in flight. Heard it land though so it is around here somewhere."

"I know it is around here," said Benton irritably.

"We've got three minutes to find it from when Benton arrived," said Martin checking his watch.

Eight pairs of eyes scoured the rough, but with no luck by the time Martin called out "ten seconds left."

"Ah, found it," cried Benton who had detached himself from the main party. "It has ah, ahem bounced on further on than you had thought. You were looking in the wrong place. I've been lucky, it's sitting up on nice tuft, too. Quite easy to see if only you lot were looking in the right place."

"My that is a mighty blow from the tee to there," remarked Willoughby.

"It must have got a good bounce. But it was ah, ahem a very good shot."

"You hooked it, so you can't have hit it that well," rejoindered Willoughby as he walked away.

"The ball didn't go there," said Anun as Willoughby passed him.

"Bit unlikely to have ended that near the hole."

"His ball was 30 yards back. I know as it has been in my pocket these past three minutes," whispered Anun.

From his fine lie sitting up in the rough, Benton was able to reach the green, which was beyond the vicar doing so from where he was on the fairway, and Benton won the hole to leave him only one down. The 9th was also halved, leaving the vicar one up at the turn.

"Anyone want anything to eat or drink?" asked Martin. "I am going to have one of your mother's excellent Chorley cakes," he said to the girls.

"What's this," asked Rikki, "a little cafe?"

"It's the halfway hut," said Harry.

"Want some elevenses Half Pint?"

"Rather! I am feeling a trifle peckish. Are you having some elevenses to go with your half past nines?"

"Do you wish owt, Anun?" Willoughby asked.

"Not for me thanks."

"I didn't know this was here," said Rikki. "Do golfers always stop for elevenses?"

"Ha, you are looking at the game in a new light aren't you," laughed Harry.

"Which is the bunker Lord Hankley stuck his traction engine in?" asked Anun as they settled down to their drinks and snacks. "Have we been there yet?"

"Yes, it was that one on the 2nd," replied Jerry.

"I've heard about this story, but never been told it," remarked Harry.

"I know this one," said Rikki. "See Willoughby – I know golf. That Lord Hankley was convinced the club was swizzling him. So one night, when full to the gunnels with port, he decided to park his traction engine across the course so no-one could play the next day. But he crashed it by accident into one of those sand pits, which we forecaddies call bunkers, and it stayed there for days before he could get it fished out. The members thought it a hoot as apparently having a traction engine in a sand pit does not stop golf and it made Lord Hankley look stupid, and they liked that as they had always thought him a silly old poop. That's right isn't it Willoughby?"

"Rambo couldn't have put it better, and most certainly wouldn't have."

"Okay, everyone ready?" said Martin chivvying everyone back to the game.

The vicar missed an eminently sinkable putt on 10 to lose that hole, exclaiming "fudge and fruit salad," in his annoyance.

"I could fancy some fudge right now," remarked Rikki. "Does your elevenses hut have fudge?"

"Sorry, no," replied Willoughby. "Nor fruit salad."

"There is fruit salad on the lunch menu, too."

"Is there? I like fruit salad. But I think I will still have the strawberry pavlova. Though I suppose I could have both, but would that be greedy?"

"It would. But I think I might have both, too. This forecaddying is making me rather peckish."

Losing the 10th started a run of bad holes for the vicar, as various travails on the putting green contributed to him losing the 11th – "fuzzle wuzzle" – and the 12th - "four helpings of fortune". Benton was now 2 up.

"I don't know padre why you're worrying about your putting. I'd be worrying whether the Dean is going to boot you out in a fortnight," said Willoughby. "Losing your job is more important than losing some silly golf match."

"Oh thank you, you are a right cheerful soul," shot back the vicar.

On the next green the vicar holed a 13-foot putt, to bring the match back to him being only one down.

"Oh Benton is in Hell," remarked Jerry happily, when Benton's effort to get on the 14th green found sand instead. "That should be one chalked up to the vicar."

"Aren't vicars supposed to stop people going to hell?" said Anun. "Mind you, Benton is probably a lost cause."

"No, Hell Bunker. That huge bunker, he has just hit his ball into it."

"If you all don't mind going round the other side," asked Benton. "It's just that this could go anywhere with my bunker play and that way you could spot where it goes. I have had to play out of here several times over the years and sometimes it has flown over the green and no-one knew where it went. So if you wouldn't mind." Everyone moved off except Martin.

"Would you mind Martin?" Benton said turning round to where Martin was standing behind the bunker watching him.

"It's okay," he replied, "we already have half a dozen people watching over there, so a seventh will make no difference, but could make all the difference here."

Benton failed three times to get the ball out of the bunker and conceded the hole. The match was now all square.

On 15 the vicar holed a tricky snaking downhill putt to halve the hole. But Benton won the 16th with a superb chip over a bunker that ended up inches from the hole.

"Here, Larry-Harry," said Willoughby ushering him over. "Tell the padre when you get down the fairway and are out of Benton's earshot not to hit onto the out-of-bounds part of the green. Tell him to play for the front of the green and far better to be short rather than long."

The vicar played first to this green and his ball ended up just short of the green. Benton then hit his shot over the back of the playing surface of the green onto the part which was closed. "Ah well just have to drop in the drop zone, ah, ahem wherever that might be," said Benton, looking happy. But when he got to the green, to his consternation, he saw that the drop zone, rather than being at the front of the green, as he knew it would be, was now at the top and involved playing down the trickiest part of the slope. Moreover the flag had been moved from earlier that morning to a new position.

"Yikes, the greenkeeper has done no favours there with that drop zone. That's one heck of a tricky shot," said Martin. "Cor, anyone'd do extremely well to get down in two from there. Flipping Nora. What a sadistic place to put it."

The vicar had a relatively simple putt off the fairway up a small slope to the flag. Benton was faced with a shot nigh on impossible to execute well: he had to nudge a tricky putt across and down a steep, slick slope, knowing if he over hit the ball would skate off the green and down the fairway.

This is exactly what happened, his ball ending a few inches further away than the vicar's. It was still his turn to play, as furthest from the flag. He used a putter and hit it to within two feet of the hole and the vicar graciously conceded the next putt.

The vicar now had two shots to win the hole and level the match. His putt missed but ended up several inches nearer the hole than Benton's had.

"Sorry, can't give you that," said Benton. But the vicar calmly knocked the putt in.

"All square coming down the last," said Martin excitedly to Jerry, "canna say it has always been play of the highest order, but they are serving us up an exciting finish."

After both the finalists had teed off from the 18th and both had found the fairway, the vicar on the right side of it, Benton on the left, Rikki asked Willoughby: "is that our duty finished, can we have lunch now? I am feeling a trifle peckish."

"Not necessarily. Depends if they halve this hole."

"What happens if they halve? Do they halve the cup?"

"No, then we go to sudden death."

"What one of them has to kill the other? Are vicars allowed to do that? Or does it just mean the first player to die of boredom loses?"

"No, they go onto the 1st and carry on playing until someone wins a hole."

"Does sudden death involve forecaddies or are they allowed to go to lunch?"

"Forecaddies carry on until the match is over."

"Oh hang on a mo, Harry wants me for something," she said seeing that Harry was approaching and beckoning her over. Harry had a quick word with her and Rikki marched off towards the green.

"Where you off to Half Pint?"

"Harry wants me to spot by the green, as he says you can't see where shots go from here."

"True. I'll come with you."

"He says you are to remain with the vicar to give moral support."

"Oh this is like what's it, the 3rd one," remarked Anun to Jerry. "You can't see the putting area from here. Where's Rikki off to? Has she given up and gone in?"

"I think she is going to see the balls land," replied Jerry.

"Oh do we need to, too?"

"No real need if she is."

The vicar played first. "That'll do nicely padre," said Willoughby, "Probably on the green."

His opponent's shot looked equally accurate. "Good riposte Benton," said Willoughby, "reckon that's on as well." No-one could see where either ball had landed due to the lie of the land, and Rikki had disappeared out of sight, also.

As soon as Benton had played Harry had marched off to the green well ahead of the rest of the party. When the players reached the top of the slope they could see that both balls were indeed on the green. "Splendid shots the pair of you," said Martin.

"It comes down to a putting competition now," said Benton deliberately loudly enough for the vicar to hear.

"Where would they send you?" asked Willoughby of the vicar. "Some grim inner city dump I suppose?"

Harry was crouching down behind the ball nearer the hole. "Tricky shot that, vicar."

Benton took a long time lining up his putt, as holing it would mean the vicar, with his notoriously erratic putting, would have to hole his putt just to stay in the game. Benton's putt looked a good one, but it shaved the hole, coming to rest two feet beyond the cup.

"So this putt to win the Shack," murmured Martin under his breath to Jerry.

"Oh, this isn't my ball," said the vicar looking at it. Mine has a red cross on it. "Oh dear I thought my shot was on the green – did you see where it went Rikki?"

"Only two balls came over the first one which Mr Snivelgate has just hit –"

"The first!" exclaimed an anguished Benton.

"– and that one which you are standing by."

"Oh yes," said the vicar, "this is my ball," he said indicating the one now two feet from the hole. I regret to say that you appear to have hit my ball, Benton. Oh dear."

"Sorry Benton, you lose the hole," said Martin, "for playing the wrong ball."

"But Harry was lining up that putt," said Benton accusingly.

"Doesn't matter," said Martin. "It is the player's responsibility to check he was or she was playing the correct ball before making the stroke. Ah well, it was an exciting match. Shame you ruined it for everyone at the end, Benton, but never mind," said Martin, looking anything but disappointed.

"I know where the ball was so we can just replace the vicar's ball and we can ah, ahem just play on. Shame, as you said, for an important match to end in anti-climax."

"Sorry. But the rules are quite clear: you lose the hole," said Martin.

"Is that it over, then?" asked Rikki of Willoughby. "Can we have lunch now? Oh, who won by the way?"

Chapter 17

"Ah Willoughby," said Martin, at the celebratory lunch, "this new competition of yours. A slot has opened up in a couple of weeks' Pirbright tells me. I know that's a trifle soon, but how about we stick it in then?"

"Two weeks? Gosh."

"If you wait for perfect conditions, you will never get anything done," counselled the vicar.

"Who I am to argue with the good book," replied Willoughby. "No, let's do it. More fun to have it in the dregs of summer than mid-autumn. Just need to spread the word rapidly to get people aware and signed up. You will play in it won't you Martin?"

"Of course. Put my name down for it. You'll play Jerry won't you? Jerry?"

"Yer what, what?" said Jerry, who had been talking with Anun, oblivious to others.

"That new club competition we talked about, in two weeks. You in?" asked Martin.

"Yes I'm free then, sure Jack'll be too – yep pencil us in. Foursomes isn't it?"

"Modified foursomes, that idea Willoughby was telling us about when Rambo rugby tackled the Steward."

"Harry's idea," corrected Willoughby. "Yes, it's foursomes and each team member still has to tee off on half the holes, but it doesn't have to be one on odds and one on evens; they just have to decide beforehand which nine tee shots each will take and mark it on the scorecard they give their opponents."

"Oh that sounds fun, so if one of you is better on par 3s he can play all the par 3s, for example," said Jerry.

"Precisely," said Martin, "brings a new tactical dimension to proceedings" and, smiling, he added: "And if one of you doesn't fancy clambering up to the 4th and 13th tees, he can give that shot to his partner. We better have a name for these new rules – be easier than explaining it each time. We'd better invent one for it. Willoughby – you're good at invention."

"I had been thinking," said Willoughby, "that the system devised by Dr Stableford was called Stableford so we'd better call this one a King competition."

"Er that could sound a bit rude when yelled across a fairway," pointed out Martin.

"How about King Harry rules?" suggested Rikki.

"King Harry rules. I like that!" said Willoughby.

"Well. Er," said Harry, "it's kind of you but be a bit awkward if it is named after me, as I have arranged to write an article for Golf Fortnightly about it and, well, if it was named after me would look like I was blowing my own trumpet."

"Very prudent, Harry," said the vicar. "Everyone who exalts himself will be humbled, and he who humbles himself will be exalted."

"What about the inventor and where it was invented?" suggested Willoughby. "King Tangents has a ring to it."

"Yes it does," said Martin, "that okay with you Harry?"

"Yes, that works well."

"Got a commission out of it, have you Harry?" said Willoughby, impressed. "You'll make us all famous yet."

"That trophy you're donating for it, Willoughby," said Martin, "please make sure it's not solid silver – be more restful all round."

"I will. But it will still count as one of the silver competitions won't it?"

"Yes of course. Er, who decides these, is it us or some other committee?"

"I don't know. Must be us as the Competitions Committee, mustn't it?"

"Suppose so."

"That means it gets an honours board."

"Ah but that decision will be down to the House Committee won't it?"

"Will it? Or is it Estates?"

"Or us? After all it's a board about a competition."

"Who is going to authorise payment for the board?"

"Perhaps it's a Finance Committee matter then?"

"Doesn't new expenditure on something have to be okayed by the Fundraising Committee?" chipped in Jerry.

"I think that only applies to proposals which come from the Membership Committee," said Martin. "You were thinking of having a beano afterwards – does that mean we have to get it agreed by the Social Committee?"

"Yes definitely should have a buffet afterwards," replied Willoughby enthusiastically, "make a real occasion of it. Play in the afternoon, revel in the evening sort of thing. The Steward is off that week on his hols shrimping in Herne Bay or whatever he does, so we might be allowed to enjoy ourselves."

"A buffet?" said Rikki, her ears pricking up. "When?"

"Two weeks' time," Willoughby replied to Rikki, then to Martin and Jerry he said: "We'll have a shotgun start so everyone will get back to the clubhouse at the same time for grub."

"A shotgun start?" asked Rikki. "Is it one of those sudden-death competitions?"

"No, Half Pint, it means that all the players start at the same time."

"Won't that make it a bit crowded? How will they know which ball is whose?"

"No," explained Harry happily, "they start on different holes, and play all 18 holes in order starting from whichever one they started at. A shotgun is fired by way of a starting pistol so each group tees off at the same time."

"And shotgun starts have buffets afterwards, do they? Does the club have many shotgun competitions?"

"We'll get you interested in golf yet," laughed Harry.

"Shotgun competitions don't require forecaddies do they?" asked Rikki nervously.

"No," laughed Harry.

"You'll be playing, of course, won't you Willoughby," said Martin.

"Well my partner isn't available that day and, well, someone will need to be there to do the organising and whatnot."

"Nonsense," said Martin, "the organising will all be done by then. The kitchen can cope with the buffet, and you can't collate the scores until the thing is over and as we'll all be finishing at the same time there's no advantage to not playing."

"You will want to play in this competition," said the vicar softly, "when you look back, you'll be glad you did. For your sake and his."

"You are quite right padre. Of course I should play."

"Why don't you team up with Harry?" suggested Martin. "That would be appropriate: the founder of the competition and the creator of its rules. That okay with you Harry? Or have you already a partner?"

"I would be honoured," replied Harry.

"The honour would be all mine old boy," said Willoughby. "And by the way you are teeing off on 4 and 13."

"Ah, Rambo," Martin hailed the passing member. "Two weeks' time: an important King Tangents Foursomes competition, you going to sign up to play in it?"

"Yes, well, yes. But my recent foursomes partner, Todd, said playing golf gives him earache – odd thing, never heard that before about golf, normally it's backs or knees – and so he is taking some time off foursomes golf. So I will need to find a new partner."

"Well if you can't find one, just sign up on your own and we'll pair the singletons up. That's a point, I better go and see Miss Murtle and organise a sign-up sheet, and maybe some posters and things," said Martin getting up.

"King Tangents," said Rambo, "who is he? I can't remember a King called Tangents, I am sure I would have."

"Oh he is one of those lesser-known ones," said Willoughby. "I think he is one of the more ancient kings you probably weren't taught about at school. Ethelred the Unready, Orlo the Organised, Ivar the Boneless, Napoleon the Boney – you know one of those chaps."

"What has he got to do with golf? Golf, didn't exist then."

"Well it is quite an interesting story actually," said Willoughby.

"Yes," prompted Rambo when he realised Willoughby had stopped.

"And you can read all about it in Harry's article in Golf Fortnightly." Then he added after a pause: "See, that's how you do it Rambo."

"Oh can't you just tell me? I will not tell anyone, you know me."

"Sorry, Mr Ramsbotham," said Harry solemnly, "strict embargo imposed by the magazine I am afraid."

"That's the way the professionals do it, Rambo," said Willoughby. "The pros don't give away their material for free, they make people buy the publication. Two weeks' time, the Godfrey Flower Trophy: spread the word, tell the members to sign up for it."

"I will, I will, thank you Willoughby," and with that Rambo bustled off.

"Oh, you do fib so," said Rikki.

"But I have piqued his interest. He won't stop talking about it now. That'll get some more people signed up," chuckled Willoughby.

"Is Dumbo good at recruiting people then?" asked Anun dubiously. "I'd've thought most people would avoid anything to do with him."

"Oh yes, he'll be excellent. Get a twattle basket like him to tell people that there is a competition to be signed up for, and this gives everyone the perfect excuse to excuse themselves from his company saying they have to go and sign up."

"Oh that's clever," said Anun. "I got stuck with a tedious turnip the other day who would insist on giving me a blow-by-blow account of his round. All of it fairly incomprehensible to me of course. Any tips on how I should have got out of that?"

"I have a technique," said the vicar, "when people start doing that to me. I wait til they have got onto the 2nd and then I say, I hear that 17 and 18 were playing particularly trickily today – how you get on there and what did you hit at 18? Works almost every time."

"Two weeks. That really isn't much time is it actually," mused Willoughby.

"Don't worry," said the vicar. "It will be a great success."

And he was right. It was.

Chapter 18

The vicar saw a distinctive figure sitting outside on the bench beside the putting green. He stood for a period, hesitating whether to join him, before silently sitting next to him. After a while he said softly: "You miss him don't you?"

"Oh hullo padre, didn't see you there."

"I've only just arrived. It is a noble thing you have done in his honour."

"Yes, I do. Funny thing is, I have known Godders, knew him, all these years – since we were children. But I never really knew him, or maybe there wasn't much to know. But he was a constant in my life, an affable companion around the course and in the clubhouse, never likely to over stimulate one with his conversation maybe, but a kind, decent, generous soul with the good stuff in him. A chap you were never unhappy to see. He had no raging ambition, never did a mean thing, never trampled over anyone to get what he wanted. When he left a group you rarely noticed that he was gone. No-one was ever going to write his obituary in the papers. But he deserves to be remembered, his life acknowledged by more than a few friends and family."

"I think this proves that when he has left a group some people do notice that he has gone," the vicar remarked gently.

"Never realised how much I would miss him," said Willoughby. "Had genuinely never occurred to me. If you add up the hours I have spent with him – I have just been having a wee stab at it – I reckon it comes to years. Literally. All of them at the golf club. If it wasn't for golf I would never have known him. I have never been to his house, well once, when I was a child and his mother invited me to tea."

"Lovely tea it was. We had a jolly nice cherry cake, iced it was, lovely thick icing. My mother never iced cakes unless it was Christmas or a birthday. I think Godders' mother wanted to meet her son's new playmate – his parents didn't golf, just as mine didn't. I think I was being given the once over. It was literally the once as I never got invited back. Shame for it was darn nice cake. Cherry; iced it was."

"There were fewer things to do here in those days when you were young, none of these gameboys or tweeping or whatnot, no opportunity to send someone a virtual horseradish or whatever the youth of today do. We had to do real things with real people. So in the holidays my mother would dump me down at the golf club as it struck my parents as a place where I could come to no harm, I'd have something to do and they'd know where I was. She would leave me with some money to buy a bottle of pop after the golf and she'd come back for me later. It was there that I met Godders – I think his parents had had much the same idea as mine and so we just palled up. More fun trudging round the course with someone than on your own. That's how we started playing together, as children and, well, we just sort of carried on playing together. Have I ever told you the story of how we won the first of those Junior Foursomes?"

The vicar was about to say yes, but realised that his friend wanted, needed, to talk, so said no.

"It was when old whatsisname was chairman. Not the one who looked like a bemused chipmunk, what was his name, Duchy Originals that's it, er, hang on no, Duchy Holland, but the one before him who looked like a tenacious toad – Richard somebody that was it, or was it somebody Richards? Anyway he was called something.

But he had the idea that the club should be doing more to boost junior golf. He saw juniors as the future of the game and the club; quite rightly, too. Most of the old members saw us youngsters as a pain in the proverbial – paid little in the way of subs and annoyed them by playing what they saw as their own personal course. These people would be the same ones years later grumbling that the membership was declining and that the subs were going up as we had too few people in the club."

"Anyways old Richards had this idea of introducing a competition for children in the summer hols. A knockout, as we were still in the era of match play. He decided it should be foursomes as that was more sociable, more promoting the club ethos as he saw it. Only three pairs entered, and Godders and I were the ones who got the bye in the semi-final, as I suppose it was, and we were to play the winners from among the other two pairs."

"The pair that won, one of them was an exchange student over here for the summer or part of it, he was Swiss or German or something – he came from one of those foreign countries. Anyways, the date of the final was set, and a couple of days before it he was called back home – his grandmother was ill or something, so we had no-one to play in the final."

"We had to turn up and play as Richards had arranged for some local paper coverage as part of his efforts to encourage the young into golf so it was decided that we could only win if we teed off – bit like the idea behind the Captain's Drive In, I suppose. A photographer was there to record it for a story in the paper, so we had to tee off. Well only one us had to, obviously, being foursomes. My mater and pater had not turned up, and Godders' had, so it was decided he would hit the drive. The snapper snapped him doing so. Mr Richards, if that was his name, then presented us with the cup, and the snapper snapped that, and that was it."

"I literally hadn't hit even one shot in the whole competition."

"Always rather looked on our entries on that honours board as a bit of a joke; but now I am very glad my name is up their next to Godders'. Very glad indeed."

"Quite right he was old Richards," Willoughby continued. "Look in the clubhouse many weekdays and all you see is a collection of coffin dodgers with the odd exception like young Harry." He paused a little, as though something had struck him, before continuing quietly, "I suppose Godders was one of the exceptions, he didn't manage to dodge did he. Poor soul."

"That is why you haven't been playing isn't it," said the vicar gently, "not your ankle."

"Haven't really found any enthusiasm to get back out there. Didn't always play with Godders, of course; just seems that way. But he was always my foursomes partner in any of the comps. Somehow, dunno, can't really face being out there with some young shaver who gets all annoyed cos he's played a bad shot, or someone whose view of golf is all about getting his handicap down by whatever by whenever. Godders never worried if he played a bad shot, and why should he. There's plenty of things to get worked up about in the world if you are so inclined, but hitting a bad golf shot shouldn't be one of them. And perhaps just as importantly, he never worried if I played a bad shot."

"Silly game when you think about it. What is the purpose of golf – it is to shoot as low a score as possible. But why do people play golf? Presumably cos they like hitting a ball with a golf club, so what do they do – they try to do it as little as possible. Makes no sense, if you think about it. Cricket it's how many runs you score, the more the merrier. Now that's a sensible sport – they stop the game for afternoon tea. Probably the most sensible game there is. But then in most sports you win by how many times you do something; golf you win by how few times you do something. Whole darn game's potty."

Willoughby laughed: "Well Godders and I certainly got the hang of it that first foursomes victory. One shot! You can't hit fewer shots than that." He chuckled at the memory.

"There's quite a party going on in there," said the vicar. "Looks a big success your Godfrey Flower Trophy day. You've done well by him. Just as you have done well by Rikki. She has turned into a fine young lady. You should be proud. That sermon she wrote – very interesting, very perceptive."

"Yes she's always had brains and looks," replied Willoughby, "though somehow she's never had the brains to realise she has the looks. She has been lucky in that respect. But she can be very literal, she sees life very straightforwardly, and that has always made me feel particularly protective towards her for life is not always straightforward."

"She has never really shown any interest in boys before Harry," Willoughby continued, "and I'm not even sure how interested she is in him – poor Harry. Anun went one way, she another I suppose. For Rikki it was always animals, still is – those tits she feeds, that pig of hers and whatnot. She had a pony when she was younger. Borrowed or was lent, I forget now, a riding hat for her which was too big for her tiny bonce, so padded it out with newspaper. Hat was still much too big for her, of course, and I remember leading her on the rein about the field and the hat gradually slipped down so she couldn't see where she was going –

didn't matter too much as I was leading the thing – and all you could see was this hat and below it the most enormous smile you could ever imagine. To see someone as happy as that, such a natural and unaffected happiness, well it does something to a chap."

"She has always had this great innate ability to love life," Willoughby went on. "It's a wonderful gift and I never want her to lose it or have it taken from her. I feel protective towards her. Very protective. That was why I was glad to play today with Harry. Golf reveals a person's character, as you know."

"She is here now," remarked the vicar. "Saw her at the buffet. She is a good trencherman, as my mother would have put it."

"Likes her grub, always has. Mind you, probably helps that her mother is such a good cook. Her cakes have gone down a bomb so it looks like she'll get the gig here permanently. Good news for that family has never exactly been flush with money. That smallholding has never been much of a revenue earner and she has had to bring up two girls on her own."

"She must have done alright for she managed to send them both to private school," remarked the vicar.

"It helped that they both got scholarships – they are bright girls. But that was family money. Money from a distant relative or something."

"How distant?"

"Distant enough. But yes," said Willoughby to change the subject, "Rikki loves her grub. Always has."

"She can carry it well now," said the vicar, "she is such a pretty girl. Just hope when she gets older she doesn't run to a certain stoutness, like her father."

"I doubt she will. She puts it away, but it never shows,

and anyway, a jolly, pretty plump woman is a fine sight. We are designed to have curves. It's stick insects who are supposed to look like stick insects. If we go round looking like stick insects, how would that make them feel? They'd lose their sense of identity and I doubt they can have much sense of pride in being a stick insect at the best of times. But she'll be okay – her father remained a wiry fellow all his all-too-short life and he must have had all the joys of his wife's cooking when he was on land."

"Oh, yes I forget. Odd how she and her sister are so unalike in many ways."

"That's nothing. What about me and my brother."

"I didn't know you had a brother."

"I don't. I exist, he doesn't – you can't get less alike than that."

"Sorry, I couldn't make your inaugural Godfrey Flower Trophy, but I had my meeting with the Rural Dean."

"Oh padre, please forgive me, I totally forgot. How did it go?"

"Very well indeed, our church is to remain open."

"Oh I am so glad. Oh well done vicar."

"The management consultancy report was most complimentary in a slightly bizarre way. Talked of the imaginative way our church involves itself with the local community and the long hours and personal sacrifice I put in on my outreach programme and pastoral care."

"You look after us well, padre. I'm glad they respect that."

"I think in this respect it is more a case of me being looked after by my parishioners; one in particular."

"What goes out on the tide comes back on it," remarked Willoughby.

"The Bible tells us that two people are better off than one, for they can help each other succeed. If one falls, the other can reach out to help. But someone who falls alone is in real trouble. A person standing alone can be attacked and defeated, but two can stand back-to-back and conquer. I am very glad you stood back-to-back with me. I am truly fortunate to have you as a friend. When you feel like taking to the course again on a regular basis, I'd be delighted to be your partner. But only if you like."

Willoughby said after a lengthy pause: "I think I would like that very much. Thank you."

"We could play this Tuesday, if you like. I'm free now on Tuesdays."

"Oh, I thought you chaired your diocesan whatnot then?"

"I have been relieved of those duties."

"Been sacked?"

"No, I have been asked to take on the newly created role of the diocese's Director of Outreach Programmes, so someone else is being landed with that committee chore. I mean been asked to steer that important aspect of the diocese's work. Oh, sorry, on Tuesdays you do your yoga don't you?"

"Not anymore."

"Been sacked?"

"No, Mrs C has ended it."

"Really? Why?"

"Winnie and her, I mean yogi and her had a falling out."

"Oh dear. Why?"

"She is always jolly enthusiastic and encouraging our yogi, always giving us new positions to try that she says we will be good at, and at which we seldom are. As far as I can make out, the animal kingdom must spend its whole time contorting themselves into the most unlikely poses when my back is turned. One of the new positions we had to do last week was to make a face like a cow. She told

Mrs C she thought she would be very good at that and Mrs C took it the wrong way. Or possibly the right way, I am not sure. Anyway the upshot is Mrs C was not a happy bunny, and has decreed we are no longer doing yoga with yogi."

"Oh dear. Did you ever discover if there is also an upward dog?"

"Oh yes. You lie on your front and raise yourself up using your front paws and the idea is to get your torso into a near vertical position – makes one feel a bit like an arthritic seal at feeding time. And talking of seals at feeding time."

"Hallo Willoughby, hallo vicar," said Rikki who was carrying a plate piled high with food. "May I join you?"

"Of course," replied the vicar.

"Oh, happy birthday Willoughby for yesterday. Did you get my card?"

"Yes I did you cheeky young pup."

"I thought it was very funny," said Rikki, touching her nose with her hand as she laughed.

"Ah Willoughby, there you are," said the Secretary, "there is quite a party going on in there, haven't seen the place so heaving of an evening. Most excellent. Lots of bar profits. Oh I have good news for you about your eligibility to stand for the Competitions Committee. You have to have played in at least three silver competitions or to have made an exceptional contribution to club competitions in the previous year and I think this most certainly counts in that category, so you will be eligible to stand for re-election."

"Oh goodie," said Willoughby.

"Yes it is good, isn't it," said the Secretary. "So now there will have to be an election. Well if you will excuse me, I think I will sample the buffet – a most handsome spread it looks."

"Talking of good news, have you heard about Harry?" asked Rikki. "He is going to move into Paddock's Farm when we go back to uni, to help Mumsie. She had been going to get a Wwoofer in to help her."

"How would a dog have helped?" asked Willoughby.

"It stands for World Wide Opportunities on Organic Farms," said Rikki. "It's a scheme whereby foreigners wanting to improve their English get free board and lodging in return for helping out on a farm."

"Does that pig of yours speak perfect Queen's English then? Or is the ducks?" enquired Willoughby.

"But now Harry is coming instead. I am so pleased as I did not like him being at Winnie's Place. Not with winter coming. Horrible what happened there wasn't it?"

"Yes, indeed," agreed both the vicar and Willoughby.

"Also it saves him rent," added Rikki. "I don't think there is a lot of money in being a freelance writer."

"Happy Day-After-Your-Birthday" said Anun, bounding up and planting a big kiss on Willoughby's cheek. "These are from Rik-pig and me," she said indicating a box of chocolates, "and this is from Mummy," she said giving him another box.

"Oh thank you my dears, most kind. Oh this is intriguing," he said opening up the box. "Ah, macaroons!" he cried delightedly. "Oh thank you, Anun, thank you Rikki, and please do thank your mother. I am a lucky feller." Then he asked anxiously: "Ludo isn't here is he?"

"No," laughed Anun, "if you mean Bingo."

"Would you like a celebratory chocolate padre?" he said offering the box to him.

"Oh thank you, yes."

"Do I get one, too?" chirruped Rikki.

"Willoughby, I have been researching King Tangents and I don't think he exists."

"Oh hallo Rambo," said Willoughby. "Can you research something that doesn't exist? And how do you know when you have stopped doing it?"

"I think you have got that wrong. I don't think there was a King called Tangents."

"Maybe he ruled under a pseudonym, perhaps for security purposes, or because he was shy," suggested Willoughby.

"Oh, do you think so? Are you sure? I have not heard of that before."

"Oh yes, lots of Kings used a different regnal name to their own – Alberts are notoriously shy, or perhaps just embarrassed at being called Albert. That why they always rule as Edward or George. And queens for that matter. You don't think Queen Victoria was called that did you? She was christened Princess Alexandrina Sharon."

"I didn't know that. I came across quite an interesting story actually in my researches into King Tangents."

"Here have a chocolate," said Willoughby hurriedly.

"I am allergic to nuts."

"Well don't have a nutty one then. There's a card somewhere explaining what they are, oh Rikki's got it."

"It's okay there's probably a key on the bottom of the box," said Rambo as Rikki proffered him the card.

"No!" Willoughby and Anun cried simultaneously, but it was too late, as Rambo had turned the box upside down.

"You cretin!" shrieked Anun, into whose lap most of the chocolates had fallen.

"It wasn't my fault, it wasn't my fault," shouted Rambo angrily. "Rikki had the card."

The vicar got up and calmly ushered Rambo away. "Have you been to the buffet yet? Shall we go together, looks rather good."

"Oh look," said Rikki, "now we have given you two presents in one. Now, you have got a toddlers' jigsaw," she said helping Willoughby identify and replace most of the chocolates in their black plastic tubs.

"That one's a strawberry cream," said Willoughby happily, "I know exactly where that one goes," he said popping it in his mouth.

"It's like that farmyard jigsaw you gave me when I was very little where you had to slot all the animals back into their spaces above their names. I loved that."

"Yes, I remember. Have you managed to work it out yet?"

Rikki stuck her tongue out at him. "Did you get any other nice presents?"

"Yes I did, thank you." And he had. Yesterday morning his wife had left for him a large wrapped parcel, with the message that it was for his study. When he had unwrapped it, it was the painting of toddler Rikki with Squeak.

The sounds of revelry from within the clubhouse reached two ladies walking along the road by the golf club. "I wonder what's going on there," said one of them.

"You don't want to know," said the other. "All sorts goes on there. The stories you hear. They once kidnapped a nun and took her there and poured milk all over her."

"Did they! Why?"

"It's some sort of initiation ceremony, all these clubs and societies have them don't they before you can become a member. The vicar was involved. But then he gets up to all sorts of things, that one. They were going to close his church a while ago because he was running dogging sessions in the church car park. Instead the Archbishop of

Canterbury decided to close the car park instead. He discussed it with the Pope, I heard."

"Oh yes," she continued, "all sorts goes on at that golf club. There is a room which has its windows high up so no-one can see in. They claim it is the billiards room. Well the window cleaner told me that there isn't even a billiards table in there. It is quite obvious to me what they use that room for. But then they are quite shameless, about it – I have heard members brazenly admit they are going to the club for a foursome. Some very odd people are members of that club."

The End.

BRINDLE BOOKS

Brindle Books Ltd

We hope that you have enjoyed this book. To find out more about Brindle Books Ltd, including news of new releases, please visit our website:

http://www.brindlebooks.co.uk

There is a contact page on the website, should you have any queries, and you can let us know if you would like email updates of news and new releases. We promise that we won't spam you with lots of sales emails, and we will never sell or give your contact details to any third party.

If you purchased this book online, please consider leaving an honest review on the site from which you purchased it. Your feedback is important to us, and may influence future releases from our company.

Printed in Great Britain
by Amazon